What Lies Ahead

What Lies Ahead

MARCI HENNA

Also by Marci Henna

When We Last Spoke
Now a major motion picture

"Inside the heart of everyone lies a gemstone of kindness waiting to be polished."
—Ruby Cranbourne

For my beloved husband, Louis, in thanksgiving of his
loving kindness and encouragement throughout
these many years. What a blessing he is to
all who know him.

Also for those who served during the Vietnam War
and their loved ones who worried back home.

One

My name is Juliet, and I swear on my great-grandmother Itasca's grave that nearly everything I am about to tell you is the gospel, according to me. If I give you my word, then "You can Shake 'N Bake it" and eat it later just like they did in those General Foods commercials. I can't say what Evangeline's or Jewel's take on it might be, but that problem belongs to them.

If you had lost your parents like dominos in a row when you were seven and nine and a half years old, as Evangeline and I did, your heart might be like hollow, bitter dark chocolate, without sweetness or depth. Instead, we were tended to by our grandparents, Walt and Ruby, like two small pots of bubbling *dulce de leche*. Now, what we have become is a mixture of sweet caramel and cream, with only shavings from the old, bitter, dark past sprinkled on top.

I have come to realize that whatever age you were when you were orphaned is the age you remain inside, forever. So it is with Evangeline and me. What I have to say about all that is this: two good people with loving hearts can make a difference that cannot be measured. Now that I am forty-five and Evangeline is trailing right behind me, I can look back and see what their goodness cost them.

Years later, in February of 2003, I am beginning to discover that my life was like a box of Crystal Wedding Oats with a treasure inside I could take out and examine once I blew the dust off it. Take Jewel Gemburree, for instance, who had been sparkly like cut glass until she broke one day. After college, except for phone calls, occasional holidays, and funerals, she vanished from our lives so completely that Evangeline and I could hardly remember the way

1

she smelled of cinnamon and brown sugar from morning toast or the way she'd once held a tambourine waiting for her cue on station KOFF.

Our grandmother Ruby had maintained that Jewel had a special calling on earth, that her mission was different from ours, but that it was important nonetheless. Whatever Ruby said, our grandfather Walt generally agreed with, and they'd both treated her as though she was just like us girls. Jewel was Pearl's daughter, her only child, and Ruby and Walt's only niece. It was her sudden reappearance, however, that took my breath away.

I had just gone into Densesky's Groceries and Dry Goods to try to buy some nutmeg because I had whirls of cooking to do for Valentine's Day. Among other things, I planned to make heart-shaped lebkuchen cookies to give away to my House of Cranbourne customers. My store is located in downtown Fireside, just around the corner from station KOFF, where I also broadcast *The Cranbourne Variety Hour* every Saturday afternoon. Next thing I knew, who should wheel right up and touch me on the shoulder but Jewel? Seeing her out of the blue was startling and got me to thinking about how much I missed my grandparents and Ruby's sisters, Pearl and Sapphire. My conscience burned when I remembered how I had failed them all.

"I didn't know you were in town," I said, dropping the plastic container of nutmeg into the red store basket I carried over my arm. In her wheelchair, Jewel looked thin and brittle, like fall leaves. I reached over and hugged her gently, almost afraid I'd break her.

I felt suddenly overcome with worry about why her condition had deteriorated so much since we were last together. Furthermore, how would she feel about seeing me after all these years? Would she hold the past against me? Were there silent grudges festering in her heart?

"Just got in this afternoon," she said. "I came back to spend a little time with Charles, the best father on earth. I found a picture of him and Chuck Yeager standing next to Glamorous Glennis in forty-six, not long after World War II was over. It was in the *Boston Globe* archive. I had it blown up and autographed. You know he'll be eighty-four years old come July, right?

"Time has gotten away from me. I didn't realize he was that old because there's something about him that just doesn't age. His mind is as good as ever. What a sweetheart he is too."

"Time? You may remember, that's what I teach in Cambridge. I guess I've got as good a grasp on it as anyone. Charles can't have much left, even if he seems fine. But you're right, Juliet. He is the sweetest man in the universe." Jewel smiled, looked away at the rack of spices, vegetable oils, and boxes of Jell-O and then back at me.

"That picture ought to mean the world to him, Jewel. That and seeing you."

Jewel shrugged and gestured toward her wheelchair. "I'd have come a while ago, but as you can see, it isn't easy for me to get around. While I'm here, I guess I might as well close up Mama's house."

"I'm so sorry. I know how hard that must be. We all loved your mother, and Charles has meant a good deal to all of us, hasn't he?" I managed to say something, at least, although her acknowledgment of her condition pricked my heart like roses at a funeral.

"Yes, indeed," she said. Her eyes teared up briefly.

"Pearl's been gone, what. . . three years?"

"As of February 26," she said. "Should have done it a while back but just couldn't. Thank you for checking on the place from time to time and keeping it going until I could face it."

"Pearl was a wonderful person. I was glad to do my part. Was the least I could do, really."

Our good friend Selma came around the corner of the aisle and said, "Now what do we have here? Jewel Lee Gemburree, did you just pop into the air like Samantha Stevens from *Bewitched* or what? Oh my stars! I cannot believe my eyes."

At seventy-nine, Selma was still the fashion icon of Fireside. What with her beaded chandelier earrings, apricot jersey dress, long matching sweater, and high-heeled chocolate leather boots, she was a walking advertisement for the fashions at Densesky's where she'd worked for so many years.

Densesky's had once had a sizable yard goods and sewing notions department but now had quite a selection of smart ready-to-wear outfits. The women of Fireside had shifted their attention from the sewing machine to the workplace. Now they worked outside the home at the Fireside Electric Cooperative, in the local bank, at the courthouse, or at the Fireside Inn and served as school board members on the Fireside ISD. Where high school girls once practiced home economics, they now studied computers and circus arts in PE. In Selma's opinion, girls no longer knew how to thread a needle, much less sew on a button. Maybe the boys could learn how to do that, she once pointed out.

Now Selma was patting Jewel on the arm and saying, "Shug, so glad to see you."

I studied Jewel, now in her early thirties. She wore a silver bracelet, a white T-shirt, and jeans with holes in the knees. Her wiry black hair was long, parted in a zigzag, and ironed straight as a board. She lived in Cambridge, Massachusetts, and taught a course entitled "Advanced Time Evolution, Wave Function, and the Schrödinger Equation" at the Massachusetts Institute of Technology. In her spare time, Jewel had also taught German literature until the hectic schedule eventually overwhelmed her. Due to her demanding career Jewel had simply not traveled to Texas often. Moreover, Pearl had died suddenly from having failed to look both ways before crossing the street while visiting Jewel. She had been cremated, her ashes scattered around the Ryman Auditorium in Nashville, where she'd played percussion on several occasions.

Jewel was therefore both familiar to me and yet a stranger as so many years had passed since our last good visit. We froze awkwardly, examining each other, and the silence made me nervous. Long absences, Pearl's death, and Jewel's poor health had put a strain on the ties that bound us. Like rubber bands, we had been stretched to snapping position.

Then the Dixie Chicks' "Long Time Gone" came over the store's speakers and filled the silence. I couldn't think of a blessed thing to say to Jewel, and so I just turned to Selma and said, "Quick, Selma. What did you have to eat on this date in February of 1946?"

"Oh, honey. Do you think I'm old enough to remember 1946?" she said, putting her hands on her hips and sending me a mock frown.

"Probably not, but just supposing you are."

She winked, laughed, and tilted her piled-to-the-sun blonde hair in thought. "Well, I was out of sorts due to hormones that day and ate an entire box of Moon Pies, plus one piece of fried chicken, just to balance things."

After we all laughed, Jewel reached over and held Selma's hand, saying, "I've been waiting years to ask you a question." Jewel had never walked again since the accident when we were kids. Had her spine not been involved, she might have realized her dream of becoming a dancer. Seeing her now made me ashamed as I remembered the role I'd played in it.

"What's that, Jewel Bug?" said Selma.

"Can you do the Lindy Hop?"

"You mean that swing dance?"

"Yes, that's the one."

"Well, I used to could. Been a good forty-five years since I last tried. I did win first place at the Victory Falls Annual Dance Competition. Norman and I still shake a leg every Saturday night of the year. Mainly the Electric Slide and your basic two-step. Why are you asking, girl?"

"I like to go to downtown Boston and watch couples practice sometimes. Love their costumes, how fast they move. All those dips, tucks, and aerials make my heart race."

"That a fact?" said Selma. She looked at me and smiled. "Juliet, why don't you and Evangeline bring William and Jacob over to Diamond's Dance Hall on Saturday night, and we'll show Jewel Bug a good time? I think the Lindy Hop is coming back to me." Selma hugged us both good-bye, and headed over to the soda fountain to dip ice cream for customers.

"See you later, Jewel", I said, reaching down to pat her shoulder. "Got to get back to the ranch and locate some memorabilia for our next broadcast. Let's talk soon."

An hour later, Evangeline and I climbed shaky steps into the cobweb-covered attic to search for some of Ruby's old stage costumes, Walt's felt Stetson, and some photographs. I wanted to take them down to station KOFF and put them in the window to promote the coming Saturday's program on the history of *The Cranbourne Variety Hour*.

In the scheme of things, it hadn't been very long since Evangeline and I had placed the twin-hearts headstone on Walt and Ruby's graves, and we were still missing them something awful. Dedicating a program to honor their enduring love for each other, for us, and their devotion to the broadcast seemed like the perfect way to celebrate Valentine's Day.

The attic was covered to high heaven in granddaddy longlegs, moldy cardboard boxes, and pink cotton candy–like exposed insulation. There were decaying trunks that dated from the 1800s through the twentieth century. However, one of the newest had no doubt been purchased by Walt after Ruby's passing. It was lined with cedar, heavy as an anvil, and stuffed to the brim with things he'd thought important.

There was a somber photograph of Ruby's mother, Emerald, in her billowy, faded black dress with its high collar, as she sat stiff-backed in the family heirloom chair that dated back to the Civil War, and Ruby's father, Angus, with his long white beard and black coat standing behind her.

The chair had been placed outside, next to the cottonwood tree that is located next to the windmill, and alongside it, the water tank with the date November 25, 1905, scrawled in concrete by a stick. The cottonwood tree was much smaller then—not much more than a sapling—and gave little hint as to its future magnificent glory. You see, the Cranbourne ranch had once belonged entirely to the Gemburree family. Gradually, they had deeded over land to each of their three daughters, but Walt and Ruby had eventually bought out her sisters' portions.

I gathered all the pictures I could find of Ruby and her sisters and put them into one pile. But the sweetest photograph of all was of Ruby. Ruby as a barefoot three-year-old in overalls with unruly red hair, feeding maize to baby chicks and smiling shyly at the camera.

Next, I found another of my favorites: one of Ruby and her sisters all dressed in various versions of black taffeta with elbow-length white gloves and bodacious satin headbands. They were the famous Gemburree sisters, who'd one by one fallen in love with the music industry and it with them.

Ruby, Sapphire, and Pearl had draped themselves over the hood of Ruby's red Thunderbird, looking as if they were about to ride in the Fireside Butternut Squash Fall Festival parade. What they were really up to was promoting their new album, *The Fireside Book of Love*. The one-and-only Pearl had wiggly blonde hair that some called naturally marcelled. She leaned against Ruby's right shoulder, and raven-haired Sapphire leaned against her left. Both sisters had an arm wrapped around Ruby's neck.

Ruby's hair was the flame igniting every picture, always making her the shining star in the pile of baby photos, newspaper clippings of her showing off her prize-winning vegetable garden, and of course, a snapshot of her smiling brilliantly as she cozied up to her beloved Walt. He was leaning against his coal-black 1968 Chevrolet truck and had pulled her toward him like a star to the sun.

His summer straw Stetson was set way back on his head the way James Dean sometimes wore his. Khaki sleeves were rolled up to his elbows, and his shirt was unbuttoned one down. He held his hand up to his lips and blew a kiss to Ruby that hung in midair, frozen in time for all these years. I pictured her reaching up to catch it a second later. Like wedding roses in the family Bible, they are forever pressed just so in my memory.

Underneath the pictures of the Gemburree sisters was a snapshot of Pearl and our mother, Marguerite. They were fishing in the Pedernales River and wore blue jeans rolled up just below their knees, old cotton blouses, and scraggly straw hats. Pearl had caught a decent-size catfish, but Marguerite leaned up against a boulder with her cane pole propped up beside her and held her nose, as though the stink of fish and old moss was more than she could bear. In the other hand, she held a lit cigarette and looked at it as though it was her one sure thing. But Pearl smiled broadly, as though that catfish were the best ever caught. Although their friendship was based on a mutual love of music and a dozen or so songs they'd written together, they were as different as river water and red clay. Where Marguerite impulsively flowed this way and that, Pearl was thoughtful and stuck to her bedrock foundation.

It was the same day when Walt's old ranch truck nearly ran over Pearl that cemented their friendship, however. She had parked not far from the river's edge and walked in front of the rusted 1953 Ford to inspect some broken fence line. Like an old warhorse, it jumped out of gear and headed right toward Pearl. When Marguerite saw it coming, she dropped her cigarette and shoved her out of the way. I kid you not, this may have been the only moment our mother's impulsivity served others well.

That day became the bobbing cork in their friendship and was what helped it stay afloat through strained times to come. They spent long hours swapping newspaper clippings of Patsy Cline and Loretta Lynn and playing Yahtzee in our living room while Evangeline and I were just old enough to play Go Fish. When Marguerite whined about how boring her life had become, Pearl would just say, "There's nothing boring about raising two girls. Why, every day is packed to the gills with love." Then our mother would roll her eyes and reply, "If you say so."

Marguerite counted upon a somewhat older Pearl for guidance and validation. It was no wonder, then, when Pearl, our mother's go-to support system, began to go on long tours and devote herself to music that Marguerite floundered. If Pearl wanted to get her career back on track, then so did Marguerite. But Pearl didn't have any children to raise, and therein lay the difference. So when our father, James, went off to fight in old Vietnam and Pearl left on tour, the cork that had kept Marguerite from drowning disappeared completely under water.

It was Sapphire who most quickly threaded the worm on life's hook while others cut bait. She was the middle of the Gemburree sisters and always cast her lines wherever she thought it made sense, without worry whether the fish's feelings got hurt. She said Marguerite was a needy person—that she'd soak up all the water from a sponge just by standing next to it—that she couldn't help herself from taking every last drop of all to be had. She did not care much for our mother, but as a Gemburree, she stood by us anyway.

Later, when Pearl returned from tour, Sapphire pointed out that it was easy to see that her sister's most endearing quality was found in her determination to rescue others. This ultimately meant that she sometimes found herself in difficult positions as she repeatedly tried to save our mother from drowning in mistakes created by a self-absorbed world view. Our determined Pearl simply paddled forward, no matter the challenge, by demonstrating how to hold her head up despite the depth of rising water.

I blew a kiss to the picture of Pearl and my mother and then stared upward at the naked attic beams, counting granddaddy longlegs until my eyes crossed, fighting back the tears. Memories of how Ruby and her sisters had ruled as queens over the Fireside Gem Society, Maitlin County, and the rest of us were so strong.

"Evangeline, do you think the rumors about Pearl were true?"

My sister rolled her eyes and toyed with her silver hoop earrings. "What's the truth got to do with anything? And anyway, who's still alive to tell us?"

"Selma Davis Densesky, but I don't want to know the truth if it differs from what I believe."

"That could be a sore subject with her, anyway, on account of their friendship. I'd walk on eggshells if I were you," she warned me.

"I'll glide over those eggshells like a chicken hawk," I said.

Just then, the telephone rang. I hightailed it down the attic stairs and into Ruby's kitchen, just in time to catch the old black rotary wall phone on its last ring. Hadley's voice poured through the receiver like honey from a spoon.

"Hey, girl," she said. "Hope I'm not interrupting anything."

"Just a trip down memory lane," I replied, fidgeting with the wall-calendar picture of an old-fashioned picnic with Uncle Sam plopped down in the middle of the perfect American family on their quilt. "How's business?" I asked, referring to my House of Cranbourne store in downtown Fireside, where my longtime friend, Hadley King Hammerschmidt, worked. My store sold all kinds of unique items like ketchup and mustard dispensers in the image of George Burns and Gracie Allen, Edsel hood ornaments mounted on shellacked wooden boxes for that special Father's Day gift for the man in your life, and jars of homemade Fireside Organic Goat Chili from my range to yours.

"Business is flying just as sure and straight as Air Force One, Juliet. But there is one itsy bitsy problem, though," said Hadley.

"What's that?"

"We're just about out of those *de-lish* heart-shaped petit fours."

"You mean the orange-chocolate-coated ones that have liquid Dutch chocolate centers or the 'Your Cheatin' Heart' ones stuffed with antacids for that too-full-after-barbeque-and-chili feeling?"

"Neither," she replied. "The ones you borrowed the recipe from Selma's sister to make. You know—Tango Tangerines' Famous Cha-Cha-Cha Hearts on cabaret legs with dancing shoes—the ones that are stuffed to the chocolate shell with tangerine pudding cake."

"Oh dear. . . all right, then, I'd best get cooking."

"Don't you want to know who ordered them?" she asked, obviously dying to tell me.

"Go on. . . I know you'll tell me anyway."

"William Bartlett just came in and ordered fifty dozen Cha-Cha-Cha Hearts to send to his best clients for Valentine's.

"Is that all?" I asked, crossing my eyes and shuddering.

"No, there's the order from some gent in Oklahoma who wants you to do a special favor for him."

"And just what might that be?" I was almost afraid to ask, due to my past experience with unusual requests.

"He wants a gigantic chocolate heart dressed in a cowboy tuxedo. He asked that you give it a pocket that stays open so he can slip an engagement ring inside. Also wants you to include a card with a microchip that plays 'Hey, Good Lookin'' by Hank Williams."

"A tall order, Hadley, but I'll do anything for a couple in love." I smiled to myself, imagining how I might feel if my boyfriend, William Bartlett, ever gave me an engagement ring in such a creative fashion or any fashion at all. I surprised myself by even thinking such a thing, considering we hadn't been dating all that long. Not this time, anyway. Not since we'd broken up after high school graduation.

After I hung up the telephone, I walked back into the garage and peered up the folding stairs that led to the attic. I could just make out Evangeline as she scrutinized a photo. "What are you looking at?" I called out.

"A picture of Jewel taken when she was a baby," said Evangeline. "It was all a crying shame, wasn't it?"

"Sure was," I said, wondering whether Evangeline completely understood what I had done, as she had been so young at the time. It was a good thing I hadn't become a Catholic; confession had never been my strongpoint. "Was also a shame the way Sport went."

"Well, that was mainly my fault," said Evangeline, fishing a tissue out of her pocket. "For the love of chocolate, what were we thinking?"

"I suppose we weren't thinking at all."

Two

In September of 1968, my sister Evangeline and I were just starting to adjust to the fact that our father was dead and never coming back from Vietnam and that our mother was more partial to living in New York and pursuing her Broadway career than she was to raising her girls. Furthermore, we were busily tucking ourselves into our grandparents' lives like kangaroo joeys in pouches. We didn't want to get more than shouting distance from them most times, didn't particularly want to share the space between Walt and Ruby with any other child, and sometimes not even with my new best friend, Hadley King, who spent the night on rare occasions. If you'd been put out to the curb like the Flintstones' saber-tooth tiger, Baby Puss, you'd be worried too.

Not long after our great-grandmother Itasca died from congestive heart failure and puredee orneriness, Ruby got to missing the old days when she and her two sisters, Pearl and Sapphire, used to tour the country, singing in honky-tonks and playing music. She had been in a blue funk ever since that day in May when she'd cracked her head wide open by catching her heel on Adah Mae Applewhite's porch steps and had to go to the hospital. It had been a miserable time for her because of the death of her mother-in-law during Walt's absence and whatnot. My sister Evangeline and I had about driven her crazy due to our despair over our missing parents and our ability to make monkeys out of ourselves. Perhaps our poor behavior was due in part to the fact that we worried to no end that our grandparents would ultimately ditch us too. If Ruby went into Fireside to sell eggs on Saturday morning, Evangeline and I stuck to her like glue, just in case she aimed the Thunderbird for parts unknown and left our sorry behinds for good.

What saved and united us was the Saturday afternoon radio program we'd performed in for the past year. Ruby played her fiddle while Evangeline pushed the buttons during airtime at station KOFF, and I read all the advertising copy and just said what naturally came to my mind. This gave us something cheerful to focus on as a family and depend on during the weekends when we weren't in school.

On Labor Day, Evangeline and I were in the living room arguing over who got to pull the RCA's on button to tune in to *Captain Kangaroo*. I was especially fond of Mr. Green Jeans, but it was Mr. Moose and Bunny Rabbit who spoke to Evangeline. She loved to watch them drop ping-pong balls on the captain's head.

"I got dibs on the TV because I got to it first," said Evangeline, pouting. Her puffball bangs frizzed up over her eyes, making me think she could claim kinship to the captain if she wanted.

"You're a Pinocchio if I ever saw one. Why, your nose is growing about a foot a minute," I said and crossed my arms. My blue jeans had grown short throughout the school year, and now that I was ten years old and three inches taller, looked just like pedal pushers. I reached down to brush off a black ant that was crawling up my bare ankle. "Nothing doing. I got here first."

"Rabbit, Squirrel, you two will argue over whether the moon is round or curved," said Walt as he wedged between us and pulled out the TV knob himself.

He reached up to push back his gray hair, and this is where his resemblance to Gregory Peck comes in: He grasped both sides of his collar with his thumbs pointing upward and raised his eyebrows at us.

"Thunder!" said Ruby when she came into the living room. She was holding her fiddle and bow and looking mighty peeved. "I could hear you girls arguing from in yonder. Was trying to practice my fiddle, but I cannot hear myself think."

Ruby took her fiddle and went out to the washhouse to play, which caused me to abandon my post presiding over the TV usage. I picked up my Brownie camera and decided to follow her. You see, I still worried plenty about Ruby since the day she'd fallen, and cracked her head. It wasn't like there was a spare Ruby roaming around. She was all Evangeline and I had since our mother had ditched us like muddy shoes on the porch steps. I sat on the cellar door in the shelter of a pomegranate tree not far from the washhouse, listened to her tune up and then play "Amazing Grace."

Naturally, Ruby still pined for our daddy, her only child. She had never forgiven Vietnam for stealing James's life away, but she rarely spoke of it. I could just tell, knowing her like I did. She still got that far-off look in her eyes and would sometimes tear up whenever a man his age stood in front of the Fireside Barber Shop or if she went to deliver eggs on Saturday mornings and ran into one of his old classmates.

Once, when she drove her Thunderbird along our ranch road, a lost Chevrolet Corvair met us spewing caliche everywhere. Like a streak of lightning, Ruby turned the car around to prove to herself whether, magically, it had been James. That we all hadn't made some terrible mistake and he was still alive somehow. That he hadn't been biding his time to spring it on us like a bean sprout waiting to pop up through her garden soil. Evangeline and I just sat in the back and buttoned our lips. You know what they say, *Miracles happen every day*, and we were desperate believers.

Directly, Walt appeared in pursuit of Ruby and went in the washhouse just as she quit playing. I left my perch on the cellar door, hid behind the rain tower, and watched them. Ruby sat on a rusted green metal chair by the wringer washer. A bucket of clothespins rested on the cement floor to her right, a pile of old *National Geographic* magazines leaning like the Tower of Pisa to her left. She looked forlorn, like a lost fiftysomething-year-old child. However, she perked up when Walt entered the tiny room and wrapped his arms around her. Ruby smiled and hugged him back harder.

"What's the matter with my girl?" he asked.

"Aw, I don't know," she said sadly as the smile left her face. "Just can't wrap my mind around a few things, I guess."

"What might that be?" he asked.

"How quick things change."

"Like what, Ruby, darlin'?"

"Take James, for instance. Seemed like one day he was being born, and the next he was taken from us."

"I know," said Walt, his voice growing softer. "Wasn't fair."

"Then when you went up to New York to track down Marguerite, your mother passed away one night. By the afternoon of the next, I was in the hospital with my head broken like an egg on the sidewalk," she said, reaching up to touch the back of her head.

"Things do take a turn faster than we can blink sometimes," said Walt. "You got to keep your sights where your aim is, though. Straight ahead."

"I know," she said. "You're right, but my heart is having a hard time believing."

"Why don't you go on and play the fiddle with Sapphire and Pearl, like you done when you was girls?"

"I couldn't do that anymore than the man in the moon," said Ruby.

"Well, why not?" he asked.

"Because they're going on tour this fall and won't be back until the holidays. Heading out to Nashville, Memphis, Kansas City, and who knows where all, to promote our new album. No telling how long they'll be gone. . . Maybe Christmas before they get back. Can't say for sure."

"Well, why don't you go on with them? They can't make it without a good fiddle player. And you sing twice as pretty as Patsy Cline or Connie Francis. Now that I think about it, you sing like an angel. Remind me again, Ruby, honey, the title of your album is. . .?"

"The *Fireside Book of Love, featuring the Gemburree Sisters: Ruby on fiddle, Sapphire on steel guitar, and Pearl on percussion,*" she said, smiling, pretending she was announcing their show.

Walt clapped and whistled when he heard that, as though for the first time. He knew it gave her a powerful boost to think about her work.

Now I could see Walt's back as he leaned up against the screen door of the washhouse. At six foot four, he was a good big man. He lifted his arms and pulled Ruby toward him. I could see nothing of her but her tiny shoes in between his size 13 ones. She was no more than five feet with shoes on, so it wasn't surprising I could virtually see nothing else of her.

"But what would I do without you if I went?" she asked, sniffling.

"You'd get along," he said. "I'd take care of the girls. We'd be waiting for you, Ruby, darlin', when you got back. It would be good for you to have some fun. And I'd teach them a thing or two about cattle and checkers. Maybe we'll tune in to some Gene Autry pictures or watch the Lone Ranger and Tonto ride into the sunset one more time."

"I don't know, Walt," said Ruby.

"Well, think about it. I promise to make your homecoming extra special if you do. Say, did I ever tell you that you're one good-looking tomato?"

"No, don't believe you ever phrased it quite thataway."

"My blue-ribbon girl."

Like her award-winning garden, Ruby's life had been ripe. Ripe for sainthood long before she'd tended and buried her mother-in-law, loved us girls to pieces, and saved Adah Mae Applewhite from the mold and mildew that had rotted her life from the inside out. Then there was her champion fiddlin' onstage and on *The Cranbourne Variety Hour* on station KOFF.

The thought that Ruby might leave us for a while choked the breath outa me. I had a big coughing fit right there on the sidewalk outside Ruby's washhouse. Then they both popped through the screen door and faced me where I'd been hiding, pressed against the side of the rain cistern like a chameleon. I now hid my camera behind my back.

"Squirrel," said Walt, calling me by the pet name he'd given me. "Were you listening in on our conversation?"

"It was on accident," I said when I finally quit coughing. "I just wanted to know where you were and came to find you."

"From now on, you need to speak up straightaway when you find us. Eavesdropping is against our family code," said Walt, frowning.

"What is our family code?" I asked, thinking about the Morse code mentioned in my Nancy Drew novels. "Does it involve tapping?"

"No, it's our understanding of how a Cranbourne ought to behave."

I suppose it's fair to say that both of us girls had made Ruby lose her last marble. Evangeline was now eight and ripe for pranks and oddball collections of Dubble Bubble gum wrappers that started to stink after a while, paper labels from vegetable and soup cans that were folded and bound by a rubber band, and Betty Crocker points from cake mixes. Then there was an envelope stuffed with all those sticky S&H Green Stamps. She thought she might redeem all her collections for cash somehow and that she'd be living high on the hog thanks to her persistence and planning ahead.

She'd become too ambitious, however, and removed every single label from the Campbell's Soup and Pork 'N Beans cans, Green Giant Wax Beans, RO*TEL Tomatoes, Spam, Dole Sliced Pineapple, PET Evaporated Milk, Sugary Sam Sweet Potatoes, Musselman's Applesauce, and Vienna sausages before they had been opened. So now, when Ruby opened her cabinet, she saw a sea of fifty-three naked tin cans with tiny white scraps of paper stuck to remnants of glue.

Please understand that when I say Ruby's kitchen was her domain, it was also part of her personal identity. Every item in the cabinets, from a tin of cream of tartar to jars of maraschino cherries, pickled pearl onions, tins of smoked oysters, and cans of sauerkraut had been perfectly organized, with labels facing outward. It saved her time and frustration to operate in a tidy, thoughtful fashion, and it annoyed her to no end if anyone messed with her system.

That evening, dinner was unusual, to say the least. Every time Ruby opened a mystery can Evangeline had unwrapped, she simply put the contents into a bowl and served it to us for dinner. While Walt got to eat something special she had cooked, Evangeline and I ate our fill of canned black olives, sauerkraut, Spam, and pineapple. We stared glumly at our plates.

"Mamaw, why are you making me eat this too? It was Evangeline who done it. I was just an innocent bystander," I said, pouting.

"Well, Squirrel, you were standing by, so I'd call it guilt by association. Next time you stand around and watch Rabbit make a mess of my kitchen, you might ought to think about coming to tell me. Furthermore, you are in trouble for following me out to the washhouse and spying this afternoon."

I glared at Evangeline and kicked her shoe beneath the table. "Dagnabbit, Rabbit."

"Who do you think you are, Yosemite Sam? I'm gonna tell on you for kicking me," she muttered. "Mamaw!"

Walt told us to put down our forks on the table and head off to bed if we couldn't act any better than that. We could go to bed on hungry stomachs and see whether it improved our attitudes. He expected us to be shipshape bright and early and to go let out the chickens, which had been shut up at night to be protected from predators, before we walked to the school bus. This was a job that could prove messy when we traipsed through droppings in the chicken yard. Furthermore, it was some distance from the house.

And if that didn't change our attitudes, he said, we could shovel manure in the barnyard until we felt good behavior coming on.

That night, after Evangeline and I had gone to bed, I could hear Ruby and Walt's soft conversation coming from their room.

"Think you might be right, Walt. Maybe if I go with Pearl and Sapphire to promote *The Fireside Book of Love*, I could pull myself out of the dumps and be more fun to have around."

"Seem plenty fun to me, Ruby, darlin'," said Walt, kissing her loudly.

"Oh, Walt," she said, giggling. "That tickles."

"Remember how much fun we had when we were courting and entered into that twenty-four-hour dance contest over in Longhorn Caverns?"

"Do I ever," giggled Ruby. "Pa sat right there in a chair and watched every step we took, just in case you got out of line and danced too close."

"But he fell asleep, and I snuck in a good kiss," said Walt. "Do you remember the song we were dancing to?"

"'On the Sunny Side of the Street.'" Ruby sighed happily. "It was the first time you ever kissed me."

"That was a forbidden kiss, where now all our kisses are sanctified. In my book, each one tastes even better than the last. Ruby, darlin', you were fun then, but you're just as much fun now. When you get back, we'll make up for any kisses we might have missed out on while you're gone."

"Promise?" asked Ruby, softly.

"I do."

Three

As was our custom, on Saturday morning, Evangeline and I helped Ruby wash the hens' eggs, grade them, and place them in cartons. Then we took great care to meticulously bathe, dress in our going-to-town clothes, and head out in Ruby's Thunderbird.

Like chicks following a mother hen, we followed Ruby out to our usual nests in the red car. I sat in the front, and Evangeline draped herself across the back seat, propping up her feet on the side window. When Ruby gave her the eye, she put her feet down and smiled with false innocence.

"Straighten up and fly right, Rabbit," said Ruby.

"I will, Mamaw," she said sweetly. "You can depend on me."

As we barreled down the caliche road toward Fireside, Ruby turned on the radio to liven things up. Soon, she began belting out the lyrics to Buddy Holly and the Crickets' "Maybe Baby." Evangeline and I couldn't help but get into the act, although we were sorry singers.

We had a trunkful of eggs and Ruby's fiddle so she could play on our Saturday program at station KOFF as usual. She had been teaching Evangeline, who showed some talent right off the bat, but she knew better than to even try with me.

My talent was talking, and that was my portion of *The Cranbourne Variety Hour*. So when we finished delivering eggs to Ruby's customers at the drugstore, various businesses in town, and Densesky's Groceries and Dry Goods, we went straightaway to station KOFF, in a two-story yellow cupcake of a building that stood facing the Maitlin County Courthouse.

While Evangeline and I argued often and loud, we mostly behaved when we were on the air. Mostly. I began the broadcast the way I normally did: "Hello, this is Juliet Cranbourne broadcasting *The Cranbourne Variety Hour* to you from station KOFF. Welcome to Fireside, Texas—where no strangers are known! We are the home of the free and the brave and the everlasting polite persons. We never take the last cookie, except maybe Evangeline does sometimes. Even during a bake-off, we always hope the other person wins. Most importantly, no one here eats beets, but we thank the hostess for them anyway.

"The following is a paid announcement by the Maitlin County Ornithology Welfare Department. Join us next Thursday at twelve noon in the Fireside Hardware Store break room. Please remember to bring a sack lunch. Noted buzzard psychologist Weldon Rhodes will speak on a topic of national and local concern: Buzzard depression—do they get more than they bargained for on our highways?

"This is just a reminder from the Cranbourne family to be kind to buzzards this weekend, and all days, especially those feathered friends who are under a lot more stress than their ancestors were. Put yourself in their claws for a moment; just when they dive down for breakfast, along comes a car. Remember, if you can be a good friend to a buzzard, you can be a good friend to anyone. Just one of life's little golden lessons.

"Next, we have Ruby Cranbourne striking up the fiddle with Roy Turk and Lou Handman's tune, 'Are You Lonesome Tonight?' It is performed in the style of Elvis Presley, whom we all know and love here in Fireside, Texas, despite his marriage to Priscilla last year."

After the show ended, Ruby pulled me aside and said, frowning, "Juliet, you do rip the pages right out of *Emily Post's Etiquette* now and then. . . and you also press some of my buttons on a regular basis. I think I'd better not take too much for granted while I'm gone. And please don't speak of my dear friends Elvis and Priscilla that way."

Later, Ruby discussed every Saturday show that was to occur on station KOFF in her absence and laid out detailed program instructions for us, as well as what would happen if we didn't behave ourselves on air. She said if we minded Walt and our manners to a T while she was gone, upon her return, she would drive Evangeline, myself, Hadley (my new best friend), and another child of my sister's choosing to Austin to view a taping of *The Uncle Jay Show* and to eat at the Piccadilly Cafeteria.

Evangeline and I crossed our hearts and hoped to die or stick a thousand needles in our eyes and swore we would mind our p's and q's. Ruby smiled at us, although she didn't look convinced.

"Will Packer Jack be there too?" asked Evangeline. "'Cause he is my favorite man in the world."

"Really?" said Ruby, looking surprised. "If Uncle Jay is on the show, so is Packer Jack."

"Groovy," said Evangeline.

When we went to the Methodist Church on Sunday, Ruby made certain we sat in the front pew. We saw Selma Davis and Mr. Densesky across the aisle from us. I supposed Ruby prayed fervently ahead for our good behavior in her absence, although she didn't say so. She did, however, insist that we shake hands with the minister, who gave us the eye on our way out. I was left with the feeling that the entire town of Fireside would have us in their crosshairs should we step out of line.

On Monday, Ruby busied herself with a jillion errands in preparation for her absence. There were bags of chicken feed, a card of safety pins, a box of Duz Detergent, S.O.S pads, Dove soap, sugar, Noxzema, Jell-O, Chiclets, Dr. Pepper, and apples to buy.

All those items, except for the chicken feed, could be bought at Densesky's. When we went into the dry goods section to buy safety pins and some lavender thread, Selma was dancing to Bobby Freeman's "C'mon and Swim," unaware that she had any customers at all. She was wearing a black lace mini dress with matching go-go boots and looked like a forty-something-year-old version of Nancy Sinatra, with piled-up hair and pearlized lipstick.

Evangeline doubled over laughing. "Looks like she's got a cat in her drawers fighting to get out every time she wiggles."

Ruby tried to suppress a smile and said, "Keep your thoughts to yourself, Rabbit."

Selma quit dancing when she realized we were watching and had a good laugh at herself. "You'd be dancing, too, if you were wearing this rock on your finger." Selma held up her left hand to show off the biggest diamond ring that had ever been seen in Fireside, Texas. "I'm engaged!"

"Well, who on earth bought you that ring?" asked Evangeline.

"Mr. Right, that's who! He proposed yesterday after we saw you in church. Look, I'm gonna try out my new last name on you: Selma Louise Davis Densesky. Isn't that beautiful? Just the sound of it makes my heart go pitty-patter."

Ruby cocked her head and smiled. "It does have a nice ring to it. Sounds right pretty. When do you aim to marry?"

"Valentine's Day," Selma said. "Just five months away." She fairly glowed with excitement. "They say the second time around is a charm."

"I want to be the flower girl," shouted Evangeline in excitement. "I've been waiting my whole life to be a flower girl, and I'm nearly growed up past it. It's now or never for me." Evangeline's little face was filled to overflowing with desire to be the showboat show-off she'd always wanted to be. All of us could see that.

"And I want to be a junior bridesmaid," I said, smiling broadly as I pictured myself in a smart, short red velvet dress with my black patent-leather Sunday shoes, because wouldn't she choose red for a wedding on Valentine's?

"Squirrel, Rabbit," said Ruby, trying to control her embarrassment. "That will only happen if she asks you. It's poor manners to invite yourselves, as you've just managed to do. Un-der-stand?" She enunciated each word slowly, as though she were chewing every syllable for extra emphasis.

"Yes, ma'am," we said, although I was already working up a scheme to get Selma to ask us herself.

Selma just smiled at us, said how sweet we were and that she and Mr. Densesky hadn't yet gotten down to wedding details. She handed Ruby a card of safety pins from a spin rack and got a spool of lavender thread down from rows of thread, all arranged perfectly, according to color.

After Ruby had paid her, we got into the Thunderbird and headed back to the ranch. We nagged her incessantly about being in Selma's wedding. But Ruby would make no concessions on our behalf. "Furthermore, this is not Miss Davis's first marriage. It's her second, and often second marriages are supposed to come with fewer frills, which means there may not be a flower girl or junior bridesmaid at all."

I asked her just who had come up with that outrageous rule? Wasn't it more important that Selma have her really big day made the most beautiful imaginable, especially with the added frills of Evangeline and myself? It was our *dream,* I said. Otherwise, we might as well just lie down in the middle of the highway like the buzzards I'd mentioned in my station KOFF broadcast.

"That's right, Mamaw," said Evangeline, who would have escaped our tirade in better shape had she not then added, "Now, don't be a square. Just give us what we want!" She smacked the back of Ruby's seat to dramatize her words and stared a hole through Ruby.

Ruby pulled the Thunderbird to a stop in front of the garage and said slowly, "E-van-ge-line, I ought to take the paddle to you."

We knew, however, that Ruby's threat had no whack behind it. She had never paddled either of us and, we were quite confident, never would. It was on the heels of that certain knowledge that Evangeline giggled. "Miss me, miss me, now you gotta kiss me."

Just then, Walt came out to the car to help Ruby unload the groceries. He was wearing his going-to-town khakis and Stetson. The toes of his brown lizard Tony Lama boots had a thin layer of caliche dust on them, which looked alien against the otherwise perfect shine.

Walt hadn't said a word as Evangeline wiggled out of the back seat, so she didn't realize he was behind her. She threw herself into a full-fledged go-ahead, I-dare-you-to-paddle-me performance, petulantly saying, "Oh, Mamaw, you wouldn't paddle a cute girl like me."

Walt loomed over Evangeline and tapped her on the arm. Surprised, she whirled around to see our grandfather not looking all that happy.

"Rabbit, I'd better not catch you giving your sweet mamaw a hard time. I'll tell her to give your dinner to the goats. Shame on you. Your mamaw has done nothing but take the very best care of you, and now you're treating her worse than most folks would treat a mangy dog. Straighten up and fly right—all the way to your room."

Walt lifted a bag of groceries and the large box of Duz out of the Thunderbird's trunk. He cocked his head in the direction of Evangeline as she disappeared through the screen door into the house.

"Just don't know what's gotten into Evangeline of late," he said, sighing.

"Well, I do," I piped up, lifting out a gallon of Clorox and a pack of toilet paper. "She's gotten too blessed big for her drawers. That's what!"

"She's not the only one," said Ruby as she dropped her car keys into her black patent-leather purse.

"That a fact?" said Walt, looking me in the eye.

"It must be contagious 'cause I didn't start it." I smiled angelically. "Evangeline done that."

"*Did* that!" said Ruby.

"Yes, ma'am." I hung my head and tried again. "Evangeline done did that."

I looked up just in time to see Ruby wince.

"I just think, Squirrel, that it wouldn't hurt for you to go keep Rabbit company in your room and to, well. . . just think a bit." Walt pointed toward the house and nodded his head. "Go on inside."

I felt confused about my banishment and whether it was on account of my recently acquired knowledge of grammar or if I had been sent because Ruby was just flat-out tired of listening to me. Like a turtle on vacation, I crept ever so slowly up the back steps and into the house and sat down on the bed.

After the death of our great-grandmother Itasca, we'd moved back into our old bedroom instead of having to sleep on the sofa bed in the living room. It had been repainted to give us a fresh start on account of her having died in it. Where the walls had once been cream colored, they were now the palest of lavender. We had a purple gingham bedspread with an actual dust ruffle and accent pillows, and on the wall was an honest-to-goodness poster of the Beatles with John Lennon wearing a furry vest. *Sergeant Pepper's Lonely Hearts Club* had always spoken to both us girls. Ruby had given it to us on Christmas the first year we came to stay for good.

Evangeline lay on the other side with her legs in the air. She repeatedly lifted and dropped her feet against the headboard with a dull thud.

"Get your foot off the headboard, Rabbit. You trying to get us grounded?" I asked indignantly.

"Nope, you dope on a rope," she responded.

"Listen, knothead—if we both don't shape up, Ruby and Walt might just haul our sorry behinds out to the city dump—and then where'd we be?"

"In a heap of a mess," she replied haughtily.

"You can bet your allowance on it!" I added.

"All fifty cents?" she asked incredulously.

"Maybe a whole month's worth—two dollars."

After Ruby put away the groceries in the kitchen, she stopped by our bedroom to make eye contact with us. We stood up tall and promised to shape up if we could just get out of our room.

"Fiddledeedee," she said, putting one hand on a hip.

"Don't worry, Mamaw," I said. "This time if Rabbit just doesn't do right, I'll set her straight."

"Walt will be in charge while I'm gone," she said emphatically. "If either one of you makes a mess, you'll have to answer to him. Remember, if you do well, you'll get to go to Austin. If you don't, I'll have you clean out all three chicken houses, and there'll be no dessert after dinner until you go to the university and get married. Do I make myself perfectly clear?"

"Yes, Mamaw," we said, as visions of a trip to Austin floated through our brains.

Moments later, just as Ruby was making a bowl of cherry Jell-O with fruit cocktail, the sounds of Pearl and Sapphire's voices came from the back door. The screen door opened, and Sapphire came through first, carrying a plate of icebox cookies and a pitcher of cinnamon mint iced tea, which was her specialty. Pearl was singing a verse from Jeannie C. Riley's "Harper Valley P.T.A.," and Sapphire turned to say, "No, don't sing that. We sung that just a while ago. Since we're near the Pedernales, let's sing, 'Shall We Gather at the River?'"

Ruby smiled bright as could be and joined in singing the hymn. After they finished singing, Sapphire handed us the plate of cookies while they sat around the kitchen table and drank iced tea.

My sister and I soon lost interest in adult conversation and went into the living room to watch the Beatles on an *Ed Sullivan Show* rerun. We started eating cookies as fast as we could and arguing over who was gonna get to marry George Harrison. My feelings had suffered some since Elvis had gone and married that Priscilla woman and left me out in the cold. I'd thought he would wait until I grew up and then marry *me*, but there's just no telling what caused him to cave in to another woman like he had. So now George was receiving most of my affection.

Evangeline said, "Squirrel, you can't have George because I saw him first."

Then I replied, "You're way too wet behind the ears for him, Rabbit. What he'd be looking for is an older gal like me. What he'd want with a child like you?"

Then she replied, "Oh yeah?" and snapped off the TV. "Bet you my entire bubblegum-wrapper collection he'd rather marry me."

I hitched up my high-water plaid pants that Walt and Ruby had given me for my birthday the previous March and straightened my shoulders underneath my iceberg-blue ruffled blouse. "I'm the one with style and who might could look British thanks to this hip Beatles' blouse I'm wearing. George would way rather marry me."

"Oh no," I overheard Ruby tell Pearl in the kitchen and set her glass of iced tea down on the table with a thud. Something about her voice caught my attention, causing me to abandon my argument with Evangeline. Next thing I knew, Ruby was crying. "It can't be."

"It's a tough old world we live in, sometimes," said Walt, who'd just come inside from checking on the cows. He'd thrown his hat on the counter and was washing his hands in the sink with Lava.

"When did you find out the rabbit died?" asked Ruby.

"A few months back," said Pearl.

Evangeline looked at me as we watched from the living room, peeking around the sofa. A look of horror crossed her face. "Mamaw said something about Rabbit dying, but I didn't die. And I ain't about to, because nobody can make me. Think I ought to go in the kitchen and show 'em I'm still kicking?"

"Nobody thinks you're dead, Rabbit. Hush up and put on your listening ears." I motioned for her to stay down behind the sofa and put my finger to my lips.

Sapphire said, "I can't believe you've kept this news all to yourself. You, who has never kept a secret in your entire life. Who's gonna raise the baby?" She raised two open palms and lifted them in question.

"Good golly, Miss Molly, this is some situation," said Ruby, sniffling.

"Did she just say *golly*, Rabbit?" I whispered behind the sofa.

"Gol-ly, she did," said Evangeline, doing her best to imitate Gomer Pyle.

Ruby said, "Maybe Walt and I should do it. We have a good marriage, and, well, we're in the child-rearing business again anyhow. We should be the ones to raise it."

27

"No, I want to," said Pearl. "Now's my chance to be a mother. I never found the right man to marry, but I always knew I wanted to have a child."

"Hardly a soul in Fireside would cotton to this," said Walt. "You being a single mother without a husband might not set well. This is a wonderful burg, but everything has its time and season here. It isn't a good idea to get things out of their natural order."

"I've never cared one whit about what other folks have thought about me. I'd sooner worry about whether doodlebugs had a dry place to burrow than to worry about the strange notions in other people's noggins," said Pearl.

"People wouldn't make a ruckus if Walt and I was to raise it," said Ruby.

"She's right," said Walt. "Always is."

"No, Ruby, I got my mind made up. Anyhow, it won't be just me. Sapphire will be there to back me up and help out with it."

Sapphire sighed. "Well, I have to admit we don't know doodly-squat about raising a child just yet, but we'll learn. You betcha. I'll be there to help love this little tyke."

"I believe we can do *anything* we set our minds to," said Pearl. "It ain't gonna be easy, but nothing worth having ever is. I've wanted and waited for this my whole life, and the time has finally come. Please don't get mad at me. I know I ain't going about this in the traditional way, but I need your support."

I heard sniffling from the kitchen, and presently, Ruby said, "Well, you're both Gemburrees, same as me. I don't know who among us is more ornery or stubborn. Guess we'd have to draw straws to figure that out. All I can say is, I'll stand *with* and *by* you."

"One thing's sure," said Walt. "It wouldn't help the girls if everybody in Fireside was to know where this baby come from. There'd be questions they ought not to have to answer, and tarnation, it just isn't anybody else's business. I think we need to tell the girls the truth when the time is right, but nobody else ought to know."

"That's right," said Pearl. "I'd appreciate it if you would all keep it locked away in your hearts for the baby's sake too."

"Let's light a candle to seal the promise, just like when we was girls," said Sapphire.

I heard Ruby's kitchen chair scooting back from the table and her footsteps as she walked over to the kitchen counter to retrieve her honeysuckle-scented candle and matches from the decorative metal box that hung above her electric stove. Presently, I heard her return to her chair, strike the match, and the sound of its brief *pssst* as it lighted.

"Oh, heavens, does this ever bring back memories," said Ruby. She paused for a moment and then said, "I hereby open the reunion session of the Fireside Gemburree Girls' Society. I see we have a quorum and a potential new member by the name of Walt Cranbourne."

"Sure do," replied Sapphire. "But he don't look much like a girl."

"Then we'll have to change our name," said Pearl. "How 'bout the Fireside Gem Society, males included?"

"We have a motion on the table," said Ruby. "All those in favor sing, 'He's the yellow rose of Texas.'"

Everyone laughed, and Pearl said, "Now, don't nobody make Walt feel unwelcome."

"The motion is carried," said Ruby. "Now for the rest of our new business. This is the real serious part. All of us who are in cahoots on this new baby must solemnly swear to never tell anyone about where he or she came from until we gaze upon the face of the Good Lord in Heaven or until voted otherwise by the communion of members in the Fireside Gem Society. Are we in agreement?"

"We are!" said everyone in the kitchen, including Walt.

"Well, then, hold out your palms while I drip a little wax to seal the deal," said Ruby. "Next, press your palm against that of the person next to you. Sapphire, you press Pearl's; Pearl, you press mine; and Walt, I'll press yours."

After everyone had obeyed her instructions, Ruby said, "Repeat after me: *nobody, not Chickenman, not Superman or the Shadow, can make us break our silence about this.*" They all snickered but repeated it word for word.

"Well, then, we're bound together by wax and promise until hell freezes over." Ruby pushed her chair back, stood up, and said, "How about we make a mess of fried chicken, green beans, new potatoes, and have a little coconut cake to celebrate? We've all got to pack for the tour before we go to bed tonight, so let's get the lead out of our drawers!"

Four

When Ruby and her sisters drove off in the brown American Motors Ambassador station wagon pulling the Airstream trailer at dawn the next morning, we all tearfully waved goodbye. Our mamaw had always been a looker, but now, in her emerald-green shirt-waist traveling dress, she looked like the queen of stage, screen, and the world of music. She took a deep breath, let a tear slip as she blew us all a kiss goodbye, and then pulled herself together.

We had the sinking feeling there would be no good meals until she returned, and certainly, she wouldn't be hugging us when we needed it. It kind of made me mad, really, to think that her music and whatever mystery baby they'd talked about were more important than the three of us she'd left behind.

Soon as they were out of sight, Walt said, "OK, Squirrel, we've got to head to the barn and milk the cow. When we get through with that, you can help me cook breakfast. Rabbit, you go on out to all three chicken yards and let the hens out of their coops. Pour a bucket of feed into their troughs. Afterward, they need to peck and eat. They've got worms to scratch up. Look out for chicken snakes, and don't step in a pile of mess."

Rabbit just stood there on the back porch, frozen and pale. "But you know I can't stand the thought of snakes, Popo."

"Just pay attention where you put your feet and your hands. It's part of living in Texas. I've taught you which ones are poisonous and which aren't. Just respect them, and they'll respect you."

Evangeline slowly made her way toward the chicken yards while Walt and I went to milk Ruby's cow, Jessie. I knew that nervous creature really well because Evangeline and I had spent many a morning on top of the milk shed, eating range cubes while Ruby worked. Jessie liked to kick, quick as look at us. Any noise unnerved her so badly that Ruby had to snub her close and put blinders on her so she wouldn't be as likely to kick her or knock over the milk bucket. I couldn't figure out why Ruby kept her because, in my book, any cow with bad nerves was bound to give sour milk.

Walt gave me a short milking lesson, although I had watched it done many times. I did what he told me to but said I didn't much like it and that I was going to be replacing Miss Kitty on *Gunsmoke* when she got too old to play the part and wouldn't need to know how to milk cows because, well, cows just weren't groovy.

"Squirrel, we all have to do a lot in this old world that we might not cotton to," said Walt. "We do it so we can serve other folks and take care of ourselves. Sooner you learn that, the better off you'll be."

That night, I helped Walt boil potatoes, eggs, and venison sausage. We opened a package of Ruby's frozen peas and boiled them too.

I thought several times that I would ask him straight out about the rabbit that had died and whose rabbit had it been anyway, but I didn't. I knew if I mentioned it, he would know Evangeline and I had once again been listening to adult conversation when it wasn't meant for our ears and that sure as the fleas on a dog's back, I'd be in trouble again.

After dinner, Walt and I sat out on lawn chairs in the front yard, watching stars and listening to coyotes howl in the distance. Evangeline was sitting by her lonesome in the makeshift tractor seat swing, twisting its chains tightly as she spun and then letting them fly undone. But mainly, I just ignored her.

"Do you think she'll ever come back home to us?" I asked.

"Who, Ruby?"

"No, our mother. . ."

Walt looked sad and studied the ground before he looked back up at me. "I'm sorry, Squirrel. There's some things I know the answer to, but I sure haven't got the answer to that. I just flat don't know."

"Then what *do* you know?" I asked.

Walt looked toward the North Star and stared at it as though divining inspiration somehow. Then he shifted in his blue metal lawn chair, picking at the peeling paint of its arms for a moment before rubbing the back of his callused hand over his five o'clock stubble. Finally, he cleared his throat and looked over at me. I raised my eyebrows to let him know that during his silence I hadn't forgotten what my question had been and that I was waiting for an answer.

Out of his love for me, he made himself tell me more than made him comfortable. "I've heard she married another fella after your daddy died. Then that old fella got sick and took to his bed. I hear he's unable to work, that your mama is taking care of him and trying to earn a living, and you might say that money is real tight. Can't say what will come to pass in the future. Guess all we can do is pray that the perfect thing happens for you and Rabbit."

Tears welled up in my eyes just thinking about the fact that our mother had married another man. Even if our father was dead, couldn't she have just held on until she got to heaven so as not to mess up our family tree? I was sure our daddy would have been biding his time up there in a wooden swing, patting the seat next to him. I pictured what it would have been for them to have been reunited in death if not in life. *Sit down next to me, honey. I've been waiting ages for you to join me* is what I think he'd say. I'd even bet my favorite picture of Donny Osmond on that if someone didn't take my word. So even if our mother lived to be an old woman and went to the sweet bye and bye at the age of a hundred and one, our daddy would have been worth the wait. Wouldn't he? I didn't want to upset Walt, who looked worried enough as it was, so I just tucked these things into my heart. I kissed my grandfather on his cheek and went into the house, thinking what it would be like to have Ruby back home, holding out a plate of warm oatmeal cookies. I heard Rabbit following me in her hippity-hoppity way of playing hopscotch as she walked when acting silly.

"Want to play Red Rover on the front porch?" she asked. "We can tie one end to the rail and take turns. Or maybe Popo would like to jump rope."

"No, thanks, Rabbit. I'm not in the mood."

"Party pooper," she said, twirling her hair around her fingers.

"Let me alone," I said.

Evangeline stuck out her grape Nehi–stained tongue and said, "You're not my real sister. My real sister would. . ."

I went into the bathroom, locked the door, drew myself a hot bath, and stayed there until my skin was pruney and the water was cold. It was the only place I could go inside and Rabbit couldn't follow.

Eventually, Walt knocked on the door and said, "You all right, Squirrel?"

"Yes, sir," I said. But I was not all right. I felt sadder and lonelier than ever.

But the following day got me to really thinking. While Walt was trying to patch a flat tire on the ranch truck, Evangeline talked me into conducting an experiment on Jessie the cow. She had a theory that if she fed her a bag of Hershey's Kisses, she would just naturally give chocolate milk.

"Should we chase her around the barnyard so the milk and chocolate mix up good?" asked Evangeline after she'd unwrapped every single Kiss and stuffed the wrappers in her pockets should she decide to make a collection of them alongside her bubblegum and canned goods' label stashes. Jessie had loved the chocolate and was now following us around like a gigantic puppy. She used to be a tad cantankerous but was now eating out of our hands.

"I wouldn't do that, Rabbit. What if all that running around causes her milk to curdle? Then where would we be?"

"Ew," she said.

Unbeknownst to us, silver wrappers and paper Hershey labels were being whipped from Evangeline's overstuffed pockets by the wind. Walt found several in the milking stall the next morning and tricked me into confessing.

"What have you and Rabbit been up to?" he asked, holding out his hands with at least a dozen tiny foil wrappers. "You monkeys been hiding out here eating tons of chocolate? I'm surprised you didn't have a bellyache last night when you went to bed."

"No, sir," I said. "We didn't eat them."

"Who did?"

"Jessie."

"Squirrel, I didn't just fall off the turnip truck."

"No, sir, I guess you didn't. Turnips are cousins to beets, aren't they? No one on this ranch would be caught dead eating beets or being on a turnip truck."

"Squirrel, don't beat around the bush or try to make me forget my question. Did you and Rabbit eat all this chocolate without permission?"

"We didn't do it. Jessie did."

"You fed Mamaw's prize cow a bunch of chocolate?"

"Yessir. Cross my heart, hope to die. Stick a thousand needles in my eye."

"All right, I believe you. The question is, why would you and Rabbit do such a thing?"

"It was an experiment to see if she'd make chocolate milk."

Walt turned his head, trying to hide his laughter, but his shoulders shook, giving him away.

"How about we give you the first glass when it comes out?" I said.

"I understand what you girls have been up to now," said Walt. "I'd just as soon you asked permission in the future before you feed any of the livestock something out of the ordinary. You don't want to make poor old Jessie sick. It would break Mamaw's heart to lose her. And Jessie's calf, little Miss Annabelle, would miss her mother, just supposing something were to happen to her."

I couldn't help myself but started crying, just thinking I understood exactly how little Miss Annabelle would feel if her mother were to up and disappear all at once. After all, it had happened to Evangeline and me.

"It was Rabbit's idea, but I went along with it. I'm sorry, Popo."

"I think Jessie will live this time. Now let's see what color milk she'll give."

After we'd snubbed Jessie and put her blinders on, I put the metal bucket under her and started milking. To my disappointment, the milk was as white as could be.

"See there," said Walt. "If she gave us the color of milk according to what she'd had to eat, we'd be getting green or brown milk all the time.

We don't always get from life what we think we will. There's something good about that. Think on it."

I thought about it for days but just got to missing Ruby more and more. Had she been at home, she'd have been milking Jessie instead of me. Furthermore, she'd have put a stop to Evangeline's candy wrapper collection, which was beginning to draw ants into our bedroom. We all needed Ruby's help, her guiding presence, and love. But no one needed her more than Walt.

For the following week, Walt tried his hand at cooking. He put barbeque on the pit, mostly beef and venison steaks, and was pretty good at making the sauce to go with them. Everything else was a disaster. Scorched creamed corn; black-eyed peas that burned and stuck to the bottom of the pan, creating black smoke; and baked potatoes that blew up all over Ruby's oven. Take it from me, if you don't stick a fork into a potato before you bake it, it will come back to haunt you.

Then he put a pan of eggs on to boil and went outside to check on Jessie, who'd been running around the barnyard like a horse doing laps since she'd eaten all that chocolate, and forgot all about them. Let me just say that the way all that smells up a kitchen is worse than smelling a sulfur pot. Probably you didn't know that an egg cooking in a pan dry as a bone will actually blow up on you. It can send you to Mars, I'm quite certain. Nearly every time Walt set foot in Ruby's kitchen, something bad was bound to happen.

I didn't want to hurt Walt's feelings but had to get my message across. So I told him, "Popo, you're splendiferous at blowing things up. Maybe you ought to stick to anthills outside in the garden. I'll take over the cooking while Mamaw's gone. I'll even try to make you some pecan cookies with cherries on top." Pecan cookies were Walt's favorite and the best bribe I could think of to get him to quit cooking.

He looked a little sheepish but said, "OK, Squirrel, suit yourself."

I started looking for my favorites of Ruby's recipes but soon discovered she hadn't written many of them down and that they were mostly in her head. "Evangeline, come on in the kitchen and help me figure this out, will you? I aim to make mashed potatoes, fried chicken, garden peas, and pecan cookies," I called to her where she played jacks on the living room floor.

She flat out ignored me, so I tried again. "Do you want to eat Popo's cooking again tonight, or do you want to eat real good, like you would at 2-J's in Austin?"

"Jiminy Crickets, Juliet. Can't you see I'm working hard at this game?"

Evangeline bounced a red rubber ball with one hand and scooped up old black metal jacks with the other. Her blue jeans were worn at the knees, and her little belly peeked out from underneath the red prairie blouse she wore. A trail of chocolate stained the red eyelet lace that trimmed her blouse and made me worry that even Duz couldn't soak it out.

Clearly, Evangeline was no help at all. Determined, I delved into Ruby's cookbooks, which I'd rarely seen her use. I thought perhaps she'd memorized the ones she wanted and ignored the rest. I found a copy of *The Progressive Farmer's Southern Cookbook* and pored diligently over its pages. Oh, there were recipes for things that made me shudder, like one for "Coon with Collards" and "Roast Opossum" and "Son-of-a-Gun Stew" made out of marrow gut, but the one that made me gag was for beets. Anyone in their right mind knew beets were practically illegal in Fireside and always a sign of bad taste.

After laboring over a dinner that was a tad too greasy and made more of a mess than I cared to think about, Dixie Flagg's mother, Delta Mae, called up and asked to speak to Walt on the telephone. Everyone in Fireside knew that she was the queen of TV dinners and had managed to never cook a complete meal in her life. I decided that made her a smart woman in that there were no messy dishes to clean up after a meal like that. Just eat and toss the mess away. That idea sounded especially appealing now.

"Yes, ma'am," said Walt. "I know who you are. You and your husband work at the Fireside Meat Processing Plant. You'd like what. . .?"

My thoughts traveled back to the night Evangeline and I had spent in the Flagg home during the previous school year. It was right before our grandmother Itasca died and was the time that Ruby grounded us for toilet papering Selma Davis's house. No thanks to Dixie, whose wild imagination got us in a heap of trouble, we swore to never hang around her again. Just after Evangeline burst into the kitchen with our dog, Sport, on her heels, Walt said, "That'd be fine. They'll see you then." He replaced the receiver back in its cradle and smiled broadly at us.

"Squirrel, Rabbit, Mrs. Flagg has invited you girls to spend the night with Dixie. Something about the semiannual meeting of the Fireside Spy Club." He beamed broadly, looking so pleased with himself.

"Popo, are you crazy?" asked Evangeline. "What's she got up her sleeve? They say apples don't fall far from the tree. Mrs. Flagg is the tree. . . they think alike."

"Rabbit, what a thing to say. I thought you'd be pleased as punch to get an invite like that. But to tell you the truth, she did say she didn't want her daughter without something to occupy her time this Friday and thought she'd invite you two."

"Dixie is bad news," I said. "Her name is spelled t-r-o-u-b-l-e."

"I gave Mrs. Flagg my word you'd show up," said Walt. "I'd hate to go back on it." Walt cocked his head and looked straight into our eyes to make sure we didn't miss his point. Then he reached down and patted Sport on the head. The dog rolled on his back so that he could beg for a belly rub.

"Well, she is kinda fun," said Evangeline. "But don't say we didn't warn you, Popo."

On Friday night, Walt drove us to Dixie's house just before dinner-time. Knowing we'd be fed TV dinners, I had packed a box of Oreo cookies and peanut butter and grape jelly sandwiches and put them inside our red vinyl suitcase. He helped us carry the bag to the front porch and then as soon as Delta Mae appeared, he said his goodbyes and was gone lickety-split.

When Evangeline and I went and climbed the stairs, egg cartons and old newspapers hadn't budged from the steps from the previous year. On top of these piles was an old moth-eaten monkey that had sawdust leaking out of one side. Upstairs, Dixie, sprawled out on her bedroom floor, was peering through a magnifying lens at a shoebox with a plastic covering punched with air holes.

"Welcome to the Fireside Spy Club headquarters," she said. "I need your password before I let you in on top secret information."

"What kind of password?" Evangeline rolled her eyes and flopped over on Dixie's bed.

"Ok, I'm gonna remind you this once, and that's it," said Dixie, clearly put out that we couldn't remember. "Gumshoe."

"Gumshoe," we said.

"Don't forget next time," she said and peered again through the magnifying glass at her shoebox.

"What are you up to, Dixie?" I asked.

"I'm conducting a top secret experiment for the US government, of course. There's thirty-seven geckos in this box. I read that you could train them to follow a beam of light and that they can detect whether a person is lying or not. If they perch on a commie's nose and turn flaming red, they're lying. If they turn blue, then the truth is being told by a person who's a direct descendant of George Washington and cannot tell a lie."

"Those are just some of Milton's geckos that are trained to sit on the nostrils and stop snoring by exerting just the right amount of pressure," I said with my hands on my hips. "We advertise them on station KOFF all the time."

"Don't underestimate the power of these little creatures to defeat communism once and for all," said Dixie.

Evangeline peered into the box. "They stink something awful, Dixie. Who'd want to have them sit on their nostrils when they smell like a hog pen, but way worser?"

"Well, they do smell bad. Let me think, what should the commander in chief of the Fireside Spy Club do?"

"Give them a bath?" asked Evangeline.

"You're a smart thinker. But I'm even smarter. We can wash them in the sink on the second floor in the visitor's area of the jail. Then if they was to accidentally get out and crawl on the inmates, it would be easy to tell if they were communist spies or maybe double agents."

"No, I don't want to go to visit the jail for any reason, Dixie," I told her.

"Me, either," said Evangeline. "Let's just give them a bath in your tub."

"Good idea, Evangeline. Follow me, Spy Club members," said Dixie, as she led us down the hall. Light streamed through the hallway's dormer window onto a wood floor that squeaked when we walked. Evangeline followed closely behind Dixie, tracking her larger shadow with her small white Keds, as she carried the box of stinky geckos. She set them on the linoleum floor and held her nose while Dixie drew bathwater in the chipped clawfoot tub.

"Who knows? Maybe I'll pay a visit to the jail after you girls leave," said Dixie.

Oh, trust me, never put lots of geckos in a bathtub and expect them to stay there. Dixie squirted an entire bottle of Mr. Bubble into the tub, and soon geckos were leaping everywhere. They crawled up the bathroom walls, darted across the floor and up our bare legs. In no time at all, Delta Mae Flagg was pounding on the bathroom door.

"What in the tarnation are you three girls up to? Bubbles are coming up the kitchen sink, the lavatory, the bathtub drain, and the toilet downstairs."

"We'll clean it up," yelled Dixie. And we did, every last bit of suds. There was an art to catching geckos that involved using the old hairnet Dixie had found in Selma Davis's trash can the year before. I guess it sometimes pays to never, ever throw anything away.

By the time Walt picked us up the following morning, we practically hated Dixie. Her mother, who never cooked, had forced a smile and even made us cinnamon toast, a fried egg each, and several strips of bacon for breakfast. Either she was extra glad to get rid of us or was in some way apologizing for Dixie's wild behavior.

"How'd things go?" asked Walt when Dixie led him into the kitchen.

Delta Mae sat at the table with her hair still in curlers, looking tired and defeated. She wore a giant pink housecoat and was applying salve to the bags underneath her eyes as a gecko squatted on her nose doing push-ups. "These critters have been popping up everywhere all morning. Well, it could have gone worse," said Delta Mae. "And I guess there's one thing to be grateful for; the house is still standing. Things always go berserk around here on weekends." Don't hold me to it, but I could have sworn the gecko turned blue as she reached up, plucked it off her nostril, and shuddered.

40

Five

eeks passed slowly during Ruby's absence. The windmill pumped water at the rate of a trickle an hour, and the peacocks complained throughout the night, calling "Help! Help!" when they weren't suffering at all. We sometimes awoke with circles beneath our eyes due to their orneriness. In my book, we were the ones suffering.

Pill bugs rolled into piles in the corners of the house, but we counted them when we were bored. We shot flies with red rubber bands in competition with each other on the front porch. Evangeline quickly became a sharpshooter and killed three flies in a row, but I killed none. Walt tried his best to keep us busy, but we dragged our feet. When we grew sullen, he gave us chores.

"Squirrel, get out the broom and sweep up those pill bugs, would you?" he said.

"All right, I will," I said unenthusiastically.

"Rabbit, please dry the dishes and put them away," he added.

"Gol-ly," she said and rolled her eyes.

Then Ruby called from Nashville and saved our sorry hides from getting into trouble due to our generally poor attitudes. She spoke to us girls first, and just hearing her voice made us pine something awful for her. We both started to cry, and finally Walt took the phone and told us to go outside and eat a Popsicle to calm down.

"Ruby, darling," he said. "We sure been missing you, girl." I could tell Walt was feeling sad, too, as Evangeline and I headed out the back door with our banana Popsicles.

Later, when we came back inside to wash the sticky off ourselves and treat chigger bites on Evangeline's ankle, Walt updated us on what Ruby had said.

She'd told Walt that they'd been hand delivering their album, *The Fireside Book of Love*, to radio stations all over the South, and one song in particular, "Fireside Women," got everyone's heart pumping. Like cream in a milk bucket, it rose straightaway to the top. Within no time at all, it was number seven on the charts, and that fact was enough to get them an invitation to be on the Grand Ole Opry for the second time, alongside Cousin Minnie Pearl. But, like Ruby said, it had taken them a lifetime of hard work to get that lucky break twice, and their journey had been along a road filled with potholes. There was nothing fast about their rise to the top, in the scheme of things. She went on to say that they'd somehow talked Minnie Pearl into playing guitar and singing along with them this time.

"Minnie Pearl!" I said. "The one who wears the big hat with a price tag hanging down?"

"The very one. Ruby says she's already practiced with her, and Cousin Minnie says to tell you and Rabbit, '*How-w-w-DEE-E-E-E!*'"

"She's a champion hog caller," said Evangeline with round eyes. "Also bet she could call up our heifers in nothing flat. Takes a woman with a lot of talent to do that."

"Rabbit, I'd bet my allowance you could call up a bunch of hogs, too, because you like to waller in the mud," I said, rolling my eyes. "They'd think you was a sister piglet."

"Before you girls get tied up in yet another round of name-calling," said Walt, "you might want to hear the rest of the story."

"What's that?" I asked.

"Ruby, Sapphire, and Pearl are gonna be live from the Grand Ole Opry this very Saturday night. We can tune in the radio to WSM and listen to them right here in our own living room."

We whooped and hollered like we'd lost our minds. Rabbit tried to whistle but just managed to spit a lot. All our commotion caused Sport to begin howling and scratching on our front door. He always was a poor sport when it came to missing out on something exciting.

After we let him in the house, I asked Walt, "Can Hadley come and spend the night while we listen to Mamaw sing on the radio? We can put on our fancy-dress costumes she made and pretend we're part of the Gemburree Sisters. We'll have us a real good time. Please, Popo?"

"Sure she can!"

"What about Davy Ottmers, my new best friend?" said Evangeline. "Can he spend the night?"

Walt's face went crimson with embarrassment. "Well, Rabbit. It doesn't work like that. You're a young lady, which means no boys can spend the night here, now or ever!"

"But, Popo, he's got talent. He can stick his hand in his armpit and pump his arm up and down to the tune of 'The Star-Spangled Banner.'"

Walt smiled. "Is that a fact?" he said. "The boy sounds like other eight-year-olds I've known. He's a prize pig, ain't he? Even so, no boys are allowed here overnight. Tell you what I can do. I'll buy us some cans of beans 'n weenies, sauerkraut, and some chocolate milk to go with it." Walt pulled out a handful of Hershey's foil wrappers from his pocket and winked at Evangeline. "Don't guess your experiment with Jessie paid off well, did it, Rabbit?"

"No, Popo. It didn't. I wasted all my candy on a cow that didn't give us a single glassful of chocolate milk."

"Gosh almighty. How do you like them apples? Guess it just goes to show you, you can't make a deal with a cow and have her hold up her end of the bargain," said Walt.

"Don't I know it!" said Evangeline, who then sat down at the kitchen table and slumped over, putting her head down on her arm.

"Don't take it too hard, Rabbit. For dessert, I'll get us one of those Sara Lee cherry pies. Is that a deal?"

"Deal," we said. I felt guilty, thinking it wasn't a meal that would make Ruby happy and was probably going to get us all in trouble if she ever found out.

Come Saturday morning, Evangeline and I washed and graded all the eggs by weight like our pants were on fire. We were eager to get to town, do our *Cranbourne Variety Hour* show, pick up Hadley, and get back home to listen to our beloved Ruby and her sisters perform.

To share my excitement with station KOFF listeners during the broadcast, I said, "Welcome to Fireside, Texas, home of the Gemburree Sisters, Ruby, Sapphire, and Pearl. You ought to go straightaway and buy their new album, *The Fireside Book of Love*, at Densesky's this afternoon before tonight's appearance on the Grand Ole Opry show, broadcast by WSM radio in Nashville, Tennessee. I'm sure they'll be glad to autograph your album cover when they get back from their tour. And for every purchased album, Evangeline and I will let you pet our dog, Sport, next Saturday down here at the station. Remember, we don't just let anyone pet him for no good reason. Every hair on his head is precious to us.

"I want to remind our listeners that the Fireside Butternut Squash Festival and Parade are coming up in two weeks. If you have a parade float you want to register, call Billie Mac Wilson, and he'll put you on the list. He says to tell you that this year's theme focuses on the existential value of growing a twenty-plus-pound squash. Just apply that thought to your parade float in the most creative way and see if you don't win the blue ribbon.

"Next, after Evangeline plays 'Turkey in the Straw' on her violin, is Davy Ottmers, who's going to perform 'The Star-Spangled Banner' with his one-man show."

Just after Evangeline launched into a squeaky performance, I cued in little Davy. He was wearing gold corduroy pants and a striped navy-blue-and-white knit shirt that was four sizes too small. He had a cowlick that stood straight up on his blond head and the bluest blue eyes you've ever seen. He smiled with delight when I said, "Warm up your armpit, Davy boy!"

Davy hammed it up good. No one had ever played his armpit half as good in the history of broadcasting, I was quite sure. Before he was midway through, however, the switchboard began lighting up with callers who had a different take on things.

Davy's mother called to tell him to come home, do his homework, and quit performing immediately. Seventeen mothers called to tell us we ought not to broadcast such a concert as that and wanted to know if we had lost our ever-loving minds. Some added that they would be sure to buy Ruby, Sapphire, and Pearl's album but thought they wouldn't make it over to the station to pet Sport next Saturday.

One thing for sure was that station KOFF listeners had an opinion and a voice, a fact that I complained about bitterly to Walt, who just said I'd taken quite a risk by inviting Davy Ottmers to play his special concert for all the mothers out there in radio land and that I had to take it as it came to me. That Ruby had warned me to stick to the programming she'd laid out but that I'd paid her no mind.

What I wanted to know was, didn't my opinion matter too?

"Course it does, Squirrel. But you still have to live with the results. I suggest you stick to what Ruby told you next time."

"I will," I promised, with my fingers crossed behind my back.

By some miracle, Walt still let my new best friend, Hadley, come over and spend the night. He must have felt sorry for Evangeline and me, on account of us being so blue about missing Ruby in general.

When Hadley's folks dropped her off at 5:00 p.m., we had just enough time to put maize out for the chickens, close them up in the henhouses, feed Sport again, and check on the sick mother and calf in the barnyard. They looked pretty good, so Walt told us to open the gate and let them out into the south pasture.

From there, we went straightaway into the house, washed up, and heated up the canned beans 'n weenies, sauerkraut, and Sara Lee cherry pie in Ruby's kitchen. Evangeline poured out three glasses of chocolate milk and managed to overflow two of them so that the counter fairly flowed with a chocolate river. It trailed off the counter and down onto the linoleum floor into a puddle.

"Look!" said Evangeline. "It's a cascading pool, like we learned in geography last week, same as they got on the island of Kauai. Except it's chocolate, not blue."

I studied the mess on the floor and noted that it had formed in the shape of a school bus. "That's odd," I said.

45

"Heavy!" said Hadley as she leaned over to look at it and twirled her dark pigtails. "Far out, even!"

We decided to put on our fancy-dress costumes that Ruby had made us, so we might pretend we were onstage at the Grand Ole Opry too. Walt had turned up the radio loud so we could hear it all over the house. In the living room, he settled into his old office chair and leaned up on its back two wheels against the wall. It looked precarious at best, but that was how Walt liked it.

Mr. Roy Acuff and Cousin Minnie Pearl made their appearances first and got us all revved up. When Minnie said, "*H-o-w-w-w-DEE-E-E-E! I'm just so proud to be here,*" Evangeline, Hadley, and I got so excited, we had a hard time settling down enough to listen to her tell one on Brother. We thought Ruby, Sapphire, and Pearl would never appear, but the Gemburree Sisters were introduced just as soon as the comedian finished kidding the audience.

Ruby said, "We'd like to dedicate our new hit, 'Fireside Women,' to our loved ones back home, Walt, Juliet, and Evangeline." Then she counted, "One, two, three, go. . ." and the music began.

At the sound of Ruby, Walt quit leaning his office chair back against the wall on two rollers and landed on all four with a thud. He whistled at her like she could hear him all the way from Nashville and said, "You can do it, Ruby, darlin'! I'm rootin' for you!"

They played the best they ever had, and I couldn't help but feel naturally proud. I felt certain, somehow, that she knew we were all back in the living room watching her every move and missing her more than ever.

Hadley, Evangeline, and I danced in our costumes for the remainder of the broadcast, drank grape Nehi, and ate Cheetos like we always did. Then we went outside and twirled around, making the yards of colored tulle swirl around us. Our feet were bare against the blades of grass as the sun dipped below the horizon. We felt dizzy from joy, from spinning, from excitement and were about half-sick. None of it sat well on top of the beans 'n weenies, sauerkraut, and chocolate milk, so we went inside to take Pepto-Bismol and lie down with a cool rag on the back of our necks to settle our stomachs.

Six

With Ruby gone, we were all getting a little sick and tired in general. Our spirits took a dive through the next few days, and Evangeline and I picked on each other more than ever. Walt had to send us to our room umpteen times, but it did no good. It wasn't until after Columbus Day that we straightened up and flew right.

October in Central Texas meant warm days but cooler nights and mornings. Flowers still bloomed but with less enthusiasm than during spring. Squirrels and rabbits occasionally scampered across the dirt road, and a white-tailed doe watched us and snorted before hightailing it away.

We walked to the bus stop early that morning after a breakfast of Walt's burned pancakes and black bacon. I should have cooked but over-slept and awoke groggy and half-peeved due to a nightmare about being chased by a feral hog. We spied a chicken hawk perched on the fence post, so Evangeline pulled out one of twenty-five thick red rubber bands she kept ever ready to kill flies with from her jumper pocket and took aim. She pulled back on the rubber band and let it fly. Although it fell short, it enraged the hawk, which made a dive for Evangeline's puffball hair. It pulled out several strands with its beak before flying away to safer ground.

"Serves you right!" I said, swinging my book satchel in a circle as we continued to walk. "Poor chicken hawk."

"Poor, my foot!" said Evangeline. "That's the wicked, *evil* enemy of Mamaw's chickens. That hawk can swoop up a chick so fast, it'll make your head spin completely around, Juliet. Not that it would be anything new; it spins all the livelong day."

"It most certainly does not!"

"Spins like a washing machine, around and around."

We argued until we reached the bus stop and began chucking rocks at the gatepost instead. We could hardly wait for the bus to come around the bend and pick us up out of our vexation with each other and to deliver us into better humor. This could only be accomplished when we were out of each other's sight.

School at the Fireside Elementary was good entertainment. At least we knew our friends would be there, waiting for us. Hadley King might regale me with her latest tales of roller-skating in San Angelo over the weekend while visiting her aunt Violet. The boys would be trading baseball cards and plotting against the substitute teacher. I would try to teach a group of friends how to do the Swim, and Evangeline would just be her annoying self.

When the bus finally arrived, it was thirty minutes late. It dawned on us that there would be no time before the bell rang for us to engage in important social activities. As soon as the bus door screeched open, I saw that our old bus driver had been replaced.

"Where's Mr. Roper?" I asked as I climbed up the steps.

"Had a heart attack and died yestiddy. Name is Seymour. Y'all girls get on up the steps, and do not let the doors hit you on the backside. What do you think this is, Ken Kesey's party bus?" he said and laughed. His hair was greasy and hung long down both sides of his face, but his head was crowned by a ball cap worn backward. He wore a long, tired-out shirt with holey elbows and a frayed hem. He hadn't buttoned it but was wearing a stained, muscle shirt underneath. He smelled of that sour, sweet, stinky stench of old, wet maize.

I hesitated behind Evangeline as we climbed on board. She squinted at him and said, "I hate chicken hawks," which must have seemed random to Seymour.

Seymour just glared at her, took a cigarette and matches out of his tattered shirt pocket, and lit up. "They don't pay me enough to put up with snot-nosed brats," he said. "In Nam, I put the Vietcong in their places every chance I got. Went down in the tunnels and come out a decorated war hero because I didn't put up with no nonsense. Go take a seat at the back of the bus, chicken hawk girl."

"What did they decorate you with?" asked Evangeline. "Glitter?"

"Move it!" he barked. "Get outa my face!" He glared at her like he was about to eat her alive.

Evangeline slinked toward the back, just behind me. When I plopped down on the picked-at green leather seat at the very back, Evangeline slid down next to me, her nose wrinkled like she'd just smelled a stinkbug.

Up front, Seymour sat in his driver's seat, puffing on his cigarette and taking swigs out of his thermos. He talked to himself and answered both sides of the conversation.

"I said, 'Lieutenant Dawson, we got us an Alpha Bravo going on. Boo-koo Charlies outnumber us seven-hundred-sixty to one.'"

Little Lilly Malone raised her hand and said, "Excuse me, Mr. Seymour. What's a boo-koo Charlie?" When Seymour glared at her in the rearview mirror, she quickly shoved her tiny hand back into her purple jumper pocket.

"None of your beeswax," he said. "Just listen to my story and you might learn something. No more questions, shortcake." Seymour took another swig from his thermos and appeared to ponder something.

"Where was I? Oh yeah. Because we was air cav, I radioed for a chopper to come on and get us outa there. Wasn't no way we was gonna survive. Too outnumbered. So when I told them that, why didn't they come and get us?

"Nobody said nothing, zip, nada, except no enchilada. Left us down there to fend for ourselves. Was down in them tunnels with just a few grenades and a round or two of ammo. Charlies thick as thieves, coming from every which direction.

"We didn't know which way to go. Should we go left; should we go right? '*What* should we do?' was all I wanted to know. When I got shot at and hit in the belly, my life flashed before my eyes. I swear on a stack of Bibles, I saw my daddy appear right in front of me, even though he died in the Pacific War when I was an ankle biter."

That got my attention. Although I didn't like Seymour much, I did feel right sorry for him on account of losing his dad. I nudged Evangeline and raised my eyebrows to punctuate what he'd said. She shrugged her shoulders and looked away.

"Didn't turn out so hot. So today, I'm still asking the same question. What in the name of the good ol' US of A should we have done?" Seymour tossed his cigarette butt out the bus window and immediately lit up another one. He threw the match out the window, too, and I grew afraid he was about to set the whole world on fire.

"You ought not to be a firebug," said Luke Schwartz, a freshman who wore thick glasses and had gone without a haircut for months due to his disdain for the process. "You know what Smokey Bear says: 'Only *you* can prevent forest fires.'"

"Next time I'll put it out on your head, bush boy," yelled Seymour.

Twenty-three unruly children had somehow suddenly become star citizens. No one moved a muscle; we were too scared to breathe. "He ain't right in his head," I whispered to Evangeline.

"And. . ." she said, "I wish he'd used Dial soap like they say in the commercials, 'cause he smells like a hog, but way worser."

"Shut up, you girls in the back!" Seymour roared. "I hate commotion. I'm about to get going, and how you 'spect me to drive when you make all that confounded racket?" After Evangeline and I pretended to lock our lips and throw away the keys, he finally put the bus in gear, and we meandered toward the highway and school.

However, when the bus finally rolled to a halt at the stop sign on the highway, he turned the bus in the wrong direction and began to drive fast.

"Wait, Mr. Seymour. You turned wrong!" yelled Clayton Bossier. He was a high school senior with sandy hair, freckles, and a letterman jacket that he wore even when it was hot. He worked sacking groceries on weekends and in the summer at Densesky's and had always been kind to us girls.

"I don't give a flying monkey's derriere whether you think I'm going in the right direction or not," Seymour said. "One thing's for sure, I will take you anywhere I have a mind to go."

"What are you gonna do with us, Mr. Bozo?" yelled Evangeline as she stood up in the aisle.

"Sell you back to your old man and lady. Running outa Mary Jane and A-bomb, not to mention the fact that I'll need fuel for the King Air I'm gonna win on *Dialing for Dollars*.

50

"All you brats are now my hostages. I've been held hostage before and *surprise*, now it's your turn. Capisce? You better pray your people want you back. If they don't, I'll have to sell you to someone else. Let's face it, none a' you are all that good looking. You ain't pretty like me, so I guess I'd have to sell you to the lowest bidder." He laughed like it was the funniest thing he'd ever heard. But none of us saw any humor in it at all.

"We'll see about that. Our popo's gonna fix your wagon," said Evangeline. Although she'd tried her best to be brave, she puckered up and started crying.

"Hey you, chicken hawk girl. Stop flapping your lips. Sit down and shut up."

Seymour pulled on his thermos, drained it, and tossed it on the floor. "Man, this is heavy monkey poo. Another dead soldier," he said sadly and shook his head as the metal thermos clanked down the bus steps toward its closed doors.

Evangeline and I held hands, which we'd hardly ever done in our lives. I pressed my nose against the bus window and looked out at the farmhouses, fences that protected buffalo and exotic game animals, miles and miles of live oak trees, Aermotor windmills, and abandoned stone buildings. We were headed toward Stonewall and passed acre after acre of peach orchards, which were now covered in brown, shriveled leaves. I started to wonder whether we'd ever see Ruby or Walt again, and tears streamed down my face.

Evangeline, however, had a plan. She shoved her hand in her dress pocket and pulled out a wad of thick red rubber bands. "I'm gonna take him out with these," she said.

"You've got to be kidding me," I said, wiping my nose with my hankie. "You can't even kill a rat with one of those."

"Put your thinking cap on, Juliet. Seymour's a way bigger target."

"You can't kill him with a rubber band, fathead. You're not even in range to get him."

"I'll inch up on my belly like a queen snake."

"There's no such thing as a queen snake. You mean a *king* snake."

"Yes, there is such a thing. They got 'em in Ohio. I read it in a library book and saw a picture of one."

51

"So even if you snake your way all the way to the front and zap him on his neck, then what?"

"Then he'll get mad as a hornet and pull over. Then the rest of you can launch an attack."

"With what?"

"Book satchels, of course. There are about twenty-three overloaded book satchels on this bus. We're a force to be reckoned with."

Seymour managed to light another cigarette as we hurtled down the highway at sixty miles per hour, which was about all the old bus could manage. Its engine groaned, and the bus jerked as he shifted gears. Then he pulled a wrapper out of his pocket that looked like Dubble Bubble with free comics and fortunes. Seymour licked that cartoon wrapper like it was the best candy he ever had. Evangeline said she was an expert on bubblegum-wrapper collections—hers numbered 274 in total—and what he was licking was no gum wrapper. So I just naturally had to believe her.

"Turn this bus around and take us to school!" shouted Pete Olson, rising up in his seat. He was a high school senior who served on the debate team and had never lost a contest. "If you do that, things will go better for you in a court of law."

"Well, ain't that nice of you?" said Seymour in a sarcastic voice. "Sit down and shut up! You're interfering with the voices in my head!"

Little Tommy Schaefer, who sat directly in front of me, turned around and said to me, "Do you want me to bite him?" He put his chompers together and smiled so we could get a good look at his teeth. The front four were missing.

"Thanks, Tommy," I said. "I don't think it would do much good."

"You've got no teeth. What are you going to do, gum him to death?" said his sister, Jill, who was seated next to him.

"Then you bite him," said Tommy forlornly.

We roared past Stonewall like it was a speck on the road and lurched and swayed toward Fredericksburg, fence posts blurring as we went by. I got to thinking that all us children might not live to see our next birthdays. Evangeline and I might never make it to a Beatles concert, and Petula Clark might never get to sign my autograph book. It was possible there wouldn't be any more broadcasts on station KOFF, and we might never, ever have the chance to see our mother again either, supposing she wanted to see us. It was then I quit being scared and just got fighting mad.

"Evangeline, let's use your idea. It's the only one that makes sense, now that I think about it. Go ahead and pass out some of those rubber bands to the other kids, the ones with aisle seats. Tell them that when I yell out, *Stop the bus; I need to go to the bathroom,* they're to pelt him on the back of his neck, shoulders, and arms with the bands. Bet you he pulls the bus over to whack us after we've done that. Next, we're all gonna rush and smack him with our book satchels until he's done for. I wanna see stars coming out of his eyes when we're finished, just like Wile E. Coyote."

"Then what?"

"We'll all pile out of the bus, run as fast as we can, and flag down a car to help us. Pass the word to all the riders. Make sure the high school kids ambush him first. They're the biggest." As I said that, I noticed that a cardinal-red Chevy truck pulled up even to the bus in the passing lane and that Seymour's attention was on the passenger.

Evangeline sent her thick red rubber bands down both sides of the bus aisle, whispered our instructions, and told everyone to pass it on. Every child was poised and ready to fire, but Seymour had other ideas. He leaned out his window and flirted outrageously with the blonde, who was doing her best to ignore him. "Hello, darlin'. Ain't you lookin' sweet today?" She turned to glare at Seymour through big white sunglasses, and I was struck by the familiarity of her frosted pink lipstick. Her teased hair was piled up high, and an autumn-print scarf that was tied around her neck flapped in the breeze when she rolled down the window. She wrinkled up her nose at Seymour as though she could smell him from where she sat, rolled up the window, and looked away. I was sure it was Selma.

I took off one of my white socks, stuck it out the bus window, and waved it like an SOS flag, but Selma didn't seem to notice. She was too busy trying to ignore Seymour and anything to do with him, including the likes of us. Then I ripped a piece of notebook paper out of my spiral, wrote HELP on it, and held it up to the window. That didn't work either.

Seymour started yawning and shaking his head as if trying to stay awake. "I need some coffee," he said as his head started to nod. The bus swerved several times into the left lane and then across onto the road shoulder, but he soon startled, awoke, and got back into the right lane.

"He's about to fall asleep and kill us all," I said.

"Crazy old buzzard," said Evangeline.

"You move into position and take the first shot."

"OK. I'll aim for his ear." Evangeline dropped to her knees in the swaying bus's aisle and began crawling to the front, out of Seymour's eyesight in the rearview mirror.

I yelled, "Stop the bus; I need to go to the bathroom." Instantly, every child poised their red rubber bands and sent them flying through the air, like rubber arrows, aimed at Seymour's scruffy head, neck, and shoulders. Some fell short of their target and landed in the aisle, while others snapped at the windshield. Plenty hit Seymour, though, who became mightily perturbed.

"What are you snot-nosed brats up to? I'm gonna pull this bus over and wale the tar out of each and every one of you v-a-r-m-i-n-t-s."

Next thing you knew, the bus started swerving into the left lane and then back into the right, into the left again and back into the right. Then old Seymour went straight to sleep like he'd been conked on the noggin, and the bus headed toward the guardrail.

All us children closed our eyes and prayed to the Lord we wouldn't get killed by the metal in front of us. I can't say what a guardrail is exactly for if it doesn't guard or protect you from something.

Although we left the pavement lickety-split, by some miracle, the bus rolled to a stop just in front of the metal rail. If you ask me, I think a jillion angels stopped our yellow gravel-spitting vehicle in the nick of time. Why they would help us, I can't say for sure; Evangeline and I weren't always perfect children. Maybe they had come to save all those other children, and by grace, we were saved too.

When we realized we weren't about to die on the spot, we focused our attention on Seymour. We didn't need to plow into him with our book satchels. Judging from the unnatural way he'd draped himself over the gear shift, he had to be dead, hadn't he?

You know what they say about the best-laid plans, don't you? They never work out quite the way you think they will. Before we could blink,

Selma Davis was trying to force open the bus door, but Evangeline ran up and opened it for her. Norman Densesky, whose forehead was wrinkled with concern, was right by her side.

Upon seeing Seymour slumped over the steering wheel and hearing Rabbit's tearful account, Norman grabbed some rope out of the back of his truck and tied the sleeping driver's hands behind his back.

"Ain't he dead?" asked Evangeline, sniffing.

"No, just drunk as a skunk," said Norman. "Or looped up on something."

Before long, the highway patrol found us, and not long after that, Officer Dale Morris showed up and started interviewing every child who'd talk to him. Half the kids were in tears, while a few big senior boys just laughed. Walt would have said they were flat out of line. I guess they were just nervous and didn't know what else to do. Wouldn't you be?

Selma wrapped her loving arms around Evangeline and me and drew us to her. She was wearing a tight pumpkin-colored sweater, black slacks, scarf, and high heels. Her piled-to-the-sun hairdo was fastened in the back by a hair clip covered with little faux pearls.

"Oh, dear hearts," she said. "Are you OK?"

Selma held our hands as we watched a limp Seymour being pulled off the bus and laid out on the gravel for examination.

Officer Dale bent over him, opened Seymour's eyelids, and checked out his eyeballs. Next, he listened for a heartbeat and, finding one, said, "Still living." Directly, he looked up at Selma and Norman and shook his head. "This one's a doper. We found his A-bomb wrapper and whiskey thermos on the school bus."

The officer stuck his thumbs in the belt loops of his khaki uniform and looked around at all us kids. He shook his head and said, "Now I've gotta figure out how to get all you brave kids back to your families. You might could use a hug from your folks. School can wait until tomorrow. In the meantime, I gotta take this nincompoop bus driver to the hospital."

"I can drive the school bus and take these children home to their families," said Selma. "I know where they live. In Fireside, everybody knows everybody else."

"You sure?" said Officer Dale. He looked at her with some skepticism. He looked at Norman. "How about you? Can you drive the bus?"

"Don't look at me," said Norman. "Selma used to drive a big rig for a living. Truth is, she was born in one. Furthermore, she's got the right license." Norman turned to Selma. "Show him, honey."

Selma opened her purse and pulled out her Class A CDL. Her photograph showed Selma as she always looked: pearlized lipstick and teased blonde hair piled to the sky.

"Whoa," said Officer Dale. "You weren't pulling my leg."

Straightaway, Selma began taking charge. She turned around to find us staring at Seymour and said, "Let's get out of here. Mr. Densesky and I are going to take all you kids home. We won't be going to Fredericksburg like we'd planned. We were going to run some errands for our wedding, eat some German food, listen to an oompah band at Oktoberfest, and do what they call a little dancing and romancing. But we can do that any old time." Naturally, the kids giggled when she mentioned "dancing and romancing." She winked at all of us and patted Norman on the arm as he blushed.

I hugged Selma and said, "I can't believe you showed up when you did. Mr. Roper's dead, and now Seymour is just half-alive. I can't say I feel sorry for him, but poor Mr. Roper never did anybody any harm."

"Dead? You don't say," said Selma. "I didn't hear a word at the store about Mr. Roper dying. Usually, word passes through town like lightning. All those customers coming in, scattering bits of news like jars of spilled jelly beans."

"All this mess is plumb scary to think about," I said. "Happened so quick."

Selma smiled and patted my back. "Now, Juliet. Don't fret. None of us knows what might happen next in life or what sweet or sour taste might come from it. Might make you smile, might make you pucker. One thing you can bet on is that you'll sample something different every day. You just may not get to pick the flavor. Every day is a miracle, nonetheless."

Seven

Three days later, we learned that Mr. Roper had been rescued from the grave. He'd never actually had the heart attack Seymour had claimed but rather had been struck over the head by Seymour's thermos and laid out like a marked chicken across a wood stump. Seymour, who had been working in the school bus yard as a mechanic, had seen the bus routes posted on the office wall and decided he could make some easy money by holding all of us hostage and selling us back to our folks. He'd come back from Vietnam a troubled man, on account of having flipped his lid. I think it all started with his flight back home on the Jefferson Airplane, which must have been named after President Jefferson, though I can't say why exactly. I think they played that song "White Rabbit" while he was flying across the big ol' Pacific. It somehow spoke to his concern about being chased by rabbits when he was back there picking mushrooms close to the Vietcong. Word had it that the minute he landed back on US soil, he'd walked right into a protest and been swept up by a Miss Mary Jane, let his hair grow long, and spent long hours making daisy chains because of her. Then he'd hung out at Haight-Ashbury in San Francisco during last year's Summer of Love and met his favorite old lady, A-bomb, which I'm guessing stood for Alice Bomb, someone he loved more than Mary Jane. As I may have mentioned, not all Seymour's checkers were on his board from the get-go. On the other hand, maybe he was just "Born to Be Wild," like they say on the radio.

If Ruby'd been home, I'd have asked her just how a person could fall in love with two creatures who'd clearly led him down the path of destruction. Ruby was good at answering those tough kinds of questions that explained a twisted heart.

Let me just say this one thing: even though we'd been robbed of the chance of launching our book satchel attack on Seymour, we felt stronger for having made a plan and doing something about the circumstances in which we found ourselves. If you can learn to think for yourself, you don't go around feeling like Elmer Fudd all the time, trying to outsmart a rabbit. Furthermore, we'd felt protected by an unseen hand that was not of this earth.

A part of me felt truly sorry for Seymour on account of him losing his daddy so young. I understood how that felt. Although I didn't feel like that excused his poor behavior, I knew it hadn't helped him any.

Evangeline and I were twice as grateful to be back at the house with Walt and half as cantankerous as we'd been the previous week. We combed his silver hair and made a fuss over him like he was Roy Rogers in the flesh. He just sat in his office chair with the roller wheels and let us style his hair as long as we pleased. If you ask me, I think he liked it.

"Why do you think Seymour got so sick he nearly died?" I asked Walt after having learned that he'd spent two days in the hospital under high security.

"God smote him, that's why," said Evangeline as she banged her fist on the bookcase by Walt's chair. "And wanted him to get arrested and sent to jail."

"God doesn't smite people," said Walt. "Although that rascal had it coming."

"If God doesn't smite bad folks, then what?" I asked.

"The Good Lord doesn't always give us what we deserve," said Walt. "Thank heavens. But I can't say I'm sorry he passed out when he did. Was all them no-count drugs that nearly killed him and all you kids. He's one sick fella."

Later, we helped Walt with the cows and their calves and went about the business of naming each one. There were Queen Elizabeth and Prince

Philip; Little Joe and Hoss Cartwright; Ricky, Lucy, Ethel, and Fred; Captain Kangaroo, Mr. Green Jeans, and Mr. Moose, just to mention a few of the names. I think every cow and calf stood a little taller and held their mouth a little straighter, feeling like they were somebody special. If my mama was to call me by name, I know I would feel a little better about myself too.

I often thought about the day when Hadley spent the night, the day of Ruby's appearance on the Grand Ole Opry, and how the chocolate milk had pooled into the shape of a school bus on the kitchen floor. I read somewhere that when odd things like that happen to you that can't be explained just any old way, they must be an omen.

Just a few days after the school bus incident, a package arrived for Evangeline and me. At first, I thought it was just Walt up to his old tricks again, playing Santa Claus, trying to make us believe it had really been sent by our mother, just to cheer us up, but this time was different.

Walt had come in from the post office, tossed his Stetson on the back of a chair like he always did, and plopped a brown package on the kitchen table that had Evangeline's and my names on it. He looked at it with a puzzled interest and then nodded at us.

"Well, Squirrel and Rabbit, you gonna open it?"

The package was tied with brown twine that was pulled a little too tight. It was soft and bowed a little in the middle. Evangeline lunged for it and tried to yank the twine off, but nothing budged. She threw it across the table in my direction and said, "Here, Squirrel, you do it."

I pulled at it briefly and said, "We need a pair of scissors."

Walt said, "No, you don't" as he opened his bone-handled pocket knife and slit the twine like a surgeon.

Inside the package were two T-shirts that advertised the off-Broadway show *The Oops Girls*, starring our very own mother. Both shirts were way too small for us, which made us sad. She had no idea how big her own girls had grown. I picked up a folded show program, and inside it was a letter written on lime-green stationery. It smelled just the way I remembered her, of lemon cologne and Fruit Stripe gum. I held it up to my nose and inhaled her scent briefly before I began to read.

October 10th, 1968
Dear Girls,

I meant to write you a while back, but just couldn't. Never have been sure what to say. I'm up here in New York, as you can see by the things I've sent you. Sorry that I left you back when I did. I'm sure you didn't know what to make of that. I was boiling mad at your father for going to Vietnam, when I felt sure he could have gotten out of it. Now, he's never coming home.

It seems that I've gotten myself into quite a pickle. Well, it wouldn't be the first time. Guess I can blame some of my hasty decisions on a wild Irish temperament mixed with my Gypsy nature. I can't come home just now. You are probably having such a good time with Walt and Ruby that you don't think about me much anyway.

Be good girls and study hard. Brush your teeth well, so you don't have to get them all pulled like my mother did. You won't take a good picture without teeth. A good picture is a girl's best friend in my kind of business.
Love,
Mama

This was too much information for us on the one hand and not enough on the other. Like pots of angry grease burning on the stove, Evangeline and I started sizzling and popping. We wailed. I took off my shoes and threw them one at a time at the square hot water heater that rested next to the wood and electric stoves. Evangeline walked up behind me and bit me on the shoulder in frustration with her rabbit teeth. She only ever did that when she was stretched beyond her limit.

"Quit it, Rabbit!" I yelled. "I'm gonna get my shoe and whack you with it if you don't."

Walt just stared up at the ceiling, like there was bound to be an answer from heaven written on the stained ceiling tile and said, "Dad-burn it, where's Ruby when we need her?"

The following morning, Walt could see we were down in the mouth about our mother and still suffering from our excursion with Seymour.

Walt passed me the jar of mustang grape jelly I'd asked for while buttering my breakfast toast at the kitchen table.

"They put that old cuss in the Fireside jail after a short stay in the hospital. He'll be there until he goes to trial. It might help you girls to go give him a piece of your mind. Could make you feel better to have your say."

"Can he hurt us?" I asked.

"You won't be going in the cell with him, just talking to him through the bars."

"Yes sirree Bob, I want to set him straight," said Evangeline.

After we'd done all the chores, we climbed into Walt's truck and roared off to Fireside. As we drove up to the jail, I got a knot in my stomach and nearly decided to stay in the truck to avoid the entire situation, but Walt coaxed me out.

"C'mon, Squirrel. I'll take care of old Seymour if he gives you any trouble."

When the sheriff led us to the cell, he banged the bars with his college ring, making a sharp, ringing sound. Seymour, who'd been sleeping on his cot, popped up and said, "Is it lunch yet?" He was wearing jail clothes, which actually improved his appearance. He didn't stink and had apparently even washed his hair.

I saw that there were dozens of geckos on his cell wall and knew that somehow, Dixie had struck. One speckled gecko crouched on his left sleeve.

"No, it's ten of the morning," said the sheriff. "You recognize these girls who've come to see you?"

"Oh, it's chicken hawk girl and her squirrely sister."

"I ain't a chicken hawk girl," said Evangeline. "I'm a rabbit girl."

"What you did to us children was terrible," I said. My words were brave, but my knees were shaking so hard, I could barely stand. "What made you do such a thing?"

"Well, I guess the A-bomb and Jim Beam got mixed up with the Vietnam in my head," he said. "I didn't hurt none of you anyways."

"You hurt our spirits, and that's just as bad as if you'd beaten us."

"C'mon, sister, wasn't that bad," he said. Then he turned to the sheriff and said, "I need a cigarette. How you expect me to talk to these kids without a cig?"

"This isn't a hotel, and I ain't from room service," said the sheriff.

"Well, I hope the sheriff grounds you for a long time," said Evangeline. "You might be a hundred before you get ungrounded."

"That's a fact," said the sheriff.

"Well, what of it?" said Seymour. "I got no family. My wife run off with a barber when I was in Nam. My only son died of a brain infection when he was two, and my daddy's dead. I got nothing to live for in the outside world."

"That's too bad," I said. "What about your mother?"

"She's long gone," said Seymour.

"I don't feel sorry for you one little teensy, weensy bit," said Evangeline.

"That's your call, chicken hawk girl. Guess I don't blame you. But them's the breaks."

While standing there looking at Seymour, who seemed to have lost all hope for living a decent life, I wondered what had happened, beyond what we already knew, to bring him to this place. Not only was I curious about the things he'd done, I wondered what had been done to him? If someone had been really kind to him at some point, would it have made a difference?

All these things I pondered after Walt, Evangeline, and I left the jail, went to eat at the Fireside Café, and then onto station KOFF for our broadcast. It was hard for me to make heads or tails of everything that had happened. I tried hard not to worry, but that was just part of my nature.

Eight

"Hello, this is Juliet Cranbourne, broadcasting *The Cranbourne Variety Hour* on station KOFF. Welcome to Fireside, Texas, on this sunny November afternoon. Although the weather is beautiful, Evangeline and I are a little blue. So I thought I'd play 'I'm So Lonesome I Could Cry.' But before we go to that, how about a quick word about our sponsor?

"Today's program is brought to you by Jack's Heavenly Trailer Court. Jack says that while they may not yet have hookups available for your average trailer, they can offer you a grassy space to park and a kid's playground with plenty of monkey bars, teeter-totters, and a king-size swing. Your youngsters can also enjoy the soda fountain that gives a triple dip of strawberry, vanilla, or chocolate ice cream for their eating pleasure. Jack's is located next to the Fireside Drive-In, so you can get a glimpse of today's double feature, sound not included. And without any extra charge, you can take home baby horned toads; a bumper crop have hatched this year. Remember, *For comfort to the max, stay at Jack's*. That's Jack's Heavenly Trailer Court. They've got a spot for you!

"Now, here's Hank and Audrey Williams as you've never heard them before, singing, 'I Heard My Mother Praying For Me.'"

As the record played, I considered what it would take to cheer Evangeline and me up. Two new cute puppies would do it, I decided. So, as soon as the record ended, I said, "Doggone it, Rabbit and I need some cute pups to cheer us on. Our tails are dragging, and our heads are hanging low. If you've got some pups and no use for 'em, just drop 'em on by the station, and we'll take them home."

It wasn't two seconds before I had a caller on the line.

"Juliet, this is Mamaw. I may be out of town, but I'm listening to your broadcast over the telephone thanks to Walt. You get right back on the air and tell those folks that your mamaw said you've already got a dog and don't need another one."

"But, Mamaw!" I whined.

"You be a good girl and do what I said, or you won't get to go to Austin when I get home. Do I make myself clear?"

"Yes, ma'am," I said slowly. "But what if the pups are already on their way?"

"You'd best hang the 'Closed' sign on the station door right this minute."

I thought she was about to hang up, so I said, "Wait, Mamaw. When are you coming home?"

"In two shakes of a lamb's tail or Christmas, whichever comes first."

"Good. Evangeline and I can't hold out much longer."

Five days before Christmas, I baked Seymour a plate of chocolate chip cookies and wrapped it with tinfoil and ribbon. While I was still upset with him, I couldn't help but realize he was bound to have no Christmas presents, and that alone was enough to turn him into a hardened criminal. When I told Walt my plan, he just said, "I'd be glad to drive you into town if this is in your heart to do."

"Yes, it is."

"You got a mighty big heart, my sweet Squirrel. You're gonna kill him with kindness, and that is the best revenge of all."

When we arrived at the Maitlin County jail, the sheriff inspected the paper bag of cookies, pulled one out for himself, and bit into it. "Mm, good," he said and smiled. "I can tell you're Ruby's granddaughter on account of how delicious these turned out."

When he led us back to the cell, Seymour was reading a Bible. This surprised me. I didn't know he cared a thing in the world about religion or that he could read. I slid the paper bag through the bars. He put the Good Book on his cot, reached over, grabbed the bag, and peered inside.

Surprised, Seymour said, "Thank you, sister."

"My name is Juliet."

"Thank you, Sister Juliet."

"You're welcome. Merry Christmas."

"Same back at you," Seymour said, confused by my gift. "Why would you be nice to me when I done you wrong?"

"Because you've got to forgive people before you can move on. That's what I know."

Seymour tapped his Bible and said, "Well, I guess you and Jesus cornered the market on that. I'm not sure I've got it in me to forgive what others done and what I done in Vietnam in them tunnels. Not sure I can forgive my ex-wife for running out on me, or my boy for dying, or what happened to my parents."

"Suit yourself," I said. "But you might want to think on it."

As I turned to go, Seymour said, "Tell chicken hawk rabbit girl she's a good shot with them rubber bands."

"She knows."

Three days before Christmas, Evangeline and I played in the yard, lavishing attention on Sport. We had cut holes in an old blanket and made a coat for him, although he didn't seem to appreciate it much. Then we tried to teach him how to do the two-step, but that was a problem on account of him having four legs. Next, we put Avon coral lipstick on him, but he took exception to that, bit off the waxy cylinder, and swallowed it whole.

"Now what are we gonna tell Mamaw about her lipstick?" asked Rabbit. "Sport has done gone and ruined it."

"I doubt that Mamaw would have wanted to use it again with all that dog slobber on it, anyhow. Maybe we should use our allowance and buy her another tube," I said. "It would be the right thing to do."

"No. Really?" said Evangeline. "I wanted to use my allowance to buy some Dubble Bubble and apple Jolly Ranchers."

We'd been just about out of our ever-loving minds missing Ruby when dust was kicked up down the caliche road by vehicles we recognized. Seeing Ruby and her sisters towing their Airstream trailer behind the American Motors station wagon put the color back in our palettes of imagination. They created a picture that looked more like a blue-ribbon painting than just our precious family coming home.

Sapphire tooted the horn like we played knock-knock on a door. She smiled broadly, reminding me of Jane Withers as Josephine the plumber in all those Comet cleanser commercials. You know the ones I mean, where she wears white overalls, a matching cap, and "gets the really tough stains out"?

Ruby emerged from the passenger's side perfectly coiffed, her hair held by the mother-of-pearl combs Walt and our daddy had given her years before. She wore an A-line green woolen dress that was belted at the waist and a white sweater. She was more beautiful than any fifty-three-year-old I had ever seen. Like pups, we ran to her and nearly knocked her over in our excitement. To our relief, she smelled faintly of Noxzema and talcum powder, just the way we remembered.

Then there was blonde Pearl, who stood between Ruby and Sapphire in height but was the youngest by a landslide. Pearl, who wasn't a day over forty, held a dark-skinned baby girl dressed to the nines in a white gown with lace on it. I hardly took in Pearl because my attention went directly to the child.

"Juliet," Pearl said, looking directly at me. "This here's your. . . your . . . let me think a minute what the relationship would be." She appeared to ponder the situation for a moment and finally said, "Guess she'd be your *relative*. Baby Jewel, meet Juliet, and right over yonder by Ruby is Evangeline."

Ruby had once given Evangeline and me a short explanation of why chicken eggs required both a rooster and a hen if they aspired to become anything more than breakfast. This fact resurfaced in my mind, although I little understood the actual mechanics of the miracle of reproduction as I stood and gawked at Pearl and her Jewel baby.

"Close your mouth, Squirrel," said Ruby. "I raised you with better manners. What, for Pete's sake, should you say to your Aunt Pearl?"

I closed my mouth, gave Pearl a slight hug, and said to little Jewel, "Pleased to meet you."

It was Evangeline who said exactly what I was thinking. "Where on earth did that baby come from? Had you been drinking a lot of chocolate milk to make a baby that color? Or did you find her somewhere in Memphis? Maybe at a roadside park or at the counter in Big Boy's, when you was ordering a hamburger? Or did somebody go off and leave her in the Sinclair station bathroom or maybe on your back seat when some man was giving you gas?"

Ruby closed her eyes briefly and shook her head. When she opened them again, she stared at Evangeline and said, "Rabbit, why don't you go in the house and work out some of that curiosity in the kitchen? I know there are potatoes to peel because Walt told me on the telephone you'd gotten them out of the garden."

"Thank you, Mamaw," said Evangeline. "But potato peeling ain't for me. That's Juliet's work. My line of work is digging potatoes and helping to keep the rabbits out of the garden. Why, I'd just as soon take Fletcher's Castoria . . ."

Ruby's eyes looked tired. I could see the fine lines above her lips wrinkle as she pursed them. She just stood there as though she were too tired to think of anything to say when along came Walt.

He rounded the corner from the cow pen, where he'd gone to check up on an ailing calf, caught sight of Ruby, and about half ran to get to her faster.

"My girl," he said to her, as though she were his teenaged bride. Then he kissed her smack-dab on the lips in front of her sisters and Evangeline and me. "You been gone too durned long," he said, "but are worth the wait. You're prettier than leaves on winter squash. Prettier than a June bug. Brighter than the North Star." Ruby hugged his neck and kissed his cheek. Walt picked her up and swung her around as though she weighed no more than a young child.

"Well," said Pearl, "why can't I find a man like Walt? Wish somebody would be that happy to see me every time I come home."

"There was Randy. He was always glad to see you. But then you run him off," said Sapphire, smiling and looking at Pearl sideways.

"Took me a can of Raid, but I did manage to get shed of him. Smelled like old fish all the time."

Pearl paused, looked at Walt, and said, "I'd like for you to meet Jewel."

Walt wiped his hands on his overalls and gently took the infant out of Pearl's arms. He studied her sweet face for a good long while and teared up briefly. "Yes, she's a jewel at that. Well done, Pearl. Well done."

That evening, when Ruby called us in to supper, she put bowls of peaches, creamed corn, and green beans on the table, all of which she'd canned before she'd left. Next, she brought a plate of fried venison sausage nestled on a paper towel, just steaming and juicy as you please.

I knew something was up when she let us have Dr. Pepper with our supper, as we were never allowed to have caffeine so late in the day, lest it kept us awake staring out our bedroom window at the stars. After Evangeline and I had taken our baths, Ruby and Walt came in to tell us good night, or so we thought.

Walt leaned against the doorjamb, looking like he might want to take out to get in the ranch truck if he needed a quick exit, while Ruby sat on our bed, where we lay reading.

"Girls, we've got something to explain to you," said Ruby.

"Are we in trouble?" I asked nervously, going through a mental list of what we'd done wrong during the day. There were so many things. I'd left the refrigerator door open when I poured myself a glass of milk. Evangeline had accidentally poked a small hole through the screen door when she leaned against it. Walt had to tell us twice to feed Sport, and then we'd complained about it.

"No, Squirrel," said Walt over Ruby's shoulder. "It's about Jewel."

Evangeline nudged me with her elbow and whispered, "I told you there was something funny about her. Bet she came from aliens."

"No, not exactly," said Walt. Then he muttered under his breath something like "Wish I knew what to say next."

"It will come to you, Walt," said Ruby. But it never did.

Nine

Ruby could hardly get two feet away from us for the first couple of weeks after her return from the music tour. If she went to gather eggs, we went too. If she washed her face and used Noxzema in the morning before she went to milk the cows, Evangeline and I copied her.

Whenever we annoyed her, she never said exactly that. Instead, she gave us tasks to help get ready for Christmas. She was standing next to the kitchen counter, skimming cream off a bucket of milk when she noticed that both Evangeline and I were taking up her elbow space.

"Why don't you girls go over and set the breakfast table? While you're doing that, imagine how it might look decked out for the holidays. Sapphire, Pearl, and little Jewel are coming to join us for Christmas dinner. Why don't you girls come up with the table decorations? I saw in *Southern Living* that you can make napkin rings out of the most extraordinary things."

"Like what?" I asked, studying a streak of dirt on my pants leg where Sport had jumped on me.

"For instance, you can string cranberries together, curl them into rings, and tie them with green ribbon. You can also core an apple or a pear or an orange and put a candle in the center to make a centerpiece. Yes sirree, just put a piece of fruit in a bowl with a candle in it, surround it with some pecans from our tree, and we'll have us a beautiful table—one that would have made your great-grandmother Itasca proud."

Evangeline had her own idea of how a home should be decorated for Christmas, and it apparently involved using red and green pipe cleaners, the Sears and Roebuck catalog, a can of gold spray paint, construction paper, a hole punch, Elmer's Glue, and lots of glitter.

I could just see her making an ungodly mess of the catalog, which I wished out of early every morning when I sat in the kitchen and had myself a cup of milk coffee. Lately, I'd become an early riser and, while Ruby had been gone, had helped to cook breakfast.

It always took me a while to wake up well enough to speak, so having a cup of weak milk coffee and time to look at the girls' fashions in the catalog had become an important starter to my day. So I said, "Evangeline, don't you even think about messing up my catalog."

"It ain't your catalog," she said, putting her hands on her hips. "You don't own everything in this house."

Before our argument had a chance to get going good, Ruby headed us off at the pass. "Let's see about going to Densesky's after breakfast and getting a few things to make decorations with, shall we? We've got lots to do before Santa comes, and I need to buy a few groceries. And maybe after Christmas is over, we can take that trip into Austin, visit *The Uncle Jay Show*, and eat at the Piccadilly Cafeteria like I promised before I left with Sapphire and Pearl."

"We still get to go?" I asked, surprised. I hadn't dared remind her about her promise to take us, lest Walt had told her about a few of our departures from perfect conduct during her absence.

Ruby just smiled, came over to where we were folding paper napkins on the kitchen table and hugged us both. "I'm proud of my girls. I heard how brave you were on the school bus and how you came up with a plan to try to help yourselves and the other children. You'll make fine women someday because you're quick thinking."

Where Evangeline and I had been about to launch into a huge battle over the catalog, we were now smiling and feeling good about ourselves. Our mamaw had a way of making everything better.

It wasn't long before we were loaded in Ruby's Thunderbird, heading into Fireside. She taught us how to sing "Fireside Women," like she'd done with Pearl and Sapphire so many times over the past few months. While I can't say that Ed Sullivan would have put us on his Really Big Show, I felt that we weren't half-bad.

By the time we'd arrived at Densesky's, we were all three in the best of spirits, so when we found Selma Davis cutting off yardage of tulle, we were practically over the moon with joy.

"That netting looks like something to make a wedding veil out of," said Ruby.

"You got that right!" said Selma, beaming broadly. She wore a red turtleneck, a short black skirt, and, of course, her tall black go-go boots. Her candy-cane earrings hung down low enough to touch the top of her turtleneck and took on a life of their own each time she turned her head. It was her hair bow made to match her earrings that caught my attention, however. Clipped to the front center of her piled-up hairdo, its red and white stripes mesmerized me. There was not another like it in Fireside and possibly never would be.

"I found the bridal outfit I wanted over in Fredericksburg. But I couldn't find a veil the right length, or that was full enough to cover my updo the way I wanted, so I decided to make my own."

Evangeline and I looked at each other and then up at Ruby. We wanted desperately to ask Selma if she had given any more thought to us being a flower girl and junior bridesmaid in her wedding, but Ruby could read our thoughts. She frowned, shook her head, and put her finger up to her lips. She only had to say one word, "Austin," and we were quiet.

"Hard to believe that in a month and a half, I'll be Mrs. Densesky," said Selma. Her face beamed like ours might if we'd just been told we were about to get to pick out a new puppy.

Ruby appeared deep in thought and finally said, "What can Walt and I do to help you with the wedding or reception?"

"Well, we plan to marry at the Methodist Church on Valentine's," said Selma. "And the Fireside Inn is handling the reception. But would it be too much if I were to ask you and your sisters to sing a few hymns at the church and play music at the reception?"

71

All evidence pointed to the conclusion that Evangeline and I were losing our chance to be in the wedding. If she'd wanted us to be in it, she would have said so by now.

"We'd love to," said Ruby. "What an honor to be asked."

"That would mean so much to us," said Selma, her eyes shining with joyful tears. And then she looked directly at Evangeline and me. "And I don't suppose you girls would like to be a flower girl and junior bridesmaid, would you?"

"Good golly, Miss Selma," said Evangeline, "I thought you asked some other girls by now. You betcha we would! Let's shake on it." She stuck out her little hand and pumped Selma's up and down. "Got yourself a deal."

"Will we get to wear long red velvet dresses and black patent-leather shoes?" I asked, visualizing us decked to the nines.

"I was thinking you and Evangeline could wear short velvet miniskirts, off-white lace blouses, go-go boots, and have your hair pinned up just like mine."

"Miniskirts?" I said.

"To match mine," said Selma. "That's what I intend to wear. It's what I see on the TV when it shows the runways in Paris and London. Blouses with billowy sleeves and rows of lace down the front and on the cuffs. Short sweet skirts in white leather, although mine will be red due to the fact that it's Valentine's Day and because it's my second wedding. And I think I'll wear diamond-shaped fishnet stockings to symbolize the diamond in my engagement ring and the significance of our wedding vows."

"I can see you've put a lot of thought into this," said Ruby, wide-eyed. "Do you know what music you want us to play?"

"Oh yes," said Selma. "Lots of things. I have them all written down at home. My favorite isn't actually a hymn, though. It's 'Chapel of Love.' And then there's 'O Love That Wilt Not Let Me Go.'"

"That is a pretty big variety, as far as music goes. This is shaping up to be a special day indeed," said Ruby, trying to hide her amusement.

"Yes," said Selma. "But don't worry about the girls' wedding outfits. I can whip them up in no time at all. I've got the patterns and materials all right here in the store."

We were so enthralled by Selma's wedding plans that we'd nearly forgotten what we'd come to Densesky's to buy, but Ruby got us back on track. Soon, we had a basketful of the most bliss-giving products.

By the time we arrived home, we had six paper bags of items, one of which held supplies to keep Evangeline and myself occupied over the next few days. I was to make the napkin rings and sculpt candle holders from pears. Evangeline was to make an angel out of an old Austin telephone book that was about to mildew out in the washhouse but was instructed not to touch the family's Sears and Roebuck Christmas catalog.

Evangeline and I were over the moon with excitement, not only about Christmas Day but about Selma's wedding. For the next few days, we worked harmoniously and diligently on our Christmas projects, watched *A Charlie Brown Christmas* and Bing Crosby as host for "*The Hollywood Palace*, brought to you by Gold Seal Champagne," without fighting once over who got to flip the TV channels.

When Christmas Day arrived, Ruby had whipped up meringue cookies with cherries in the middle, a coconut cake, and a Golden Westerner cake. She cooked two fat hens with dressing; a whipped sweet potato casserole with brown sugar; green beans with ham; a tomato, bell pepper, and onion salad; and baked bread and concocted heavenly hash with fruit cocktail, whipped cream, and lots of nuts. Of course, iced tea and coffee were always in abundance.

Evangeline and I set a mighty fine table, even if I do say so myself. Her telephone-book angel had been folded and sprayed into quite an extraordinary golden vision, what with her Styrofoam head, pipe cleaner arms, peacock feather wings, and a paper crown. My sister had used an entire can of gold spray paint to cover everything, and boy howdy, could you tell. Let me just say that if heaven's angels have that much gold on them, they must be a vision.

After spending hours stringing cranberries together, I enjoyed tying festive strands of them into napkin rings. Imagine the pride I felt when I tied little green bows to bind the strands and then pushed a freshly starched napkin through them—which I had ironed, remembering the instructions Itasca had given me months before her death. I whipped out my Brownie camera and took pictures of the table after we'd finished setting it perfectly. Forks on the left, knives and spoons on the right. I doubted that anyone in Fireside Elementary had set a table as beautifully as ours was.

Then Evangeline raced into the kitchen and sprinkled an entire bottle of silver glitter over the white tablecloth. "Now we've got stars to go with our angel," she said, beaming proudly.

Although some of the glitter fell on my napkin rings, I held back and didn't kick up a fuss—all in the spirit of Christmas, of course. I did, however, wrinkle up my nose at her, just to point out that her trespass upon my creation hadn't gone unnoticed.

By the time Sapphire, Pearl, and Jewel arrived, dinner was nearly on the table. We had expected them to arrive an hour earlier and had begun to worry before they finally appeared.

Pearl looked a little disheveled, and Jewel was fussing her head off. "Must be colic," Pearl said, bleary-eyed.

"She keep you up late?" asked Ruby, taking the baby out of her arms. Instantly, little Jewel quieted, a fact that couldn't help but annoy both Sapphire and Pearl.

"Jeepers," said Sapphire. "This little tyke kept both of us up all night."

"I've been down the same road before. Just draw her little knees up like this, and it'll help ease her discomfort," said Ruby, demonstrating the proper hold.

"Why didn't I think of that?" said Pearl.

Ruby looked so adoringly at the raven-haired baby that I soon felt annoyed. She was a cute little angel baby all right, but in my eyes, the privilege of Ruby's attention should belong to Evangeline and me. I was about to disappear into my bedroom, but Ruby had another plan.

"Here, Squirrel, you hold the baby while I put the food on the table."

"You want me to hold it?"

"She won't bite. Pearl and Sapphire can put ice in the glasses and take a break from looking after her."

"But what if she starts to squall?"

"She wouldn't be the first. We'll be in the kitchen if you need us."

"She smells like spit-up, though," I said.

"Do it anyhow. You smelled the same when you were a baby. Put a burping pad over your shoulder so if she starts to blow, she won't mess up your Christmas blouse. Take her on into the living room and rock her. She's likely to go to sleep, and then we can all get through Christmas dinner as one happy family."

To hold a tiny infant was strange to me. I wondered what it had been like when I was a baby and my mother held me. Had she loved me? Had she patted my back and stroked my hair? I didn't know, so I made up my best version of her.

Oh, surely she had rocked me during the wee hours of the morning and hated to part with me long enough to put me in my cradle and let me sleep. No doubt she had done the same for Rabbit, though I believed she must have squirmed much more than I. I was convinced she had sung the sweetest lullabies to us or perhaps some Broadway tune, failing that.

I imagined her rubbing Johnson's Baby Lotion on our fat arms and legs and putting pink bows in our perfect hairdos, making us admirable children through her intense devotion to motherhood. If only she would come home and see how new and improved we were. Then she would know that at least some of her efforts had paid off.

When Pearl came in and took a sleeping Jewel out of my arms, I came back to my senses. Our mother was still just as gone as she ever had been, and it didn't look like she was coming back anytime soon. And what was that about getting herself in a pickle that she'd mentioned in her one-and-only letter to us?

Evangeline and I had had long discussions about the possibilities, many of which included terrible personal tragedies.

"I bet she set her hair on fire when she was smoking a cigarette," I told Evangeline. "All that Aqua Net on teased hair might make her highly flammable."

"No way," she said. "You can't set yourself on fire 'cause of hair spray."

"Can't you read the back of aerosol cans? They always warn people about that," I said confidently.

"I can read. But I save my brain for more important things."

"Like seeing how many flies you can kill with rubber bands."

Evangeline's eyes lit up. "Well, it's important to control insects and way more funner than reading the backs of cans. I think she joined a gang, got herself tattooed, and rides all over the country eating pickles with Steve McQueen, 'the King of Cool,'" said Evangeline.

"Another possibility is that she wore her Playtex girdle out on the front stoop in the summer heat like she used to do here in Texas. Maybe folks up in New York aren't used to women like Mama."

"No," said Evangeline. "Nobody cares about seeing her in her girdle. A more realer possibility is that she's been living in a telephone booth with Mighty Mouse in Queens 'cause she can't pay her rent," said Evangeline.

"I guess it wouldn't be the first time for that either." I reached over and patted my sister on her head, but she shook off my hand and crossed her eyes.

"I ain't Sport. You can't pet me like a dog."

"I was petting you like a rabbit."

"Well, OK. That's different."

Evangeline and I had received musical instruments for Christmas earlier in the day, and after dinner was over and the dishes had been done, we got them out of their cases. Evangeline got a new violin, of course, so she didn't have to borrow Ruby's. Walt had especially chosen mine, which was a Gibson guitar in a white leather case. Oh, it was handsome, all right. But I doubted I'd ever play it well.

"Squirrel, I want you to learn how to sing like Dale Evans and accompany yourself on this guitar." Walt smiled joyfully, so delighted by his gift of music to me.

I wanted to please him desperately, to fulfill his dream. The fact that he had such faith in a talentless kid like me made me want to live up to it.

"I'm gonna get you guitar lessons in Fireside," he said. "There's a fella in town that can play like Chet Atkins. You pay special attention to every note he plays and how he does it, and pretty soon, we'll have us a star."

I smiled, held the guitar and strummed it once with the plastic pick he'd handed to me. It sounded tinny and unlikely that good music could ever come from it when I was the one playing. I thought perhaps it would have been better if he had given me dance lessons and bought me some tap shoes or ballerina clothes. I might have a fighting chance with those but was terribly worried about anything dealing with an instrument.

"All right, Popo. I'll try."

That night, Ruby, Pearl, and Sapphire sang "Silent Night" and then launched into "Santa Claus Is Back in Town" to get baby Jewel to stop crying. We were all swaying to the bluesy feeling of the music, and I could swear that little Jewel could feel it in her tiny bones. She quit fussing, her legs and arms moved in delight, and her big beautiful eyes looked directly into my heart.

It was then that I realized she was a Christmas miracle. I didn't know exactly how Pearl had come by her. Whether she'd found her someplace or landed a rooster of a man who magically poofed a baby in her, I didn't understand.

I said I thought it would be fun if we made a little manger by the fireplace and let Jewel be the baby Jesus. We could pretend she was a boy, couldn't we, just for the evening? When everyone agreed it would make no difference to Jewel whether she portrayed a boy or a girl for the next hour, we went to work.

Evangeline dumped out a dresser drawer in our room. Her bubble-gum-wrapper collection flew all over the floor, along with the marbles from her Chinese checkers set. I crossed my eyes and groaned when I saw the mess but held my tongue. Instead of fussing, I gathered up soft towels and the decorative pillow from our bed.

I talked all of the adults into posing with baby Jesus as Joseph and Mary, the shepherds, and the wise men. They wore Ruby's old table-cloths draped over their heads and held together with safety pins. As for Evangeline and me? We pretended to be fluffy angels in old, white chenille bedspreads with wings made out of coat hangers, covered in white paper and edged with silver tinsel garland. Sapphire set up a Canon camera so the timer would go off. At first, the nativity felt full, complete to me. But, as on all holidays since we'd lost our father and mother, sadness moved in. No, we weren't all present and accounted for. We could never all be together on Christmas in this lifetime. Like shards of broken pottery, our nativity set wasn't tidy. We were a patched family. I wouldn't, though, undo the family we'd become. We were the best we could be, given our circumstances.

Ten

"Welcome to Fireside, Texas. This is Juliet, the heart and voice of station KOFF, urging you to be careful where you set off your bottle rockets and firecrackers this New Year's Eve, on account of the lack of rain we've had. Go ahead with your sparklers, though; just don't let toddlers, or folks who act that age, get a hold of them. Today's broadcast is sponsored by the Lily Gilders' Association. They want you to know that if you've got a lily that needs gilding, they can help. Their offer stands to help tidy up or dress those folks who don't understand civilized attire. They can teach you how to walk, how to talk, and what to wear. No case is too tough. So if you have a family member who doesn't fit in socially or has more connection to a slide rule than humans, they can help.

"Today's special at the Fireside Café includes a roast turkey and cranberry sandwich; mustard potato salad; and a Coca-Cola, cup of coffee, or glass of iced tea for just one dollar and sixty-eight cents, including tax. Y'all go on over and tell them that Juliet, Evangeline, and Ruby sent you.

"Next on today's program, we have Ruby, Sapphire, and Pearl—all the Gemburree Sisters—performing, "Merry Christmas, Baby," in honor of their friend Elvis and baby Jewel Gemburree, the sweetest little baby girl this side of Memphis.

"But before I turn the program over to the fabulous Gemburrees, don't forget today is the last day we celebrate the Christmas season here in Fireside. Tomorrow, we all start taking down our trees. Please remember that dried-out trees are a fire hazard, and that the fire department will take all your old trees and turn them into mulch to spread around the town's gardens. That ought to make everybody happy."

Ruby, Pearl, and Sapphire began to sing and play their instruments while Evangeline pushed all the station buttons, just as she'd been taught. My sister had always been good at pushing everyone's buttons, so it was a natural fit.

And me? I just held baby Jewel. She tried to focus her baby blues on me, and I'm pretty sure she got me in her line of vision, 'cause she just smiled and smiled.

The next Monday, when Evangeline and I went back to the Fireside Elementary, Jimmy Bodine and Dixie Flagg started a rumor that passed through school like wildfire. They said Pearl was a tramp and had a tar-baby love child out of wedlock and that her sisters were just covering up for the piece of trash she was. They were passing a note through geography class calling her a back-seat hussy, whatever that was, and I just started crying. For one thing, I knew that Pearl was no piece of trash, and for another, Dixie was supposed to be my friend. We'd shared many a banana split and had gotten into a lot of trouble together when we toilet papered Selma's house that time. How could she then betray me with meanness over my beloved aunt and little Jewel? Then it dawned on me, Dixie was walleyed in love with Jimmy Bodine and was trying to earn points with that no-count boy. He was a genius at pitting friends against one another; I had witnessed this many times during social studies when he chaired the salt map–making committee. By the time he'd gotten through orchestrating a full-fledged disaster, two fist fights had broken out. But he was very handsome, if only on the outside, and Dixie was a sucker for good looks. He loved mayhem, and Dixie loved Jimmy because she loved it too. It was that simple.

William Bartlett, who sat next to me, leaned over to me and whispered, "Don't pay them any mind. My motto is don't get mad, just get even." Those words stuck in my head like gnats to flypaper. I decided I would save them for future use.

You would know that Mr. McWherter caught him whispering to me and gave him detention points. Poor Willy Billy had to stay after school and clean the chalkboard, all on account of me. I'd have thought he'd have blamed me for his having gotten in trouble, but no, he called me on the telephone as I got through drying the dinner dishes that night.

80

Walt answered the black rotary phone and said, "Now, young man, tell me your name. Uh-huh, Ermadine's boy? You don't say? Well, yes, you can talk to Juliet for a few minutes. It's seven thirty, and we have a rule: no calls after eight o'clock. You can talk for a little while, but she'll have to hang up directly."

"Popo!" I whispered, embarrassed. Now how was I supposed to hold my head up in school with a family like this? Then the room began to spin slightly. The thought that a boy had called me for the first time in my life made me light-headed.

"Hello, Juliet," he said, his voice low and soft. "This here's William Bartlett."

"I know it's you, silly. I recognize your voice."

"Oh well, then. Just as long as we're on the same page."

"Can't say we're on the same page, but we are on the same telephone line. Just hope none of the busybodies on the party line pick up their phones."

"I better hurry, then. I been thinking about what you can do to get even with Jimmy and Dixie," he said.

"What's that?"

"I got a magician's kit for Christmas. It's got a pack of chewing gum that looks like normal gum, only it isn't. It tastes like a skunk, turns your tongue black, and stings like pepper sauce."

"I love it!"

"We'll fix their wagons up good," he said, his voice rising excitedly. "Tomorrow's the day, OK, Juliet?"

"Can't be soon enough to suit me."

The next morning during geography class, William passed me the sticks of gum, mouthed "Go ahead. Give it to 'em," and smiled wickedly.

I turned and looked at Dixie, sitting to my right, and smiled a candy-sweet smile at her while Mr. McWherter droned on about the Soviet Union's population. Then I looked over at conniving, stuck-up Jimmy on my left and winked at him as though he was my best friend in the entire universe. I quickly threw a stick of gum at both children, but when Dixie reached up to catch hers, she missed it. A doomed missile, it slapped down on the floor.

To my dismay, Mr. McWherter's hearing was peachy keen, compared to most persons his age. He turned around from the chalkboard, saw Dixie's stick of gum lying on the floor, and caught Jimmy unwrapping his.

"Stop!" he yelled. "You children bring that gum to me. You know this is contraband in class. It's against school policy."

"It's not our fault, Mr. McWherter. Juliet threw it at us. She thinks she can get away with anything on account of her radio stint. It's what her trashy family taught her. I think you ought to expel her. That's what I would do, if—" said Jimmy.

"You're not in charge, young man. Juliet, is this true? Did you throw the gum?"

"Yessir," I said, my face red with shame.

"This is out of character for you," he said. "Perhaps even good students need a reminder. Juliet, you can remain inside during recess today."

If he had beaten me with tree branches, I wouldn't have felt any worse. I hung my head, and tears trickled down my face.

"In the meantime, Jimmy and Dixie, bring up the gum and put it on my desk," said our teacher, who then put the sticks in his blue sweater pocket. When the recess bell rang, Mr. McWherter went to the teachers' lounge and left me alone to take an extra test on the Soviet Union as punishment.

When recess was over, Mr. McWherter walked up to my desk, picked up my test, looked at it, and crumpled it up. "Perfect," he said. "Just perfect." When he spoke, I could see his tongue was black and could smell the faint scent of skunk.

Oh, do not partake of revenge, or it will come back to bite you like a snake. Two sticks of magic gum eaten by a teacher cost me a conduct grade on my report card, and that got me the joy of cleaning out the henhouse on Saturday morning when I should have been watching *Tom and Jerry* in the living room with Evangeline.

When I tell you that it's a plumb miracle that Ruby made good on her word to take us to Austin with our friends, just as she'd promised before she'd gone on tour, you can believe it. I guess in Ruby's view, cleaning out the foul-smelling chicken mess was punishment enough, and possibly I had been rehabilitated and saved from a life of future crimes. Or maybe she thought it was secretly funny that my teacher had eaten the very gum he'd chastised me for passing out.

Hadley stayed with us the night before and even brought cherry-flavored lip gloss for us to wear. Evangeline's friend who would accompany us was little Davy Ottmers, the armpit soloist king, but Walt had long since established that no boys could ever spend the night at our house. Therefore, Ruby would pick him up at the Fireside Café in the morning on our way out of town.

Hadley and I got up at 5:00 a.m. so we could have plenty of time to primp in the bathroom before we left for Austin. Although we had washed and dried our hair the previous evening, it came to us like a vision that we should use Dippity-do styling gel and put our hair up in the pink sponge rollers Ruby used. We wore corduroy skirts, turtlenecks, cardigans and go-go boots, and told ourselves that we looked exactly like Tom Jones's backup singers and dancers. Who knew but that Uncle Jay might ask us to dance for him? We had been learning to do the Watusi and the Swim, and of course we'd known how to do the Twist since we were little.

Before we left, the telephone rang. Once again, it was William Bartlett. Ruby handed me the phone and smiled. Evangeline just rolled her eyes and said, "It's lover boy *again!*"

"Hush up," I said, motioning for her to get away. Hadley came close to me, and I let her listen in on the conversation. What were best friends for?

"I was just calling to say I was sorry that my magic gum got you in trouble. It was my idea, but it backfired."

"It's OK," I said.

William breathed a sigh of relief. "Then we're still friends?"

"Oh sure."

"Great! Just checking. See you around. OK?"

"Sure. See you at school."

I had no sooner hung up the phone than Hadley squealed, "Oh, he digs you, Juliet. He's one neat-o cat. All the girls think he's cute." I didn't know what to say, so I just giggled.

"You are so lucky," she said.

83

"Spare me," said Evangeline and rolled her eyes again.

"Don't you remember the time he came to our rescue on the playground when nasty Nathan Wilcot kicked sand in your eyes?" I reminded her.

"Well, I guess he has some good points," said Evangeline.

We all piled into Ruby's Thunderbird, excited to start the journey. Hadley and I still had the pink sponge rollers in our hair, and Ruby had braided Evangeline's so that it wouldn't look like the puffball it usually was.

We met Davy Ottmers and his mother at the Fireside Café. She was a large woman who always smelled faintly of fried fish on account of her job as restaurateur and cook. When Davy hopped out of her car, his blue jeans jacket caught in the door as he slammed it. His mother had to get out of the car, walk around to the passenger side, and get him unstuck. Mournfully, he looked down at his new jacket which now had a grease stripe down its front. His hair looked like an accident, too—what with a cowlick and a rooster tail that a pair of scissors had been taken to and stood up like cornstalks. For once, however, he wore a shirt that covered his belly and pants that reached below his ankles. For all his shortcomings, Davy had a lot of confidence and a certain swagger.

Ruby said, "Now, Davy, you sit in the front seat where I can keep an eye on you." She smiled at him, but her eyes meant business. "Evangeline, you sit in the middle in the back seat, because you're the smallest. Juliet, you and Hadley sit by the doors. If everybody minds their p's and q's, a good time will be had by all."

We were no farther than the city limits in Fireside when Evangeline leaned forward from the back seat, put her left elbow up on the front seat's back, and started arm wrestling with Davy. When their jostling caused Ruby to swerve the car, she said, "Wrestling is a bad idea, kiddos. Let's sing instead."

Ruby cranked up the radio, and Petula Clark's voice came on. She sang "Downtown," and we were her backup group. Our music had a lovely beginning, but you know how Davy was. He started squeaking his armpit to the music and shouted "Downtown" a little too loudly and very off key. I wasn't surprised one whit, but Ruby had been away on tour and missed his station KOFF concert. She raised her eyebrows at him but then just smiled as broadly as you please.

When we arrived in downtown Austin, it was time for lunch at the Piccadilly Cafeteria on Congress Avenue. Hadley and I quickly took off our pink sponge rollers and shoved them in a bag. Evangeline rolled her eyes at us and didn't so much as think to pull a comb through her wild hair, which was sticking up like a baby gorilla's might. The braid Ruby'd plaited had completely come undone. Ruby caught her before she slid out of the car.

"Come here, Rabbit," said Ruby. "How'd this happen in such a short time?" She whipped a comb out of her purse and patiently worked through the rat's nest that always seemed to be present. Then she pulled her hand-kerchief out and said, "Stick out your tongue." Ruby got Evangeline's spit on the center of it and started to wipe off the chocolate spot on her cheek. Evangeline wiggled and squirmed, but Ruby had a firm grip.

"Mamaw, you're making me mad," said Evangeline. "Davy has done got out of the car and is halfway to the cafeteria. I'm gonna be late."

"You'll live," said Ruby flatly.

Davy had already opened the cafeteria door and was making a beeline toward the dessert end of the line. He plucked off a bowl of strawberry shortcake and said, "This is all I want."

"No sirree," said Ruby. "Get yourself a piece of fried chicken and some peas and mashed potatoes to go with that. . . or something else that makes sense."

Davy's eyebrows drew together. There were endless choices for us all to make, and it was overwhelming to a boy whose mother cooked the same food for her family that she did for the Fireside Café. He was used to meals that rotated from one day to another, and there were only seven entrée choices at his parents' place: meatloaf on Sunday, chicken-fried steak on Monday, chicken and dumplings on Tuesday, liver and onions on Wednesday (which all children in Fireside hated), knockwurst on Thursday, fried fish on Friday, and Mexican casserole on Saturday.

"I can't decide," he said. But when his little blue eyes lighted on spaghetti, he had to have it. Ruby insisted he have green peas to go with it, and of course, Davy got to put the strawberry shortcake on his tray as well.

Evangeline copied Davy's choices to a T. The rest of us loaded our trays with no incident and followed the hostess to a table by the window. She waited, took our trays, and there we were, five people in puredee heaven.

Davy was so short, he sat on his knees in his chair and started picking up each strand of spaghetti one at a time and slurping them. Within about two seconds he and his shirt were covered with spaghetti sauce.

"Oh no," said Ruby. "You can't wear a shirt like that on *The Uncle Jay Show*."

Davy looked down at his chest and got a gleam in his eyes. "Looks like blood, don't it? I can tell Uncle Jay I got shot by a bandit in a spaghetti western. I'll just say I fought him off and am going to get a reward from Clint Eastwood himself. You know that movie *The Good, The Bad and The Ugly*, don't you? Maybe I'll get a badge or something like that."

"Yes, I've heard of it. Oh dear," said Ruby. "We'll have to think about what to do."

Before Davy had finished lunch, he had shortcake in his blond hair and peas in his ears. It takes talent for a kid to do that in nothing flat. I thought maybe it required even greater skill than playing his armpit.

Ruby calmly whisked him away to the women's restroom, washed his hair underneath the faucet, combed it, and turned his shirt inside out so it appeared semiclean if a little bedraggled.

"You're lucky this is January, Davy. You can wear your blue jeans jacket during the entire broadcast to hide your shirt, and no one in the audience will be the wiser. Just hold one hand over the grease spot where you slammed it in the car door and freeze in that position until the show is over. That'll help keep you out of mischief too," said Ruby. But Davy could have cared less about his appearance, took one last drink of milk, started laughing, and made milk bubbles come out of his freckled nose.

By the time we got to the studio, Evangeline and Davy were trying to outdo each other making monkey faces and sounds. Ruby had tried to keep her attention on navigating Austin traffic, a whole other animal compared to tiny Fireside, which had only one traffic light and so she had to let them act up as long as they didn't get too out of hand.

Hadley and I managed to keep as broad a distance from them as possible as we walked up the sidewalk to KTBC studio at 10th and Brazos in downtown Austin. We caught a glimpse of ourselves in the reflection of a store window, checking to make sure our hairdos were perfect and our posture was board straight, which Ruby said was the key to digestion and making a good impression on television.

We had naturally thought we would be the stars of the show, but the moment Ruby walked onto the set, Mr. Jay Hodgson acted like the Queen of England had just arrived.

"Well, hello, Ruby, so glad to have you back at the studio. Haven't seen you since you and the other Gemburree gals did that special for us. When are you going to come back and do another one?" asked Jay. He was dressed in a red, long-sleeved shirt and khaki pants. Every strand of his dark hair had been combed into perfect submission.

"Well," purred Ruby, "we'd be glad to come back and do a song or two for the station any time you want."

"Is Marguerite with you?" he asked. "If so, the two of you could sing an impromptu duet."

"No, she isn't," said Ruby, letting it drop.

"Oh," he said, clearly disappointed. "I thought she would be."

The sound of my mother's name brought tears to my eyes. Hadley touched my sleeve and whispered, "It's all right, Juliet. He doesn't know." I wiped off my cheeks with the back of my hand and tried to smile, but the day no longer felt golden. It felt brownish and ugly, like the January day it was.

"Where's Packer Jack?" rang out Evangeline, oblivious to the goings-on.

Jay looked around the set and joked, "You'll smell the old rascal before you see him. His reputation always precedes him."

In another twenty minutes, thirty boys and girls were sitting cross-legged on the studio floor and on risers, watching cartoons on the monitor. Just as soon as Mighty Mouse had finished his last rescue, out walked Uncle Jay with his microphone. "Hello, boys and girls," he said. "Welcome to *The Uncle Jay Show*. Say, do you know my friend Packer Jack?"

Packer Jack had a long, frizzy beard that shifted against his chest each time he turned his head. He wore a moth-eaten black hat, a vest, and a bandanna.

Evangeline's hand shot up in the air. "I do!" she yelled enthusiastically with the other girls and boys. Her eyes were sparkling with excitement. Next to her was Davy, still in his blue jeans jacket to hide his stained, inside-out shirt. He had let his hand drop to his side, exposing a long greasy stripe on the blue denim.

Hadley and I were seated on another row with the older, taller children but I kept my eye on the pair, lest they get out of hand. Ruby stood just out of sight of the camera, giving us all "the look." We were both concerned that little Davy would launch into his armpit solo, but he just sat there with a glazed look in his eyes. I guessed it was due to that too-full feeling he may have felt from lunch at the Piccadilly.

"Let's start with show-and-tell. Have we got any talkative boys or girls in the audience?" asked Packer Jack, straightening his vest. His gray beard moved with each word he spoke.

Again, Evangeline's hand shot up in the air. "Come on up to the front," said Packer Jack, "and tell us what you got for Christmas." Evangeline made her way to Packer Jack, smiled up at her favorite TV personality in the world, and appeared completely starstruck.

"I got a fiddle," she said, and then held up seven fingers, "and seven pairs of panties with hearts and days of the week on them. There's Monday, Tuesday, Wednesday. . . but Sunday's my favorite panty of the week on account of the heart being purple, my best color."

Packer Jack and Uncle Jay tried their best to keep from laughing, their faces sweaty and the reddish color of sugar-glazed beets. No one seemed to know what to say, so I looked at Ruby for help. She was clearly dying from embarrassment and was frozen as fearfully stiff as my favorite cherry Popsicle. I had to do something to get us out of this mess, so I just did what came naturally and started talking.

"Uncle Jay," I shouted and raised my hand as though I were in the classroom with all the answers. "Fireside, Texas, has a message for you."

Uncle Jay, who was still trying to recover from Evangeline's embarrassing revelation, composed himself and then looked directly at me. "Is that so? You're Ruby Cranbourne's granddaughter? Why don't you come up and tell the audience your name?"

Nervously, I made my way toward him, nearly tripping over Davy Ottmers's foot. He was taking off his jacket, exposing his wrong-side-out, spaghetti-covered catastrophe. He stuck his hand underneath his shirt and under his armpit. I could see he was about to launch into his famous concert, so I just gave him the stink eye big time, and he grinned, raising his arm up even higher.

"My name is Juliet Cranbourne, host of *The Cranbourne Variety Hour*, which airs each Saturday afternoon at 3:00 p.m. on station KOFF. Fireside, Texas, would like for everyone here in the Austin viewing area to know we're the friendliest little town this side of heaven. We'd like to invite Austin to be our sister city, although, we'd be your much smaller sister."

"Well, that's awfully nice of you. . . and Fireside! Boys and girls, Miss Juliet is the granddaughter of none other than Grand Ole Opry star Ruby Cranbourne. Ruby and the Gemburree Sisters have performed on this very program many times. Miss Juliet, you're a very hospitable and gracious young lady and obviously a great ambassador for your community of Fireside. Would you like to add anything in closing to elaborate on why your town is such a friendly one?"

Davy slapped his arm down against his hand in his armpit and launched into "Yankee Doodle Dandy."

I don't know what possessed me exactly, but just the very idea of Davy getting me into more unpleasantness with Ruby or Walt due to his armpit concerts made me powerfully anxious. Oh, how my mouth so often got me into so much trouble, even when I was trying desperately to be good. "As a matter of fact, Fireside is such a friendly town that we're inviting all the KTBC viewers to come down to station KOFF next month on Groundhog Day. You can watch the Gemburree Sisters sing tunes from their new album, *The Fireside Book of Love*, eat cookies in the shape of groundhogs, and drink pineapple punch in the spirit of sharing our new sisterhood!"

I took a deep breath and tried to decide whether Ruby was going to kill or congratulate me when we got home. Across her beautiful face swept a strange mixture of delight and horror, sort of like what you get when you eat a dozen doughnuts and then have to lie down with a rag on your forehead.

Uncle Jay patted me on the head like his favorite puppy, then looked into the camera with a big smile across his face. "You've heard it here first on *The Uncle Jay Show*. Go on down to Fireside, Texas, and visit Austin's potentially new sister city on Groundhog Day at station KOFF.

"Now, before we begin our January spelling bee, let's have a word from our sponsor, Borax Fab!"

On the monitor in the background, we could see the Borax Fab commercial running while Uncle Jay wiped his forehead and Packer Jack made funny faces at the kids.

The commercial depicted three perfect children rolling downhill in their white outfits and getting covered with grass stains. Then their equally perfect parents rolled downhill with them, and everybody got up smiling and singing like they did that every day. It wasn't until their mother started singing, the "Oh Fab, I'm glad" jingle as she stood over the washing machine loading laundry that I recognized our mother, Marguerite Milford Cranbourne.

Evangeline was oblivious to the commercial and our mother's presence in it. She was far too occupied with Davy Ottmers's second performance, to the tune of "Comet—it makes your teeth turn green. Comet—it tastes like gasoline. Comet—it makes you vomit. So eat some Comet and vomit today!" which she was whistling without the added benefits of lateral incisors because her upper ones were missing. More spit and air came out than whistles.

Tears flowed as I recognized our mother singing with her onscreen family and smiling like she hadn't a care in the world. I couldn't help but wonder whether Borax Fab could clean up Evangeline's and my messes and make us perfect children.

Eleven

When we left KTBC and got inside Ruby's Thunderbird, our grandmother gave us mixed signals of her reaction to our visit on *The Uncle Jay Show*. She put Evangeline and Davy next to her on the front seat where she could keep a close eye on any upcoming shenanigans.

"If you two don't beat all," she said. "I don't want to hear a peep out of you all the way to Fireside. Evangeline, practice your multiplication tables on the back of this old grocery list." Ruby pulled the folded, lined paper from her black purse. "And Davy, I want you to write the name of every country in the world that begins with the letter *A*." Ruby handed him the receipt from the Piccadilly Cafeteria and doled out two old pencils with petrified erasers to her seatmates. "Not a word you two. Now get to work."

Ruby looked in the rearview mirror as she started the Thunderbird's engine. "Juliet, really! Where on earth are we going to find a cookie cutter in the shape of a groundhog? You should have talked to me first, but under the circumstances. . ." She looked over at Evangeline and Davy and shook her head. Before she put the Thunderbird into drive, she turned around and smiled at Hadley and me. "On the other hand, it never hurts to promote the new album on air one more time. Juliet, you're one smart cookie!"

Soon as we walked in the door from Austin, Pearl called on the telephone and asked to speak to me. I just had to smile; it always made me feel grown up and important to be singled out to speak on the phone.

"Squirrel, would you like to babysit little Jewel while I try to get my grocery shopping done? I don't want to take her out in public places with the flu season at its worst in years. I'll pay you fifty cents an hour. How does that sound?"

"You don't have to pay me, Aunt Pearl. I'll be glad to watch her."

"Well, that's mighty generous, honey. Maybe you could also help me with her during Selma's wedding reception."

Just the mere mention of Selma's approaching marriage to Norman Densesky filled my stomach with joyful butterflies. The thought of getting to show off baby Jewel to the wedding guests was so appealing, as was the idea that Evangeline and I were going to finally get to have our dreams come true. To get to babysit and be in the wedding party on the same day was nearly too good to digest. I nearly floated through the next few days on the breeze of anticipation.

A week later, Selma summoned us to the store to be fitted in the white leather miniskirts and blouses she was making for us to wear in our important roles as junior bridesmaid and an older-than-usual flower girl. Ruby stood with us inside Densesky's dressing room while Evangeline and I took turns standing on the wooden carpet-covered platform while Selma pinned up our hems. We could see her back in the mirror. Her hair, piled high as usual, was held together by a pencil stuck through the center in place of a clip.

"Are you excited?" asked Ruby. "Your wedding day will be here in two shakes of a lamb's tail."

"I'm so beside myself, I can't see straight. I'm just praying we won't have another ice storm like we did last year on Valentine's. No one in the Texas Hill Country except me knows how to drive on an icy road. When I used to drive a big rig, I was prepared for most anything."

"You're a gooder driver than most," said Evangeline. "And you outdone yourself the day you rescued us on the school bus."

Selma reached out, hugged my sister, kissed her forehead leaving pearlized lipstick prints, and then looked at me. She cupped my ear with her hand and said, "Oh, Sweet Pea, y'all did such a good job at not letting that old devil bus driver get the best of you. But that's in the rearview mirror. Best we keep our eyes on what lies ahead, rather than the road behind."

Our grandmother, who had been told the story of our abduction many times, teared up briefly and then got the conversation back on track. "Hopefully, it will be a clear, sunny day," she said, studying our hemlines. "Oh dear. They've both grown so much, their skirts are much shorter than I imagined. You girls need to be careful not to bend over during the wedding. If you must reach down at all, bend at the knee. Again, I repeat, do not lean over. People will see whether you're wearing Sunday, Monday, or Tuesday underwear, Evangeline. You too, Juliet."

As Selma slipped the last straight pin into Evangeline's hemline, she said, "All I really want is for all the people I care about to be there at our wedding. In some ways, I'll be feeling a tad sad because both my parents are dead. The only family I've still got living is my sister, and I'm just praying she'll be able to come. Her Tango Tangerines factory keeps her plenty busy."

"So you're an orphan too?" I asked, feeling tears well up in my eyes.

"No, I've never been an orphan because the good Lord has my back. Just remember that no matter what sadness may befall us, we're all still the children of God the Father. Furthermore, I have y'all to depend on. You're family."

"You a Cranbourne or a Gemburree like Jewel?" asked Evangeline. "We cousins, Miss Selma?"

"We're cousins of the heart," said Selma. "Family can be anyone, depending upon how you add up the folks that count."

"You are absolutely right," said Ruby. "Family is as family becomes." She looked at me and smiled. "Juliet has her work cut out for her until the wedding, though."

"How's that?" asked Selma.

"She's invited the entire viewing audience to come to station KOFF for cookies in the shape of groundhogs, along with pineapple punch. It will be interesting to see how she pulls it off."

Selma got up off her knees, dusted off her legs, looked at me, and smiled. "My money is on Juliet. If anyone could pull it off, it'd be her."

"So's mine," said Ruby. "She comes from a long line of creative, can-do people. Now let's see how she can come up with a groundhog cookie cutter and make thousands of cookies."

Later, Ruby dropped me off at Pearl and Sapphire's home. It was a two-story Arts and Crafts–style house made of limestone, with a wraparound porch and a single turret. It had a seventy-year-old pecan tree that dropped pecans as long as my thumb and a rose bush that had been trimmed back during the winter. The mailbox was attached to the limestone exterior just to the right of the front door. Two metal chairs painted green rested on the front porch, and a table made from a tree stump had been sanded and varnished. A lantern and a bowl of their favorite pieces of flint rock decorated their table. The sisters had spent many an hour on the front porch, watching passersby on the sidewalk, and waiting for the mail to come. They never knew when a residual check might arrive, or booking offers for that matter. Mail delivery was an exciting time every afternoon.

Pearl invited me inside with the biggest smile on her face. She wore a white sweater and a black scarf tied over her marcelled hair. She handed me sweet little Jewel as though she were a basket of eggs.

"Juliet, I wouldn't trust just anyone with this precious child. Take it from me, you're high cotton in my book of love. Here, and take this," she said, handing me a baby bottle with eight ounces of milk and leading us both to their floral sofa.

I nestled Jewel in the crook of my arm and said, "Now don't you worry about a thing, Aunt Pearl. Baby Jewel and I will iron out some world problems and figure out a plan for how we're gonna make a ton of cookies for Groundhog Day."

"I'm sure my four-month-old will have lots to say," she said and laughed. "After I finish buying groceries at Densesky's, I'm gonna call Charles Wesley and ask him to deliver some barbeque. We'll eat high on the hog if he can get away from the pit to do that."

"*The* Charles Wesley?" I asked. Excitement ran down my body in the form of shivers. All the way from the top of my frizzy hair, underneath my red, brown, and green–plaid dress with its white collar and shiny buttons down to my toes hiding slightly scrunched underneath my ankle socks and brown-and-white saddle shoes.

"The one and only," said Pearl. "We've been good friends for ages, if you could call it that. Anyway, I doubt he'll say no to me."

"But didn't he fly all those missions during World War II? That's what everybody at school says."

"You betcha he did. Not only World War II but Korea and Vietnam as well."

"Oh, I don't know if he ought to come here," I said, anxiously rubbing my head. "You see, I met a man named Seymour on our school bus not too long ago who'd just come back from old Vietnam. And you know what happened to my daddy in his helicopter. Vietnam makes me plumb nervous. Things happen to people over there. Some of them lose their lives, while others just lose their marbles."

"Well, Charles Wesley came out of there with his chest decorated with every medal you can imagine. There's nothing wrong with his marbles, I can tell you that, Squirrel. Every last one of his is present and accounted for. They're all still in his jar."

"All right, then, if you say so."

"Stick with me, honey pie."

"Where's Sapphire?" I asked, looking around, suddenly realizing her absence.

"Well," said Pearl, pausing. "She went to visit her good friend Violet in San Angelo. They were going to the livestock show to take a look at an ostrich somebody shipped over from Australia."

"An ostrich in Texas? Whoever heard of that?"

"Squirrel, anything can happen in Texas; don't you know that?"

"Guess I do now, Aunt Pearl."

While Aunt Pearl went to Densesky's to buy her groceries, little Jewel drank her entire bottle and burped half of it right back up on my shoulder. Well, that's a slight exaggeration. Maybe she really just burped a big one, but whatever it was went right down my collar and all over my plaid dress. "Ew," I said and wiped up the mess with a burp pad.

An hour later, after Pearl lugged the last bag of groceries in from her vehicle, she straightaway dialed Charles Wesley from her red princess telephone. "What'd I tell you, Juliet? He'll be here with the best brisket, pinto beans, and potato salad you've ever tasted before you can say 'Jack Rabbit.' Your taste buds will be singing 'Hallelujah' before the hour is up."

95

After a grinning Charles Wesley rapped rat-tat-a-tat-tat, tat-tat on Pearl's door, she opened it and then gushed all over him like Niagara Falls. He was wearing an old aviator's cap that had peeling leather and flaps over his ears. His skin was way darker than little Jewel's, and he was a tall, handsome man with a beautiful smile.

"How's my good friend?" he asked Pearl, not taking his eyes off her.

"Peachy keen," said Pearl. "Come on inside and meet my niece, Juliet. And you've already met baby Jewel."

"Good day, young lady," he said, smiling sweetly at me. "I hear you're quite a good help with the little princess." He nodded at Jewel, who was asleep on my shoulder.

"Thank you, sir. She's the sweetest baby ever. You want to hold her?"

"Sure, I do."

He gently picked her up and cuddled her in his big arms, while Pearl fussed over the pair and said she ought to take a picture. She disappeared into her bedroom and returned with her Canon camera.

"Here, I'll take the picture. You get in it, Aunt Pearl," I said, reaching for the camera.

In no time at all, the three of them posed just inside the closed front door. Charles had removed his aviator's cap and tucked it underneath his arm, all the while holding sleeping Jewel. Pearl was looking lovingly at both her daughter and Charles as if they both were the center of the universe.

It was then that I believed I knew who baby Jewel's father was. Tall, dark, handsome Charles Wesley was the only man in Fireside who fit the bill. Pearl's affection for him was obvious, as was his for her. But what I didn't understand was why they hadn't gotten married.

After Charles Wesley set the barbeque on the kitchen table and refused to take Pearl's money, he left, saying he had to get back to his pit on the double as it was time to help his assistant pit boss with the meat. Pearl gave him a kiss on his cheek, and you'd have thought she was Doris Day or somebody by the huge grin that came over his face.

"I'll be seeing you, Charles," said Pearl.

"Yes, I hope so," he replied and sighed, smiling. "You and little tootsie take care of each other. I'll be around bye-and-bye to check on you."

"See that you do," said Pearl, running a hand through her wavy blonde hair.

After he left, I thought and thought about Charles Wesley until I was bursting with questions. "Aunt Pearl, why don't you and Mr. Wesley get married? You could have a double wedding ceremony with Selma Davis and Norman Densesky if you work your cards right.

"Jeepers creepers! What brought this on?"

"Well, anyone can see Jewel needs a father and that he's taken a shine to her. You wouldn't be alone anymore, and he could take care of you both. You'd never go hungry because of all those whirls and whirls of barbecue and beans he's got going every single day."

"Except Sunday," said Pearl. "He's closed on Sunday."

"OK. You'd only have to cook one day a week."

Pearl smiled and hugged me. "Charles Wesley is the finest man I know next to your grandfather Walt. They just don't make men any better than them. But. . ."

"But what? You'd have it made in the shade," I said. "And I hate to tell you this, Aunt Pearl, but you're getting long in the tooth to still be single. What, you must be forty or so, and that's just flat-out old to still be living with your sister. Heaven knows I don't want to be living with Rabbit when I'm that old. Good gravy, that'd be downright awful."

"Why?" asked Pearl.

"Well, she's got a humongous bubblegum-wrapper collection that stinks to high heaven. No telling how many of those things she'll have by the time she gets old like you. Maybe a jillion zillion by then. Think how many ants they'll attract."

Pearl sniffled. "Well, you do have a point, Squirrel. I am a little old. But even so, I can't marry Charles Wesley."

"Why not?" I asked, not believing she would let her only opportunity vanish before her very eyes. Couldn't she see there wasn't a string of eligible bachelors lined up on her sidewalk?

Pearl hesitated, shifting baby Jewel around in her arms, "That would be a hard row to hoe here in Fireside."

"Because why?"

"Because he's a handsome black man and I'm a blonde white woman. Folks wouldn't get over it. I would have to love him a lot for our relationship to make it through all that, and so far, we're just good friends. I can't say whether I'm in love with him, although there's a lot to love about him. On the other hand, know this: was I to ever decide he or any man is the one I want to spend my life with, I wouldn't let what others think stop me."

"But you could get married same time as Selma. I'd think on it if I was you. You could eat free barbecue with potato salad and coleslaw for the rest of your life. Oh, and the banana pudding. It's not as good as Mamaw's, but it's almost as good. Like everybody always says, 'You're a pearl of a girl.' Any man would be lucky to marry you."

She just laughed and teased me by saying, "And Juliet, you're a squirrel of a girl who's about half-nutty." She reached over and tousled my wild, frizzy hair and hugged me hard around the neck. She was one of the few people in the world besides Ruby and Walt who could make me feel loved with something just as simple as that.

I wanted to ask her about one thing: If she didn't love Charles Wesley, how and why had she come up with his baby girl? But there was a voice deep inside me that said not to go there with her. She might not like the question or get mad at me, and I just couldn't take it. I loved babysitting little Jewel more than I did reading my favorite books or playing hopscotch at school with Hadley. There was a penalty to taking things too far down a road others didn't want to travel. Evangeline and I knew firsthand how that felt, and once a road was taken, there was no turning back, which was made clear by our mother. So like piles of grass burrs, devil's claw, and goat's head, I just let things lie undisturbed.

Twelve

"Welcome to Fireside, Texas, on this last Saturday in January 1969. You may have heard by now that Fireside is now a potential sister city to Austin, although we are more than a tad smaller. Think of us as the younger, shorter sister with a humongous spirit. We need to show our big sister that while we're small, we have lots of spit and vinegar. Today, we're looking for volunteers to help make cookies in the shape of groundhogs for next Saturday's broadcast, when we'll host the Austin KTBC viewers for cookies and pineapple punch. I need twenty volunteers to bake cookies at home and bring them to the station by noon on Saturday.

"We also need you to hang around the station and help mix the punch, which is being donated by Shirl's Curls and Bippity-Bop Hair Shop down on East Main, the place where all your hair shenanigans can be fixed. If you're guilty of bad home perms and peroxide disasters, come to the shop where forgiveness reigns, even though you should have come to Shirl in the first place. She'll fix you up and have you ready for your Saturday evening date in no time. Ladies, don't forget, if you need curls, call Shirl for an appointment.

"Now, for your listening enjoyment, the Gemburree Sisters are gonna sing 'Are You Lonesome Tonight?'"

Ruby, Pearl, and Sapphire leaned toward the microphone and sang, softly and earnestly. Ruby played the violin, but Sapphire played acoustic guitar rather than steel because it was much easier to cart around. Pearl had handed little Jewel to Walt, who danced with her on the other side of the soundproof glass. But when Evangeline blew the biggest bubble of her entire bubble-gum-smacking career and then burst it at the end of the song, Ruby gave her the stink eye.

"That's it," said Ruby. "You have better manners than that, Rabbit. I think it's high time you carry out your gum-wrapper collection to the trash barrel and focus on something that won't make a mess."

"Like what?" said Evangeline, pouting.

"Like helping Popo make the groundhog cookie cutters."

"But, Mamaw, those cookies are Squirrel's problem. She's the one who opened her big fat mouth on *The Uncle Jay Show* and invited every single person in the universe and the Martians too."

"You're her sister; you need to help her when she's in a fix. We're all pitching in."

"Well, that's a bunch of hogwash, Mamaw. I don't know nothing about making no cookie cutters. And you're gonna make me throw away my collection too?"

"I think it's about time, Rabbit. It stinks to high heaven, and you can't seem to remember not to pop gum on the air."

Evangeline pouted for four days solid, and it wasn't until Walt taught her to make cookie cutters not only in the shape of ground-hogs but rabbits, too, that she pulled her bottom lip back into place and smiled. They spent two full days in the shop, listening to Hank Williams sing "I Saw the Light" about twenty times on our father's turntable. When they weren't listening to Hank Williams's albums, they were listening to Tennessee Ernie Ford belt out "Shotgun Boogie," about rabbits and squirrels. Every now and then, Evangeline would break into a dance and get a little wild with the rubber hammer she was using.

"Rabbit, don't clobber me with that thing," said Walt when I entered the workshop to check on their progress. Back in the kitchen, Ruby and I had been up to our eyeballs in sugar cookie dough, and I was starting to feel peevish until Ruby suggested I go check on Walt and Evangeline's progress.

"How're you coming along?" I asked, picking dough out from under my fingernails.

"Tolerable well," said Walt, smiling. "We've made twenty-one groundhogs, one for us and for each volunteer. Rabbit has also made a few, well. . . rabbits."

"I'm worrying whether we'll have enough cookies," I said, feeling a knot form in my throat. "Guess I shouldn't have said that on the television like I did."

Evangeline wrinkled up her nose and said, "You don't always use your noodle, do you, Squirrel?"

"You're one to talk, Rabbit," I said, untying my green apron and tossing it onto Walt's worktable. "You got me into this fix, you scalawag."

"Put up your dukes, Squirrel," said Evangeline, raising her tiny balled-up fists. "You cost me my gum-wrapper collection."

"I did no such thing! You were smacking your gum on the air. You're the one to blame."

"I've a mind to get out two sets of boxing gloves and let you girls have it out," said Walt. "I've got some over yonder in the corner in that old wooden crate. Back when I drove the ambulance and worked on the Alcan Highway in forty-two, fellas who couldn't get along used to settle it that way sometimes. Brought 'em back as souvenirs."

Before we knew it, Walt had put gloves on both of us, but they were so heavy, we had to struggle to lift them into position.

"Now what?" said Evangeline, starting to giggle.

"I'm gonna count to three, and then you can both take a punch at each other. One. Two. Three."

Evangeline and I started to dance around like the kangaroos in cartoons. It felt absurd, and I thought it right funny until Evangeline popped me one in the nose. Even though I saw it coming, it knocked me off balance, and I tripped over my own shoes and wiped out on a pile of old tires.

Ruby walked in the door and frowned. "I can't believe my eyes. Who started this?"

"She did," we both said.

"And whose idea was it to put the gloves on?"

"Popo's," we said.

"Walter Scott Cranbourne! You're encouraging these girls to fight?"

Walt shifted his weight around and said, "I 'spect I did."

"Well, no wonder they fight. You know I don't like anyone hitting anyone else."

My nose started bleeding, but I wasn't sure whether it was from Evangeline's punch or that I'd tripped and fallen. I glared at Evangeline and shouted, "This is all your fault!"

Evangeline's eyes got big when she saw the blood dripping down my white turtleneck and the pink apron I still wore from making cookie dough. Tears slid down her dirt-streaked face. "I'm sorry, Squirrel. I didn't mean to."

"Walt, let's see what you can make outa this mess," said Ruby, putting her hands on her hips. "I think I'm gonna go to Shirl's Curls while you figure out what to do."

I didn't have to think long and hard to know that Walt wasn't going to be getting any sugary kisses from Ruby that day. He was in as big trouble as Rabbit and me. That took some doing.

Walt led us into the house, pulled a metal ice tray out of the Frigidaire, and ran it under the faucet. Then he twisted it until the ice popped out, half of which fell onto Ruby's kitchen floor. Then he put a cube in a rag and held it up to my nose to stop the blood from flowing. Evangeline scrambled across the floor, picking up spilled ice cubes.

"I just love ice," she said, popping one in her mouth and crunching it.

"Rabbit, I wouldn't eat ice off the floor if I were you," said Walt.

"Why not?" she said after she spit it into the sink.

"Because people walk all over the linoleum and you just never know where their shoes have been."

"That's what people say about Aunt Pearl all the time. You just never know where she's been on account of her getting little Jewel somewhere."

"Rabbit, you ought not to repeat a thing if you don't understand what you're saying." Walt kept the rag and ice cube pressed against my nose, but his sights were on my sister.

"Oh, I understand it all. Ever since that man shot Dr. Martin Luther King last year, everything has been in a terrible mess. I can't say how, but I think Jewel came out of it all. Maybe somebody lost their baby girl when all those riots happened. It would be so easy to get turned around."

"Is that what you think, Rabbit? That Jewel got lost somehow and Pearl found her during the Holy Week Uprising? Or maybe later on at the Chicago riots?"

"Don't you hear Walter Cronkite on the *CBS Evening News* say, 'And that's the way it is . . .' every night when he's winding it up?" Evangeline put her hands on her tiny hips and cocked her head.

"I do for a fact," said Walt.

"Well, that's what I think, and that's the way it is. After all, we got lost from our parents, too, if you look at the big picture the way he does."

"I understand your point, Rabbit, but not everything is always as it seems."

I repeated Walt's words of wisdom the very next morning at Fireside Elementary when the kids clustered around me in the gymnasium during assembly.

"Did that nasty Nathan Wilcot bust you one?" asked Hadley, looking at my bruised nose. "I swear, he still doesn't have enough sense to lick the right side of the spoon."

"We'll fix his wagon," said William Bartlett. "I told him not to mess with you or Evangeline ever again."

"No," I said. "Not everything is the way it seems."

"Oh," they said, not sure what to make of that.

"Did you get thrown off a horse?" William wasn't about to let the subject drop until he found out the reason for my condition.

"No. I got in a fight with Popo's workshop, and the workshop won."

"Guess that could happen to anyone," he said and patted my back. He was clearly feeling right sorry for me. I appreciated his concern and smiled.

"You could cover up that bruise with some foundation makeup," said Hadley. "Come home with me for lunch, and I'll put some of my mother's Max Factor Pan-Cake makeup on you to see if it helps."

"Great! Will your mother mind?"

"Clearly this is a makeup emergency. She never shuts out anyone in distress. She's like the Statue of Liberty in that regard. "*Give me your tired, your poor*," Hadley sang out dramatically.

103

"I get it, Hadley. Especially the part of the song that talks about breathing free." I pointed to my nose and giggled.

"Don't quit your day job, Hadley," said William. "And I mean that sincerely."

By the time Groundhog Day was upon us, seven thousand cookies in their likeness, with a few rabbits thrown in for good measure, were set up on tables outside station KOFF, and Miss Alma Webster, the station manager and regular DJ, was holding court as she stirred the pineapple punch. She wore a plaid hunter's jacket and a hand-crocheted off-white scarf, and her standard visor had been replaced with a black cap with earflaps.

"Maybe we should just have served hot coffee and chocolate and dispensed with the pineapple punch. It's too chilly to drink something that will just make you colder. Maybe it would be more popular if I spiked it with something strong."

"Oh no, Miss Webster!" said Ruby. "Think of the children. Spiking the punch is a bad idea."

"I hadn't thought about that. You're right. But my poker club would have enjoyed it."

Her white, fluffy, and often mischievous dog, Little Bit, was tied to a card table leg by her leash. She shivered, and when Miss Alma noticed that, she untied her, picked her up, and stuffed her down inside her red plaid jacket. Nothing but her head showed above the top button of Miss Alma's jacket, and I could just about swear I saw her smile. Her little black eyes sparkled victoriously from underneath all that white hair.

"Who says I can't mix punch and make a pooch happy at the same time?" said Miss Alma. "By the way, I'm going to say a few words at eight thirty to welcome folks to station KOFF and Fireside, Texas, and then, Juliet, you go ahead and talk about the Fireside/Austin sisterhood."

Straightaway, a KTBC camera truck rolled in, and the station's roving reporter, Miss Avery James, stepped out, wearing the most bodacious cowgirl outfit you've ever seen. Evangeline and I were both more than a little disappointed that Uncle Jay and Packer Jack hadn't come, and we'd been stuck with this haughty young woman instead.

"So what happened to your nose?" she asked me while powdering hers.

"I'd tell you the story, but it's way too long," I whispered, hoping no one else would start in. "Just pretend you didn't notice, OK?"

"You got it while fighting the Vietcong?" she said, wide-eyed.

"I said the story would take way too long."

"Roll," she said to the cameraman. "We've got a national interest story in the making here."

She poked the microphone in front of my face and said, "Tell us your name, little girl."

"I'm Juliet Cranbourne."

"But you can call her Squirrel," yelled Evangeline from over my shoulder. "Everybody does, on account of she is one."

"Charming," said Miss James. "Tell our KTBC viewers how you came to be fighting the Vietcong. Were you recruited for reconnaissance purposes?"

"No. I wasn't recruited, ma'am. My father was drafted."

"For reconnaissance?"

"I don't know and can't ask him."

"Why not? The viewers are waiting."

"Because he's dead. End of story." Tears welled up in my eyes, and I didn't think I could compose myself enough to go on.

"Cut!" snapped Miss James to the cameraman. She rolled her eyes and swung the microphone by its cord.

"What a disappointment. Clearly there's no meat to your Vietcong story. Not sure there's much to cover in this one-horse town."

"You're supposed to cover the Fireside/Austin Groundhog Day celebration of our potential sisterhood. It's a chance for our communities to get acquainted. Didn't Uncle Jay tell you?"

As you can guess, Miss James got in a powerful bad mood because I'd ruined her angle, so we started out on the wrong foot from the get-go. I can't even begin to tell you how relieved I was to look over and see Ruby, Sapphire, and Pearl standing with their instruments, ready to play. Right away, Miss James recognized them and said, "Well, thank heavens, there is a *real* story here somewhere." She strutted over to the Gemburree Sisters and started asking them what it was like to be on the Grand Ole Opry.

After the interview, they finished tuning up, then launched into "Fireside Women" from their *Fireside Book of Love* album. This seemed to make Miss James much happier, and she made sure the cameraman got as much footage of her as possible standing in front of the Gemburree Sisters in her sequined cowgirl outfit. Being the center of the universe clearly thrilled her.

By 8:00 a.m., cars from all over the Hill Country started to roll in. We'd overcome a major hurdle when we substituted our dog, Sport, in a handmade groundhog costume, since the real McCoy didn't exist in our burg. His job was to pop out of a cardboard box decorated to look like a giant grass-covered hole. He was to dash through the yard to symbolize not seeing his shadow and then go to Evangeline, who would be holding an Oscar Mayer wiener to entice him.

Instead, he made a beeline for Charles Wesley, who smelled like barbecue, and then leaped at Miss Webster when he smelled Little Bit hiding in her jacket. That would have worked out just fine if she hadn't lost her balance and fallen into the punch bowl, knocking it to the ground.

When poor Miss Alma righted herself, she was covered from head to toe with pineapple punch, which Sport and Little Bit just loved.

"I'm seeing stars," said Miss Alma while I tried to dab her down with paper napkins. She said, "Juliet, you need to replace me in the program. Remember, this is a regular broadcast that goes out to all our listeners. Just ad lib and it will be OK. I've got to go home and get cleaned up before I turn into a pineapple punch Popsicle."

"I wasn't planning on things going this way today. So sorry about what Sport did to you. It wasn't part of the plan," I said, trying to hold back tears.

But the crowd thought it was and had whipped itself into quite a frenzy. "More!" they shouted. They thought the punch-and-dog disaster was a planned comedic routine. So I grabbed the mic and said what came to me naturally.

"Well, howdy, everyone, and welcome to Fireside, Texas, home of the free and the brave and the everlasting polite persons. We don't eat beets, and we never take the last cookie, as evidenced by all these groundhog sugar cookies.

"I'm pleased as punch that you've driven to Fireside to help celebrate the first-ever Fireside/Austin Sister City event. You may be the bigger sister, but we were born first in 1837, thanks to the efforts of Beaufort Dieffenbachia, otherwise known as Beaufort Dumbcane. We're indebted to have been named Fireside, truly an indication of his early generosity and good judgment. Fireside, Texas, is a place where there's a fire in every hearth and love in every spirit.

"Now I'd like to introduce the fabulous Gemburree Sisters to take this celebration to the next level. That's Ruby on the fiddle, Sapphire on the steel guitar, and Pearl on percussion." A few snowflakes fell from the gray sky. Stunned by this rare occurrence, the crowd briefly stared upward, until little Jewel started to cry.

Pearl, who had held on to her daughter until the moment she needed to perform, finally relinquished baby Jewel, who was bundled from head to toe in a corduroy coat, hat, mittens, and a wool blanket, to Charles Wesley. When Fireside and the KTBC viewers saw her blonde hair briefly touch his, how the color of Jewel's skin was a blend of both adults', a hush quieter than death fell over the crowd.

Ruby saw what was happening, reached for the mic, and started talking. "I want to dedicate this song to all you beautiful children out there who are fortunate enough to have the love of your parents, but especially to those whose families may not look as though they were ordered to perfection from the Montgomery Ward catalog.

"Our good friend, Elvis, just recorded this Mac Davis tune, which will be released in April. I'm sure he'll make us proud just like he always does." She turned to her sisters and said, "One, two, three." The sisters began singing "In the Ghetto."

I can't tell you how it happened, but when I looked out over the crowd toward the Fireside Café, I was certain I saw Mama. She was leaning against the building, first holding a cigarette to her lips and then blowing smoke rings. Her brunette hair was pulled back in a ponytail, and she wore black fur earmuffs, pants, and a matching coat with red buttons.

I reached up, waved, and called, "Mama! I'm coming!" Like lightning, I took off running in her direction, not caring whether I got back to take up the broadcast before the Gemburree Sisters finished their song. There was nothing more important than getting to see her, not even Groundhog Day in Fireside.

Thirteen

By the time I'd pushed through the crowds, the Gemburree Sisters were singing the Supremes' "My World Is Empty Without You." The crowd seemed to have somewhat recovered from seeing Pearl hand Jewel to Charles Wesley, but my heart was in getting to my mother as soon as I could.

She saw me heading straight toward her, quickly ground out her cigarette, and made a beeline to her car. Like steam in air, she vaporized so quickly, I wasn't sure what to think. So I just kept heading in the direction I thought she'd gone. As I ran past Densesky's, Selma came out on the sidewalk and watched me speed past.

"What's your hurry, Juliet? Your pants on fire? Where you going?" Selma was a blur of pink and silver that I barely noticed at first as I focused on running as fast as I could. "Come on back and try on your junior bridesmaid outfit. I might need to take a tuck or two, you keep running like that and get any skinnier."

"Sorry, Miss Selma. I'll come back later. I just saw my mama, and I'm trying to catch up with her," I called over my shoulder, not pausing for a second.

Even the enticement of trying on my junior bridesmaid outfit didn't compel me to stop my pursuit. I couldn't see Mama any longer, but I imagined she would head out to the ranch, if anywhere.

For the five miles it took to get from Fireside to Ruby and Walt's yellow brick house, I kept moving, although my speed slowed to a crawl, and I grew terribly out of breath. Hearing barking, I turned around to see that Sport had taken up the chase too. His pursuit had been hampered somewhat by the fact that he was still wearing his groundhog costume.

I made a full circle of the house to make sure I hadn't missed Mama, but like always, she was gone as could be. Tied to the back door was a large bag of Red Hots but no note. I sat down on the back steps and cried my head off, and then, after Sport came up, licked my face, and started howling, I cried some more. We were both upset; at first it seemed to me that his heart was as broken as mine, but then I realized he didn't even really know her. Not really. Yet somehow, my sadness had become his.

The sweat I'd created during my long run to the ranch now made me shiver with cold in the February air. To keep from freezing as I waited for someone to come home and unlock the door, I went down into Ruby's cellar. I pulled the string on the naked lightbulb that was suspended from the concrete ceiling and surrounded by old dirt dauber's nests. On the far wall stood rows of perfectly preserved figs, peach jelly, creamed corn, green beans, and black-eyed peas in Ball jars and a discarded 1850s-era pitch-pine washstand and mirror. Resting on top were Ruby's transistor radio and the Brower Manufacturing Company egg scale she had used until it rusted shut.

I prayed forgiveness would flow abundantly when they came home on account of the fact that I hadn't finished my job for station KOFF or the community of Fireside and was about to use Ruby's radio without permission. I picked up the transistor and turned up its plastic volume dial full blast. The Supremes' "Some Things You Never Get Used To" blared out, along with a lot of static, but somehow those tambourines spoke to my spirit. I grabbed one of Ruby's potting spoons and started beating out a rhythm on the bottom of a couple of old chipped enamel pots. When that didn't help make me feel better, I started to do a dance I'd seen on TV called the Hitchhike. I caught sight of myself in the old, mottled washstand mirror through its wavy, bubbled glass that made me look funny and couldn't help but laugh. Maybe I hadn't been meant to play the guitar or even drums, despite Walt and Ruby's best intentions. Clearly, I had been born to dance on *Rowan & Martin's Laugh-In* just like

Judy Carne or Goldie Hawn. That is the way it played out in my head, at least, as I twisted from side to side and stuck my thumbs up in the air. It is easy, though, to believe you are one talented, top-notch dancer who regularly hangs out with Lily Tomlin and Arte Johnson when there is no one around to judge otherwise.

Eventually, my sadness returned as I struggled with whether to tell Evangeline that I was certain I'd seen our mother. Furthermore, finding the Red Hots hanging in a bag from the back-door handle was proof, wasn't it? And didn't the candy prove that she was a little bit sorry she'd left us?

It was almost noon by the time Ruby and Evangeline found me in the cellar. "Juliet, we've been searching all over for you. If it hadn't been for bumping into Selma, we'd still be out looking. I've never seen anyone run as fast as you." She reached over and pulled me to her and kissed my forehead. "Now, suppose you tell me what's the matter?"

I eyed Evangeline, took a deep breath, and decided to spill the beans. "I saw Mama leaning on the Fireside Café. Maybe Davy Ottmers saw her too."

"No, she wasn't, you liar, liar, pants on fire," said Evangeline and stuck out her bottom lip in a pout.

"He was with Evangeline, so I doubt he did. Why do you think it was Marguerite?" said Ruby.

"A calf knows her mama, just like lambs and puppies know theirs. Well, I just know because I know."

"Squirrel, I surely think if Marguerite came all this way, she'd have come to talk to you and Evangeline."

"Maybe she was disappointed when she saw Evangeline and me. Or maybe she's been gone so long she didn't recognize us."

"How could anyone not recognize you sweet girls? You're lovelier than the flowers in May."

"Then who left us this candy on the back door?"

Ruby looked at the bag and shrugged her shoulders. "Well, I have no idea. Could it be young William Bartlett?"

"You think a boy would leave me candy? Whoever heard of such a thing?"

"You're mighty pretty, both on the inside and out. Any boy in his right mind might just do that very thing. Juliet, you'll be eleven next month. Before many more years, boys will be paying you more attention than Walt and I will be ready for. But lest you grow up too fast, I want you to promise you'll always be our girl. You mean more than the sun, moon, and stars to Popo and me."

I put my head on her shoulder and wept until I couldn't anymore. Her hair smelled of Alberto VO5 shampoo, and there was a hint of the scent of fried bacon from breakfast still on her mint-green sweater. I wrapped my arms around her and stayed put while she patted my shoulder. When I'd dried my last tear on Ruby's handkerchief, she said, "C'mon, Juliet, let's go inside and get lunch on the table. It may only be noon, but we've all had quite a day."

The next day, I had a telephone call just before dinner from Miss Alma Webster. She sounded the same way she did over the radio but closer and larger somehow.

"This is Juliet," I said when Walt handed me the phone while Ruby panfried chicken.

"And this is Alma Webster, Sunshine. I was just calling to tell you that I appreciated you taking over when I fell into the punch bowl. Just to let you know, I listened to the broadcast at home as I wiped that sticky mess off myself. You did a real good job until you disappeared. Had there been any dead air on account of that, I'd have fired you. Not sure why you took off like a pup after a bunny, but I'm gonna ask you not to do it again. Ruby covered for you until the entire event was over. Probably has blisters on her fingers from all that fancy fiddling. Pearl and Sapphire did their part too. This is just a gentle reminder that I won't tolerate any dead air on my program, just so we understand each other."

"Yes, ma'am. I'm sorry as I can be. Won't let you down again."

"Another thing: I recommend you train that spunky Sport. I could have done without the swim in pineapple punch. Not that I don't under-stand how these things happen. Little Bit has a mind of her own too."

"Evangeline and I will give him a talking to and try to teach him better."

"One more thing. For a youngster who's barely dry behind the ears, you're a pretty neato kiddo. Keep working at your on-air presence. A natural if I ever saw one. You could work at a big station someday if you polish your act."

"Thank you, Miss Alma. I won't forget that."

After I hung up the phone, Ruby put the last piece of chicken on a platter and said, "Guess that was no-dead-air Alma you were talking to. I wasn't eavesdropping, but I could hear her monotonous voice coming through the receiver. She means well but doesn't understand what made you take off like you did. Don't let her get to you. She's right about not abandoning your post, but some situations are just what they are. . . situations."

Days later, I received a letter from KTBC about our Groundhog Day event.

Dear Juliet,

I enjoyed watching the footage of your first-ever Fireside/Austin Sister City Groundhog Day celebration. Congratulations from all of us at KTBC on an excellent outcome. How did you stage that cute groundhog dog stunt? Your event caused our ratings to skyrocket. Thanks to the Gemburree Sisters, no one ever heard better music. A good friend of mine down at the Broken Spoke here on South Lamar has asked for me to put in a good word for him, as he'd love for the Gemburree Sisters to come and play a gig. He sends a special invitation to Marguerite to join in on the performance. Tell them we'll have all of you back on The Uncle Jay Show *to help advertise "The Fireside Book of Love."*

Packer Jack sends his best to his new pal, Evangeline.

Sincerely,

Jay Hodgson

P.S. You sure can run fast. Have you thought about the Olympics?

Now, how on earth could I deliver Marguerite to the Broken Spoke if I didn't know where she was? If *anyone* could deliver her, I'd like to be the first to know.

February eighth was the last Saturday before Valentine's and therefore Selma and Norman's wedding. When we arrived at Densesky's to deliver eggs, we only had eight dozen to give them. Norman shook his head as he rang up what he owed us and took the money out of his cash-register drawer. "Hens off their feed?" he asked Ruby. He was chewing an unlit cigar and talking out of the side of his mouth. That took talent in my book. I had tried talking with whole wads of Dubble Bubble but no one could understand a word, so I gave it up.

"No, they slow down this time of year. Not much sunshine lately. Fewer hours of daylight. I've done everything but fiddle and dance a jig for them, but they're laying poorly."

"Well, can't help what you can't help. I'll supplement the supply with some from young William until they start laying again. Nobody else has eggs that taste as good as yours, though, Ruby. Not sure what you and Walt feed them, but it must make for very happy hens."

"Are you so excited that Squirrel and I are gonna be in your wedding?" asked Evangeline. "'Cause I'm feeling pretty groovy about it. It's far out!"

Norman smiled. "Yes, ma'am. I'm as excited as they come. I get to marry the most beautiful woman this side of the Mississippi and have two hotshots like you gals to help her get down the aisle. Couldn't be more pleased if you gave me a banana split on the side. Speaking of ice cream, why don't you girls mosey on over to the soda fountain counter, and I'll have Selma give you a double scoop each on the house?"

"You're the best, Mr. Densesky," said Evangeline. "I might like you even better than Packer Jack."

"Now that's a left-handed compliment if I ever heard one." Norman was smiling so big, I thought he might just swallow that stogie. I wondered whether I was tall enough to whack him on the back where it counted if he did.

"Golly wolly," called Selma as she came into the grocery side of Densesky's. "If it isn't my wedding party. Since you're here, why don't you come back and try on your leather miniskirts and ruffled blouses? This is your final fitting. If all is well, I'll send them home with you today."

"Honey, would you please give these girls a double scoop before you do that? A promise is a promise." Norman winked at Selma and looked at her like he couldn't take his eyes off her. His face beamed like it was lighted from inside. I wondered whether he was feeling all right. You've heard Elvis's song "Fever," haven't you? Seeing that look on his face naturally brought it to mind.

Some might think Norman's words were comforting. A promise is a promise? Not always. I thought about how my daddy promised he'd come back from old Vietnam just as soon as he could, and we'd watch *Dialing for Dollars* together and maybe wind up winning if we paid enough attention to the day's key word, like *wrapping* or some such. He also said he'd teach me how to tie fishing lures to earn spending money, but that never happened.

Our mother had promised to come back and get us as soon as she got settled. I thought about the two parts to that sentence: promised to come back. And get us as soon as she got settled. Unless I'd flat lost my mind, I had seen her leaned up against the Fireside Café. If you looked at the broad picture, she had kept the part about coming home but had fallen way short on getting us and taking us back.

Seeing as our father had gotten shot and couldn't come home, well, I guess that's the kind of promise made to be broken. But Mama. . . I guess I should have looked at the fine print if she'd taken the time to write down exactly what it was she was promising. Promising was one thing, delivering quite another. Much worse than promising to deliver a certain number of eggs and falling short. Perhaps Mr. Densesky was right. You can't help what you can't help.

Ruby took this opportunity to shop for groceries and walked through the aisles, pulling things like boxes of Imperial powdered sugar, black cherry Jell-O, Sun-Maid raisins, and Velveeta cheese off the shelves.

"What'll you have, girls?" asked Selma as she washed her hands and pulled a scoop out of a plastic holster.

"Two scoops of vanilla with crushed chocolate malt balls," said Evangeline. "Big, big scoops. Lots of topping."

"And you, little miss?" she asked me, eyebrow lifted. She wore a pink sweater, matching headband, and a black miniskirt. As always, her hair was teased, but this time not piled up to the sun. She'd let it down; the ends of it went just past her shoulders. She wore silver hoop earrings that were big enough to touch her cheeks and made her seem so hip.

"Strawberry, just plain, please."

"Did you find what you were looking for the other day when you were out on your run?" Selma asked me pointedly. I immediately understood she was concerned but didn't want to tell all in front of Evangeline.

"No, never did. Tried my best, though."

"Things happen when they're meant to, that's what I know. Take me and Mr. Densesky, for example. Now is the time to remarry. I wouldn't have been ready years ago when I first met him. My first husband died and, well, it took time to get my feelings in order. For years, I blamed myself. If only we hadn't gotten in that argument. If only I hadn't gotten mad and thrown my wedding ring in the dumpster. If only he hadn't gone in after it. If only lightning hadn't struck. If only it hadn't been for all those details, it might have been a different story. But then, it wouldn't be *my* story, would it?"

"Then you wouldn't be where you are today, about to walk down the aisle with Mr. Wonderful."

"Exactly. Juliet, you've got lots of things going for you. Just keep your vision straight ahead. Don't look back. All the what-if's in the world don't add up to one single tomorrow. Tomorrow will be way better."

Wanting to change the subject because it made me uncomfortable, I said, "I can't say about tomorrow, but I know about Valentine's Day. I feel like I need to practice somehow. I want to make sure I do the best job of being a junior bridesmaid anyone ever has in Maitlin County. And, Miss Selma, I promise I won't take off running.

"Pinky swear?" she asked.

"Oh, I want to join in," said Evangeline, who was up to her eyes in ice cream with crushed chocolate malt balls. It was running down her neck and covered all her fingers. It's to both Selma's and my credit that we pinky swore amid such a sticky mess. But one thing I knew in my heart: both Evangeline and I were sticky messes to our very cores. Some folks loved us anyway and stayed in our lives.

When Ruby got through spit-cleaning Evangeline's and my face with her lace handkerchief, which was destined to soak in Biz for a very long time if it were ever to be used again, we went back to the dressing room to try on our outfits.

"Oh my heavens," said Selma, looking at us in our white leather skirts and frilly, ruffled blouses through the three-way mirror in the dressing room. "You girls have grown a foot during the last month. I think this calls for white tights to go under these miniskirts. Lucky for you, we have them in stock. Otherwise, those minis would be too short, even for me. Let me just give you each a pair. They're my gift to you."

"Tights, like pantyhose but thicker?" I asked. "I haven't seen such in person here in Fireside. I did see them in *Vogue*, which I read the last time I went to Shirl's Curls."

"Densesky's specializes in up-to-date styles. I'll have you know, we sell the most fashionable items. This is a hip, happening establishment. Nothing frumpy allowed here. We don't skip a beat."

"Oh, I don't like beets," I said. "But I think I'll love tights!"

Ruby's face lit up with satisfaction when she saw Rabbit and me turning this way and that in the three-way mirror. "My stars! I've never seen two more lovely attendants. I think this wedding calls for a trip to the beauty shop for permanent waves. I'd do it myself, but let's do something special this time. I'll make your appointments for Valentine's Day, which is next Friday, the morning of the wedding."

"As for me, I'll be creating my own updo, ladies," said Selma. "Nobody can tease and pile hair like I can."

By the time Friday morning rolled around, Evangeline and I were in a state of exhilaration mixed with nerves and silliness. Thirty minutes after we awoke, we danced a jig to the *Captain Kangaroo* jingle.

"Good morning, Captain!" Evangeline said and saluted the TV screen. She draped herself dramatically across the ottoman, then shot across the room.

"Happy Valentine's Day, Captain!" I said, plopping down in Walt's old office chair, snapping across the room and back like a rubber band.

"Did you girls eat Mars candy bars before breakfast?" asked Ruby. "Or are you just excited about the big day ahead?" She smiled and patted our heads affectionately. Ruby recently had gotten her own perm at Shirl's Curls and this morning had washed and rolled her thick red hair onto metal rollers and inserted white plastic picks to keep them in place. She'd hidden the whole shebang beneath a jade-green scarf and was wearing matching green corduroy pants, white blouse and green jacket. When she put her heart in it, no one looked more elegant than Ruby, even if her hair was in curlers. She wore the perfect shade of red lipstick and looked like she should either be in a commercial for liquid Prell or Alberto VO5.

"Did you wash with liquid Prell, Mamaw? 'Cause that shiny green liquid is about the same color as your outfit. You could be even famouser than the lady on the TV!" said Evangeline.

Walt had just come in from Fireside and sauntered into the living room with the biggest grin on his face. He dropped his felt Stetson on his chair and pulled Ruby to him, giving her a big kiss square on her lips. He didn't seem to notice that her hair was pinned up in curlers and covered by a scarf. "More famous than Ruby? Don't you monkeys know she's about as famous as it gets in the music world? You ought to be asking for her autograph," he said.

"He's right," whispered Evangeline in my ear. Her warm spittle showered my skin. Because I felt it was unintentional, I wiped it off and didn't yank her hair, which was to my obvious credit. "We could sell her auto-graph at school and make ourselves a mint. You can buy a lot of bubble gum with a mint."

"That doesn't make any sense, Evangeline."

"Oh yes, it does. I'm like Yogi—'smarter than the average bear.' OK, let me go back to the drawing board. We could buy ourselves each a Tressy doll and play beauty shop with their long blonde hair."

"That would be fun, but I don't think my conscience would let me sell Mamaw's autograph unless it was for charity."

"What in the tarnation is wrong with you, Squirrel? You just ain't got a lick of business sense, like me. I say we make hay while the sun shines."

"What are you girls whispering about?" asked Ruby as she gathered her black leather purse off the sofa and put on her gloves.

"It's a secret," said Evangeline, giggling.

"I declare, your giggle box is upside down."

Walt turned on the radio to station KOFF just as Miss Alma Webster said, "And now, as requested by Walt Cranbourne for his lovely valen-tine, Mrs. Ruby Gemburree Cranbourne: Walt says to tell the KOFF lis-teners he's lucky to be married to the prettiest redhead in Maitlin County and is grateful for the last thirty-nine years of mile-high banana pie, Golden Westerner cake, tender hugs and kisses, and all the rest of that sweet stuff.

"My word to Walt Cranbourne is that he's a swell fella, and if he ever was in the doghouse with Ruby, this ought to get him out. And now, Miss Etta James sings 'At Last.'"

Walt slow danced Ruby right across our wooden living room floor as if Evangeline and I were invisible. He leaned down toward her, drew his cheek up against her, and said, "Will you be my valentine, Ruby, darlin'?"

"Every day of the year," she said softly.

"All that hugging and kissing just makes me about half-sick," said Evangeline. "Valentine's Day is about chocolate candy and cards. Anything else is flat-out icky."

Ruby sighed and said, "Walt, let's finish this dance later, when we're by ourselves. I loved my valentine message. Thank you for being all I ever wanted or needed in a sweetheart."

"Time's a-wasting," said Evangeline. "We ain't getting any younger neither."

Ruby reached up and touched her scarf. "C'mon, girls, time to get in the Thunderbird. Cranbourne women always arrive on time. If we don't, Shirl will throw us out on our ears. Nobody messes with her and lives."

Fourteen

When Shirl asked me how tight I wanted my perm, I didn't know what to say, so I just said, "Make me look like Barbra Streisand in *Funny Girl*."

"Honey, that's not a perm; that's an updo with a lot of rolls and long bangs. You trying to attract Omar Sharif?" said Shirl, and laughed.

Shirl was a great big blonde-haired woman who wore white double-knit uniforms to work and a peacock-blue headband between where her natural hair ended and her wiglet began. She always chewed gum and liked to pop tiny bubbles out of it between sentences. Rumor had it she had been married seven times, and five of those were to the same man she just couldn't get out of her system.

"Mr. Sharif is way too old for me," I said, "but he is handsome."

"Honey, you invite him to the wedding tonight, and I'll take things from there," said Shirl, winking.

"Only if he brings Donny Osmond with him," I said. "'Cause he's way more my type."

Evangeline giggled and said, "Squirrel's got a crush. Shame, shame, shame," she said, raking one pointer finger over the other.

Ruby handed each of us a magazine and said, "Why don't you girls take a look at these hairstyles and give me a report?"

It didn't take a rocket scientist to know what Ruby was trying to do—get our attention off each other so a fight wouldn't break out. But Evangeline reached into her jeans' pocket and pulled out a handful of the Red Hots I'd found tied to the back door. I had hidden the entire kit and caboodle of spicy cinnamon goodness underneath the kitchen sink

121

behind the Duz detergent. But just like a rat, my sister had sniffed her way to them.

"Where'd you find those?" I asked, glaring at her, wondering if Ruby had moved them into view.

"Right where you hid them. Finders keepers, losers weepers."

"That's stealing," I said, whacking her on the knee with the magazine while Shirl combed my hair.

"Would be if they belonged to you, which they don't," said Evangeline, putting a handful into her mouth. A thin line of red drool slid from the corner of her mouth and down her cheek.

"You're no rabbit," I said, glaring at her. "You're a grade-A candy hog. I think Mama left those for me as an apology for running off like she did."

"If Mama came to town, which she didn't, she'd have left this candy for me since I'm her favorite!" Evangeline gave me the stink eye, spit the partially chewed Red Hots into her hand, and threw them at me.

You might not think this was bright of me, but I just naturally duck when something is thrown in my direction. This was a bad idea because Shirl was in the midst of trimming my bangs. Just like that, Shirl cut off a chunk of my hair front and center, which was now too short to comb and stood straight up from the roots.

"Donkey doodles," said Shirl. "I didn't mean to do that. Evangeline Cranbourne, look at what you gone and made me do."

I got a good look at myself in the big mirror and realized life as I knew it was over. Not only could I never show my face at Fireside Elementary again, but I was going to have to walk down the aisle that very evening as Selma's junior bridesmaid, and every guest in the room would be laughing.

Evangeline had won the argument just like that, and all I could do was cry.

"My stars," Ruby said, peering at me behind the beautician's chair. We both faced the giant mirror on the wall across from Shirl's station. "You're starting a new style. Perhaps you'd like to wear one of my hats tonight. Being a junior bridesmaid and all." She forced a smile. "I do think you're old enough to pull it off."

Ruby turned and stared at Evangeline. "Rabbit, I think you've gone too far this time. How would you like it if I let Squirrel take a pair of scissors and cut a hunk out of *your* hair?"

"Wouldn't bother me, Mamaw. I'd just take the scissors and cut off all the rest to make it look like Davy's hair. Then I could be his sister for a while, and everybody would just naturally think we belonged to the same family. I could live in the Fireside Café and eat whatever I wanted, whenever I pleased. I wouldn't have to ride the school bus or share a bed with *her*," she said pointing at me and glaring through eyes closed into squeezed slits. She wrinkled her freckled nose and sniffed mightily.

"I see," said Ruby. "But because of all the commotion, I'm gathering you no longer like to eat candy. You won't mind, then, when I tell you there'll be no sweets of any nature for you for the next week. This begins tonight at the wedding. There'll be no cake for you!"

"But it was her fault," she said, jerking her thumb toward me. "She called me a candy hog and said something about our mama."

"I feel right bad about this, Ruby," said Shirl. "How about I won't charge you for either girl's haircut? And I think if I just work a little magic with Aqua Net and maybe stick a bodacious bow in the center, we can hide that rough patch. I'll make her updo look intentional, not like it is a freak accident of nature. No hat will be necessary."

"Thanks, Shirl, but I want to pay for their hairstyles. We both know this wasn't your fault."

By the time four thirty rolled around, Evangeline and I were at the Fireside Methodist Church trying to hold still enough to keep from messing up our curls while Ruby, Sapphire, and Pearl practiced their music for the wedding. I got to hold little Jewel, who kept trying her best to grab the great big bow I wore. I gently pulled her hand away when she tried since it was all that stood between me and complete humiliation.

We'd been instructed to stay in a small Sunday school room and entertain her while the others prepared for what would likely be the most unusual wedding in Fireside history. On one wall was a picture of Jesus ascending into heaven with angels and doves surrounding him.

On another was a framed copy of the sheet music to "Amazing Grace" in calligraphy on linen paper. But my favorite was of Jesus surrounded by children at his feet in a beautiful pasture. There were sheep grazing in the distance, and because I'd helped to bottle-feed lambs, they spoke to me.

"I like this room, don't you?" I asked Evangeline.

"I would if it had a snow-cone maker over yonder on the cabinet. Or maybe if they left out a bowl of rainbow-colored jawbreakers."

"You're missing the point."

"No, Squirrel. I *always* get the point. I get to the point straightaway, every time. Just like a bee and her stinger."

Jewel's face had grown plumper, and she had put on enough weight to make my arms ache. I kept shifting her back and forth from one hip to the other, which delighted her and caused peals of laughter to ring out through the room. I was quite sure I'd never seen a more beautiful child anywhere as I gazed into her brown eyes, ignoring Evangeline, who had begun twirling around the room like a dervish. She was staring at the knees of the tights she wore with her white leather miniskirt, trying to see if she could keep her eyes on the diamond pattern and twirl without losing her focus.

Evangeline cracked Jewel up too. The entire world amused her. What a privilege it was to be entrusted with her care, I thought. This proved one thing to me. Clearly, there was no one Pearl loved more than her daughter, unless she secretly loved Charles Wesley. The fact that she thought I was worthy of taking care of her made me feel important and rich beyond belief.

I'd been sad Pearl hadn't chosen to have a double wedding with Selma and Mr. Densesky, but maybe she wanted to wait for a time when she had the stage all to herself and could be the only bride at the wedding. Perhaps if they did marry one day, I could be a junior bridesmaid all over again—after my chopped-off hair had grown out, of course.

When the wedding began at 6:00 p.m., the church was buzzing with activity. Norman and his brother, best man Andy, and junior groomsman William Bartlett stepped out front in position to the right of the pulpit as the Gemburree Sisters began singing "Chapel of Love," just the way the Dixie Cups sang it.

The entire room was filled with gasping people, all unaccustomed to hearing nontraditional wedding music and seeing miniskirts in a ceremony, but this was all as Selma intended. She'd never worried about standing out in a crowd but seemed to take pride in it. A born leader and fashion icon, she was a trendsetter in every regard. Oblivious to perpetual gossip surrounding her, she simply walked through life free of worry about keeping in step with anyone else.

The first phrase of the song was my cue to walk down the aisle and stand to the left of the pulpit. I held my bouquet of red roses just so, concentrating on not tripping as I went. I'd planned to take my time and relish the moment, but my heart was beating way too hard, so I rushed down the aisle as though dragged by a horse. After I got into my spot, I kept my eyes firmly fastened on the ground until I sensed Evangeline had entered the room carrying her flower basket. She managed to make eye contact with every single guest and took her own sweet time tossing out rose petals, some bestowed like favors upon guests she liked, some thrown as though she wished they were rocks.

Then came Selma's sister, Bernice, who floated down the aisle in a short high-waist dress that looked as if it were made completely of white rose petals and had a hat to match. She owned Tango Tangerines in New York and looked like Jacqueline Kennedy, though I'd have to draw a big distinction between the two on account of Bernice's tendency to curse like a sailor.

Bernice had barely made it to the church on time due to having searched in the Austin airport for a lost piece of luggage, but she didn't seem flustered in the least bit. Salty as she was sweet, Bernice was much like the candy that made her famous: dried tangerines dipped in dark chocolate. Tango Tangerines, "the excitingly delicious candy inspired by Buenos Aires because it takes two to tango."

Although she didn't look all that much like Selma, their spirits marked them as sisters. Both had the reputation of being able to handle any adversity that came their way in an efficient manner with time left over to file their nails.

When Selma entered the sanctuary, no one's mouth remained closed. While she had dressed her wedding party all in white, which everyone knew was contrary to the rules of nature, she'd chosen to wear valentine red and carry a bouquet of white roses. Her red leather mini-skirt, fishnet stockings, veil, and hat were a first in Fireside history. There was no doubt about it; Selma's wedding would be talked about for decades.

When Mr. Densesky got a look at his beautiful bride, her blonde hair piled to the heavens and her red leather stilettos, he smiled so big I thought his lips had gone dry and stuck to his teeth. He hugged her briefly as they stood before the rotund Reverend Robby Knadle, waiting for his prompt. Then Norman and Selma claimed each other for the rest of their lives, promising never to forsake the other; to be kind, honest, and generous; to love without reservation; and to serve their fellow man as a team.

When the Gemburree Sisters sang "My Love" in the style of Petula Clark, every child in the audience went berserk and chaos ensued. This was a song we all knew and loved as it had been sung during our lifetime, not some remnant of days gone by. Children escaped their parents and danced in the aisles. Never had Fireside witnessed such pandemonium and contrariness to tradition in church.

After the song was over, Reverend Knadle ushered the guests back to their seats. "I see mayhem in the aisles, but there is strong symbolism in the midst. Clearly, as all the children in this sanctuary are in support of this marriage, so should be the adults. Selma, Norman—let's exchange the rings and seal the deal, shall we? Children, there'll be time for dancing at the reception, should you wish.

"Will you, Selma Louise Davis, take this man to be your lawfully wedded husband?"

"Did he say '*awfully* wedded husband'?" stage-whispered Evangeline.

"No, monkey girl, he did not," I said and elbowed her.

"I do," said Selma.

126

"And do you, Norman Wayne Densesky, take this woman to be your lawfully wedded wife?"

"I do," said Mr. Densesky.

"Then by the authority vested in me by the state of Texas, I now pronounce you husband and wife. . ." Eventually, he wound up the ceremony by saying, "Norman, you may kiss your bride."

I can vouch for the fact that they didn't come up for air for some time. Wally Densesky clapped and whistled for his brother and new sister-in-law as though he were attending a wrestling match.

"And now I have the great privilege of introducing Mr. and Mrs. Norman Wayne Densesky for the first time," said Reverend Knadle.

When it finally came time for the attendants to process out of the sanctuary, William Bartlett walked up to me and offered his arm. Before that evening, I had never seen him in a suit. His hair was neatly combed in place, and a red handkerchief was folded into his jacket pocket.

Old Adah Mae Applewhite came up to me as we prepared to leave the sanctuary and walk to the Fireside Inn for the reception. A hermit for decades, she had suffered from agoraphobia and grief over her deceased daughter. Only recently had she dared to leave her crumbling cottage, thanks to Ruby. Now, she wore a brocade dress covered in roses. Her gray hair was held back by mother-of-pearl combs.

"Well, that wedding was different," she said.

"I guess you're right," I said.

"Sometimes it doesn't hurt to be different," she said. "Keeps life interesting. If we were all exactly the same, there'd be no challenge to living."

"Yes, ma'am."

Walt came out of the church carrying little Jewel, who'd taken a change in attitude and was now engaged in a full-on meltdown.

"Come on, little pumpkin eater," I said, taking her in my arms and placing her on my hip.

Jewel leaned toward me and then rubbed her face on my coat. She wore a pink corduroy jacket and a matching hat with white fleece trim and dangling tie balls.

I danced her down the street to the Fireside Inn, knowing she would be my charge for the evening while the Gemburree Sisters performed for the reception. We whirled around and around past the Maitlin County Courthouse and the hardware store. I covered her eyes with my hand as we passed the county jail; thought briefly of Seymour, likely sitting on his cot; and said, "You're too young to worry about this, Jewel."

Soon, we paused in front of station KOFF and noted the Valentine's Day hearts taped to the window. I pointed out Alma Webster's mastery of red and pink construction paper, lace doilies, and crepe paper. "Jewel, someday you'll also be a whiz at making Valentine's decorations—I can teach you." She just stared wide-eyed at the window and waved her chubby arm.

Then there was Densesky's Groceries and Dry Goods Store, which was closed with a sign over the door that said "Closed for wedding, but open during honeymoon, thanks to our Fireside friends." Honeymoon? Where on earth would they go? Would they take Evangeline and me on account of we were in their wedding party?

Those were the first questions I asked Selma when we spoke at the reception. I wasn't the only one who wanted to know. I could tell by the way Jewel cooed and smiled at Selma, she wanted to go along too.

Selma and Norman had only been in the Fireside Inn for a few seconds when I hurried toward her and gave her a great big hug. We were within an arm's length of an enormous crystal punch bowl filled with lime-green sherbet and ginger ale.

"Are you and Mr. Densesky going someplace special for your honeymoon?"

Selma looked at me and giggled like a schoolgirl. "Can you keep a secret?" she asked, bending down close to my ear. Jewel reached over, grabbed Selma's finger, and tried to pull it into her mouth. She was working on getting her first tooth and was ready to gnaw on anything within reach. Drool slid down the rolls on her neck and onto her tiny smocked dress.

"You cute little dumpling," said Selma, looking at Jewel. Then she resumed her whisper into my ear. "We're going to Paris," she said.

"Paris, Texas?" I asked. "That's so far from Fireside. It will take you all of tomorrow to drive that far."

"No, honey. . . . I'm talking Paris, France. Norman and I are going to spend the night here, and tomorrow we'll drive to Austin, fly to New York, and then get on a Pan Am flight. Ever since folks started confusing me with Brigitte Bardot, I've had a hankering to see what her hometown looks like."

"No, really? Are you pulling my leg, Miss Selma?"

"Honest to goodness. We're gonna take in the City of Light and have a cup of French coffee on the Champs-Élysées. Who knows, we might even spot Maurice Chevalier at one of those outdoor cafés. Whenever I hear him sing 'Thank Heaven for Little Girls,' I want to twirl around with a parasol and feel like I'm five years old again."

"I know what you mean, Miss Selma," I said. "Sometimes I wish I were Jewel's age and had no cares in the world."

I started feeling sad about my parents all over again, but when the Gemburree Sisters started singing "Fever," Mr. Densesky whisked Selma away to dance. Ruby sounded so much like Peggy Lee, I couldn't help but be mesmerized. Norman pushed Selma across the dance floor and held her so tight, you couldn't have wedged a slip of paper between them. Oh, they were on fire with a big fever, all right.

When Ruby started singing "It's Now or Never," Pearl left her chair where she'd played percussion, moved out onto the dance floor and started dancing by herself. I thought that was a crying shame, to be alone. Next thing you knew, Charles Wesley, who'd been about to start serving the barbecue feast, removed his apron, moved to the dance floor, and started dancing with Pearl like it wasn't the first time. I have to tell you, they made a striking couple, she with her marcelled blonde hair and he with his dashing dark looks.

People gasped to see a black man and a white woman dancing and whirling together in Fireside as though they were a couple. But I just smiled, looked down at little Jewel, and whispered in her ear, "See your folks over there? I'm banking on another wedding soon."

The silence in the room soon grew thick and tough as old boot leather. It wasn't two shakes of a lamb's tail, however, before William Bartlett walked up and asked me and baby Jewel to dance to "Can't Help Falling in Love." I have to tell you, I completely forgot about anybody else in the room when Walt came over and took Jewel out of my arms so I could dance for real. It was the first time I'd ever danced with a boy, and I don't know how many times I stepped on his feet, but he didn't seem to notice as we slowly, awkwardly made our way around the Fireside Inn ballroom.

"Thank you, Juliet," he said afterward as he walked me back to my table.

"Well, I. . ." I stumbled over what to say but needn't have worried, because Evangeline and Davy Ottmers ran over and chanted, "'Juliet and William sitting in a tree, k-i-s-s-i-n-g. First comes love, then comes marriage, then comes baby in a baby carriage.'"

"Oh, grow up," I said, giving Evangeline the stink eye. "You too, Davy."

My attention returned to Pearl and Charles. Pearl was smiling more radiantly than I had ever seen, even as they parted so she could return to her percussion instruments and he to oversee his banquet helpers.

Although there had only been one marriage that day, there had been more than one love story taking place. All of it gave me goose bumps as I took Jewel from Walt's arms to give her a bottle. She was starting to fuss, and I had become the person most likely to be able to comfort her next to Pearl.

I was just starting to think I understood what love was like. Love between family members. Love between couples, love between little Jewel and myself. These were different kinds of love, but they were all important.

For the first time since the day I had last seen my mother take off, I was beginning to comprehend that love still existed. That it was bigger than I'd ever understood, that it came from someplace else and felt like heaven. That it was deeper than we realized and didn't depend entirely upon humans, who could sometimes disappoint us. That it came from another place that I only dimly grasped.

After we'd all eaten our fill of Charles Wesley's barbecue and Jewel had settled down to sleep against my shoulder, I arose from the table to watch Selma and Norman cut their wedding cake. First, photographs were snapped in front of the three-tiered cake that had been expertly designed by Mona at the Fireside Inn. On its top were Barbie and Ken dolls dressed in exact miniature replicas of Selma's red outfit and Norman's suit, topped off by a cowboy hat. Red roses lay at their feet and around the bottom of the cake. Evangeline swooped by and ran her finger around the bottom of the cake, then licked the icing. I glared at her, grateful Selma's back had been turned. She'd been spared seeing the damage created by Rabbit, aka. Wile E. Coyote.

"Keep your mitts off the cake," I hissed. "Shame on you."

"Party pooper," she said as she crossed her eyes and stuck out her tongue, coated with icing.

Unlike the only other wedding I'd ever been to, they didn't smash the cake all over each other's faces but handled everything with dignity. Seemingly, Selma and Norman were in their own invisible world, their eyes only on each other, as they gently fed each other a bite.

Charles Wesley and his team finished putting the remaining barbecue, potato salad, beans, coleslaw, onions, pickles, and iced tea into large ice chests and wiped off the serving counter. Here was a man who'd been a famous pilot during World War II, who'd flown no telling how many dangerous missions and, unlike my own father, lived to tell the tale. Now he was a businessman who made the best barbecue on planet Earth and took pride in every bite he served. Clearly, whatever mission he'd been on, then or now, he poured himself into doing a class A job.

If Pearl ever did marry him, we'd eat like kings, although we hadn't exactly suffered in that department since Ruby had returned from their tour. Everyone in Fireside knew she made the best mile-high banana pie and Golden Westerner cakes on the planet. When I asked how she made them taste so good, she said it was because she filled every bite with love. Well, looking at my grandparents sharing a kiss as Selma and Norman made their exit amid a flurry of rice flung by all of us, and seeing the way Charles Wesley looked at Pearl when she waved to Selma and Norman as they escaped through the open door, I thought I recognized the true meaning of Valentine's Day. Charles put his hand to his forehead, a second later, his fingers to his lips, and then blew a kiss to the back of Pearl's head. She couldn't catch it because she didn't know it was coming. Can you miss something as important as a kiss passing through the air and go on to lead a good life—the right life? I wondered. Or if you weren't aware of one being sent, could a kiss reach you anyway and leave its sweet mark?

I leaned over, planted a kiss on Jewel's forehead, told her I loved her and said she was my baby valentine. That I would protect her from as much disappointment as possible. That I would never leave her. She could depend on me.

Fifteen

"Welcome to Fireside, Texas, home of the free and the brave and the everlasting polite persons. This is Juliet Cranbourne, and I want to remind you that today is Saturday, March eighth, 1969, and Saint Patrick's Day is just around the corner for all our Fireside listeners of Irish heritage and for those who just wish they were. Now's the time to order your Lucky Four-Leaf-Clover Celebration Baskets from Mattie Matlock's, down on Main Street. Each basket includes two pounds of corned beef, one red cabbage, onions, carrots, and red potatoes. Just pop these tasty ingredients into a Dutch oven, and in just a few hours, you'll feel like dancing an Irish jig. As a free gift, she'll throw in a potted clover plant to bring you all the extra Irish luck you'll need.

"Now for national news. A Woodstock Music and Art Fair has been scheduled in the Catskill Mountains of New York for August fifteenth through seventeenth. Musicians Arlo Guthrie and Joan Baez have signed on for this event. Afterward, you can count on local commentary here at your very own station KOFF. The trial of James Earl Ray will commence this coming Monday regarding the assassination of Martin Luther King, Jr. Stay tuned on Monday when Miss Alma Webster will give you the latest update on whether he issues a plea of guilty or not guilty. All of us here at station KOFF send our continuing prayers to the King family for strength during these times of troubled waters.

"In other news, Apollo 9 that launched on March third, is orbiting the earth as many times as possible before it returns. Little Davy Ottmers swears he saw it flying over Fireside. Nothing like supersonic vision, right, Davy?

"Anyhow, Fireside, Texas, and station KOFF would like to send best wishes for a successful mission to the Apollo 9 astronauts James McDivitt, David Scott, and Rusty Schweickart. Woo-hoo!

"Back to local news. We have an exciting update from our sponsor, Patsy's Hose Recycling Factory. Did you know old pairs of stockings can be turned into beautiful pillows and sculptures? The ladies at Patsy's have years of experience in creating 3-D pillows in the shape of cottage roses or indoor hens and chicks and cacti gardens that never need watering and look like spring three hundred sixty-five days a year. Just a little bit of wire, old stockings, and recycled egg cartons can be transformed into treasures by experienced hands.

"Come on down to Patsy's and visit the showroom on Main Street next to Milton's Gecko's. They'll show you the many artistic items waiting for you.

"In keeping with good wishes for the Apollo 9 mission, the Gemburree Sisters will play the theme music 'Also Sprach Zarathustra' from *2001: A Space Odyssey*. And this is Juliet Cranbourne, encouraging you to enjoy our live entertainment and to keep your heads high and turned toward the sky."

After the broadcast of *The Cranbourne Variety Hour* ended, Ruby took me aside and put her hand lovingly on my cheek. "Juliet, I just want you to know how proud I am of you. You're blossoming into a talented young lady. Keep it up and you'll have a career in radio, if that's what you want."

"Thanks, Mamaw, but I don't have any talents to speak of. You're the one with talent. I can't play a single instrument."

"There are many types of talent, not just music. Your talent comes in reaching out and talking to folks. You can make them feel better by helping their spirits. That's a major talent. But if you'd like to learn something about music, we ought to line up those guitar lessons. Popo is sure you can learn to play the one he bought you for Christmas, if you'd like to give it a whirl."

I had my doubts, but the image of my grandfather smiling proudly at me came to my mind like a vision. Magically, I'd somehow learn to play the guitar like Chet Atkins and sing along like Patsy Cline at the age of almost eleven. "All right," I said. "I'll try it."

Right away, I started daydreaming about playing the guitar for my fellow sixth graders in Fireside Elementary. For starters, all the boys would finally quit teasing me and gain some r-e-s-p-e-c-t, like Aretha was always singing about. Then the girls would want to form a club and make me president of charm.

When Ruby took me to Mr. Axiom's music class the following Monday, I walked in carrying my white guitar case, so nervous my knees knocked. Right away, he told me to have a seat, took my guitar out of the case, and started tuning it.

"Nice Gibson Dove," he said. "Where'd you get it?"

"My popo gave it to me for Christmas. I imagine he ordered it from Sears and Roebuck, 'cause that's where he gets most everything."

"I gotcha," he said. "First things first. Let me show you how to hold it correctly. Right- or left-handed?"

"I'm ambidextrous," I said proudly, "but I was taught to write with my right hand, so it gets the most use."

"Good thing; this is made for a northpaw. Put the neck of the guitar in your left hand and set the body of the guitar on your right leg."

"Yessir."

"Now put your fingers around the fretboard like so." He paused, watching to make certain I held it correctly. "OK, hang on to your hat, we're in business."

But it didn't sound like I was in business at all when I played. Mr. Axiom taught me the Em chord, but I didn't like it much. When he strummed it, it sounded so fine and natural. When I tried, it sounded like a tinny, squeaky mess.

Noting my distress, he said, "Don't worry, it just takes practice."

"How about you show me how to play like Mr. Chet Atkins today, and I'll go home a happy camper?" I said. "I don't think I need to know all this fret business. Just show me how it's done. I'd like to be able to play on the radio next Saturday."

"Young lady, you'll need to practice at least an hour every day to make good progress. I can teach you how to play 'Sakura Sakura' within a week, but if you think you can play like the greatest guitar player of all time by next Saturday, you've got another think coming."

"Well, what on earth is 'Sakura Sakura'?"

"I call it the cherry blossom song."

"Well, I like cherries," I said.

He spent the next hour going over the sheet music and showing me the basics of guitar. Then he said, "Go home, Juliet, and practice your head off. See you tomorrow. Same time, same station."

When Ruby took me back to the ranch, I straightaway began to practice. I watched the anniversary clock on the mantel to make sure I stayed at it long enough to practice my head off. After ten minutes, I thought my head was nearly clean off, and Evangeline was annoying the daylights out of me. She'd thrown herself on the couch and then raced around the room using the broom for a stick horse.

"I'm a champion barrel racer. I bet I could win a silver belt buckle in nothing flat."

"You're way too old to be doing that! The only thing you could win is a blue ribbon for being the world's biggest pest."

"I could so win for barrel racing, and I'm not a pest."

"You are! That's how you got to be named Rabbit in the first place. There's no bigger garden pest."

"Hogwash," she said.

"Why'd you stop practicing, Squirrel?" asked Walt when he came back into the living room. Evangeline had draped herself backward over the ottoman and was eyeing me upside down with consternation.

"I'm being distracted something awful by her. What a stinker she is!"

"I know what a dying squirrel sounds like now," Evangeline said.

"Popo, make her quit bothering me," I whined.

"Rabbit, how about we go for a ride in the pickup?" said Walt. "We need to count cattle. We've got sixteen first-timers about to calve, and I've got to keep my eyes on them to see if they need any extra help."

"Oh, all right, Popo. Can I drive?"

"Not till you get big enough to reach the pedals and see over the steering wheel. Maybe when you turn forty or so," he said, winking.

"Not fair," Evangeline said. "I bet Davy Ottmers's family lets him drive."

"He can't even drive a plate of spaghetti into his mouth," I said.

By the time supper rolled around, so did Pearl, Sapphire, and little Jewel. Ruby was making chicken potpie and whirls of garden peas she'd frozen the previous summer. For dessert, there would be strawberry garnet delight, made of individual meringues she'd baked on a piece of paper bag at a low temperature, a scoop of ice cream, and frozen strawberries soaked in sugar, with a squirt of Reddi-wip on top. Ruby came out of the kitchen to greet her sisters, who came in through the front door like March winds. She wiped her hands on her hand-embroidered apron and adjusted the collar of her jade-green blouse. Her red hair was pinned up out of her way, but the frizz was out of control due to humidity. It had rained earlier that day, and the air was still heavy with moisture.

Sapphire was wearing denim jeans and a red sweater. She'd tucked her black hair under a baseball cap that read "Boston Red Sox," although I doubted she'd been to a game in person. It was just too far away from Fireside and all.

"Howdy, missy," said Sapphire.

"Hey, there, Aunt Sapphire."

"How's my nutty niece?" asked Pearl, smiling as she kissed my forehead. Jewel reached out for me right away, nearly throwing herself headlong into my arms. I put my guitar down on the ottoman and took her right away. Then, in nothing flat, she started wiggling as though she was trying to get down.

"Let me get a blanket, and you can put her down on the floor. I think she's trying to learn to crawl."

"Really? She's too young to do that, Aunt Pearl."

"Some babies start this young. She turned five months old last Friday. And I heard that there was a baby girl in India who crawled at three months."

"You're pulling my leg," said Ruby. "I never heard of anyone crawling before six months."

"That just goes to show you that my Jewel is talented," said Pearl, smiling.

Sure enough, as soon as Pearl placed Jewel on a baby blanket, she got up on all fours and rocked back and forth.

"She's just like a horned toad, Aunt Pearl. You've seen horned toads do that, haven't you? They rock on all fours like that before they spit blood from their eyes."

"Squirrel, my baby will never spit blood from her eyes, even if she rocks like that for the rest of her life."

"You're right. She's too cute for that. Come here, doll baby," I said, dropping down to sit by my cousin on the floor. I lay down on the wood floor beside her and propped myself up on one elbow. "When you get through rocking, I'll pick you up, and we'll dance just like we did at Selma's reception."

Now that I was lying at eye level to Jewel, she looked at me and started laughing so hard her belly rolled. I'd make a face, and then she'd get tickled again as she tried to reach over and bite my nose. I pulled back in a hurry, and she laughed twice as hard.

The following day, I went in for my second music lesson, which was continuing a week of intensive training so I could learn to play "Sakura Sakura" by the coming weekend.

Mr. Axiom sat on his stool, bent over his own acoustic guitar and seemingly unaware that I'd walked into the room. He was wearing a brown tweed jacket with patches on both elbows and worn-out loafers. His curly black hair had been oiled with pomade and his mustache waxed. He nodded his head and tapped one foot as he lost himself in playing "Classical Gas."

"That was so groovy, Mr. Axiom," I said when he finally looked up and stopped playing.

"Thank you, Squirrel."

"How'd you know that was my nickname?"

"Everybody in Fireside knows all about you."

I tried to decide whether that was a good or a bad thing. It was a tad creepy to realize I was known so well all over town, even by folks I hardly knew. Did they know I was good at talking on station KOFF, or did they know I'd gotten into trouble at school for making a C minus on my math test because I wasn't paying attention? Did they know I'd toilet-papered Selma's yard a year back and had spent all day cleaning up the mess on a hungry stomach? Did they know I liked to wear my mother's old ratty slip beneath my nightgown so I could feel close to her?

Mr. Axiom spent the entire hour trying to teach me enough about the guitar to play "Sakura Sakura." As I was leaving, he handed me the sheet music to take home and said, "Practice, practice." It made me somewhat anxious to contemplate having to learn the entire piece before my next lesson. Determined to please Walt and to keep my head up, I vowed to do just that.

Walt picked me up afterward. He wore his Jimmy Dean cowboy hat cocked back on his head. We rode along the highway back to the ranch with the window cracked, singing along with Jimmie Rodgers to "In the Jailhouse Now." I kid you not, my jaw fell right open when Walt started to yodel.

"Good gravy. How'd you learn how to do that, Popo?"

"I studied it by listening to the Grand Ole Opry regulars. And of course, I've taken a few lessons from Ruby."

We laughed and sang at the top of our lungs as we passed Densesky's. To his credit, Walt didn't seem to mind I was off key. He let me sing as long and loud as I pleased. Can you imagine? I guessed he loved me a powerful lot to let me hurt his ears like that. Had Sport been in the truck with us, he'd have set to howling something awful.

With Selma and Norman recently back from their honeymoon in Paris, marriage was still fresh on my mind. My focus on romance went straightaway to wondering how Pearl and Charles Wesley were getting along. When we walked in the house, I asked Ruby if I could borrow the telephone to call Pearl.

Soon as Pearl answered the telephone, I could hear little Jewel howling in the background.

"What's she riled up about, Aunt Pearl?"

"She bumped her noggin on the coffee table, that's what. Let me pick her up and love on her. Hang on a minute."

Presently, Pearl came back to the phone, and I could hear Jewel near the mouthpiece, hiccupping those sad poor-me noises but no longer crying.

"Well, some barbecue sauce would make her feel better. You ought to call Mr. Wesley right away and ask him to bring you some. I read somewhere that was a miracle cure for unhappy babies."

"Do tell," she said. "I'm gonna order a gallon."

"Good idea. She'll be smiling in a jiffy," I said, relieved that Pearl hadn't guessed what I was really up to.

"Did I mention she's nearly crawling, but when she gets fed up with that, she just rolls her way to wherever she wants to go?"

"How about that! She's a genius. The smartest baby I ever heard of."

"Spoken like a loving family member," said Pearl. "Speaking of loving family, would you like to babysit Jewel on Thursday night? I have some special plans."

I instantly visualized Pearl out on a date with Charles Wesley, so I said, "You bet! I'll play the guitar for her. Maybe she'd like that."

"Oh honey, I know she will! Just so you know, Juliet, nobody can do what you do. You're a one and only, and I love you, dear niece. Angels come in many forms, and here you are, so young and yet helping so many."

Pearl's words were a healing balm to my spirit. I had no reason to disbelieve her but didn't feel myself worthy of her praise that I was an angel.

Angels? What on earth was she talking about?

I can't say my vision had a thing to do with it, but before I could say "hokey pokey," I learned Pearl and Charles Wesley had made plans to go to Diamond's Dance Hall along with Selma and Norman to learn how to dance the Lindy Hop.

After we'd hung up, I was standing in Ruby's kitchen and decided to tune the radio in to station KOFF. "Yummy, Yummy, Yummy" by the Ohio Express came on, so I just naturally started dancing around the room. I wasn't a trained dancer, but alone in the kitchen, what did it matter? I had no idea what the Lindy Hop was all about, but I could dance, just to be in the spirit, couldn't I? My love of dance was the one trait I'd inherited from my grandmother Itasca, of whom I often thought.

When Ruby came in from milking a new cow, I just had to ask, "Mamaw, what is the Lindy Hop? Did you know Pearl is going with Mr. Wesley to dance at Diamond's?"

"Sure, I know the Lindy Hop. It's a swing dance that can get on the athletic side if you get serious about it. I'd be glad to show you what I know, provided you've finished practicing your guitar. And no, I didn't know about Pearl's plans."

"OK. I'll get right on it and meet you back in the living room in thirty minutes."

"I think your practice time is an hour, Juliet." Ruby raised one eyebrow and set the metal milk bucket on the counter. She leaned over it and stared at it for a moment. "Here's what I do know: there's a lot of cream in this bucket. I'll let it sit until the cream separates. Bet you anything, we'll have the makings for butter. Wynona recently had her first calf, and would you just look at this bucket of milk? She's gonna make our kitchen table a happy place to be during mealtime. Fresh cream and butter. Might churn some ice cream for Easter. . ."

"What happened to old Jessie?" I asked, thinking of the cow that Evangeline had fed so much chocolate.

"She's fine," said Ruby. "Was turned out into the north pasture is all. Ten months of milk is about all most cows can give. You might say she's on vacation until she has another calf in April." She looked at me, put her hands on her hips, and said, "Squirrel, are you trying to stall practicing your instrument? Because if so. . ."

She was still talking when I went off to work on my Em chord and the other things Mr. Axiom had taught me. If truth be told, I was far more excited about learning to dance than to play the guitar. On the other hand, I wanted to change my reputation as the only Cranbourne family member who had no musical talent. I was determined to have my moment on station KOFF playing "Sakura Sakura" and make everyone sit up and take notice that I was a force with which to be reckoned. In my fantasy, someone would ask, "What do you call a female Chet Atkins? Juliet Cranbourne, of course."

By the time Walt and Evangeline had come in from tending the cattle, Ruby had put a hen into the electric oven to bake, along with yams and peas with pearl onions simmering in milk on the stovetop. She put an old Count Basie hit called "Shorty George" on my dad's old record player and pushed the ottoman out of the way in the living room.

"Walt, why don't you help me show the girls how to do the Lindy Hop?"

Walt smiled, took off his straw Stetson, and placed it on its crown on the top of the bookshelf that stood next to his favorite chair. He wore a five-o'clock shadow over his lip and chin, and his silver hair had been molded by his hat, but he still looked as handsome as ever to me. Walt just couldn't be otherwise.

"You forgot to shave, Walt," said Ruby.

"No, my cheeks and chin are just chapped. I'm taking a shaving break today."

"The March winds have gotten my poor Walt again, haven't they?" Ruby cupped his face in her hands lovingly.

"Why should this year be different?" Walt smiled at Ruby and kissed her forehead. "Come on, Ruby, darlin'. Let's shake a leg and show these youngsters how the best swing dance ever is done. Not sure these old legs can move as fast as they used to, but I'll give it my best."

By most standards, my grandparents were young, but I didn't realize Walt could lift Ruby to do aerials and that she could slide across the floor like a schoolgirl and hop straight up to dance some more. Although the space in our living room made them extra cautious about bumping into things, they put on quite a show.

Even Evangeline was impressed, and that in itself was something rare. "Do it again, Popo. Throw Mamaw into the air again."

"That's pretty cool. How come you can do that when most grandparents can't?" I asked when the record had been played twice, and they finally stopped dancing.

"You can do a lot of things when you lift fifty-pound sacks of feed every day and throw ewes during drenching season," said Ruby. "These chores also help me build enough muscle to fiddle for long stretches. Playing music can be an endurance test."

Evangeline and I played at learning the Lindy Hop, but we mainly tripped over our own two feet and fell on the floor a lot. When it dawned on me just how many things my grandparents could do that we knew nothing about, I felt a little overwhelmed, sensing how far I had to go to learn everything I wanted. Quietly, I again resolved to practice my guitar for long hours each day. Even on Thursday, when I was to babysit Jewel, I needed to find a way to practice. I now wish I'd chosen another way to express myself. You would, too, if you'd been me. You know what they say: hindsight is twenty-twenty.

What I couldn't know then was what would happen come Thursday. How could I? You believe me, don't you? Some truths are timeless and don't come from me. They come from the stars in the universe, the hand that steers the planets, and a love that's bigger than anything I've ever known. Sadly, I must now pause to ask for forgiveness for what was to come. Please pardon me as I try to pardon others. I didn't know what I was doing.

Sixteen

Soon as I got finished with my guitar lesson on Thursday with Mr. Axiom, who had declared he was suffering from the worst headache ever, we drove straight home. As soon as we arrived in Ruby's Thunderbird, I went into the kitchen and dipped Oreos in a glass of fresh milk. I wanted to settle down, do my homework, and then practice my guitar so I could be completely free to play with Jewel as long as possible. But when the telephone rang, and as soon as I heard William Bartlett's voice, I forgot about all I'd planned.

"Hey, Juliet, this is William. I just called to see if you want to go roller-skating down at the city park on Saturday. We could skate over to Densesky's afterward and have some ice cream. What do you say?"

"That would be cool, but I can't go until I finish my broadcast on KOFF."

"Three o'clock, then?"

"Far out," I said. "I'll meet you at the park."

I was so excited, I danced around the kitchen for a good long while to every song that came on station KOFF and completely forgot about my commitment to do homework and practice my guitar until Pearl knocked on the kitchen door. When I opened it, I saw my beautiful aunt holding baby Jewel, who was wearing a pink sweater and a corduroy dress. Soon as she saw me, she lurched into my arms like she'd been waiting a lifetime to see me.

"Cutest baby ever," I said, kissing her chubby cheek.

"Even if she fusses, don't let her have more than one teething biscuit. This tot loves arrowroot."

143

"I promise."

"I won't stay out late," she said, reaching up to touch her blonde hair. "It is nice, though, to have an evening out. Thank you, Squirrel."

"You bet. Glad to do it." I looked down at Jewel, who was smiling at me. "We're going to have a great time, aren't we, Jewel?"

Pearl tooted her horn goodbye, then drove off in the Ambassador station wagon the Gemburree Sisters had used on tour the previous fall. Its tires kicked up caliche dust and excited our dog to no end. Sport chased her down the road and barked his head off. When he finally grew tired and gave up the chase, he returned homeward, panting but fulfilled. Then he wiggled back inside the yard fence without any struggle at all.

When Jewel noticed Sport through the window, she grew so excited, I couldn't help but take her outside on the front porch so she could reach out and stroke his fur. I held her on my lap as we sat on the concrete steps, and Sport put his head in her lap. He repeatedly licked her sweet cheek, which cracked her up. She laughed so hard, she couldn't even catch her breath. That's when I decided it would be a good idea if I brought out my guitar to practice and knocked two things out at once.

After we'd again settled on the front porch, Jewel on her floral blanket and me on the concrete steps with my Gibson guitar, Sport would periodically race up one side of the steps and shoot across the porch down the other. Jewel rolled this way and that, getting into any position as long as she could keep sight of our crazy dog. Then she pushed up on her knees, rocked back and forth, and began to do a sort of horned-toad belly flop. Watching Sport's antics was far better than being indoors would have been, especially with my "Sakura Sakura" music in the background.

"Would you look at this smart girl?" I said, cheering her on. As a squirrel darted across the porch toward the old pecan tree that stood at one corner of the porch, Jewel looked at me as if to say, *What in the world is that?*

Sport caught sight of the squirrel and barreled full speed onto the porch. I turned to put down my guitar so I could scoop her up, but that decision was a bad one. I should have thrown it on the sidewalk to save time. Had I done that, perhaps things would have turned out differently.

Doesn't it take more time to turn and place something down gently than to throw it?

When Sport skidded into Jewel, she flew headfirst off the porch. When I turned around toward the commotion, I saw that my precious cousin lay motionless on a patch of bells of Ireland with her eyes closed. Was she dead?

"Mamaw, Popo! Somebody, help!" My feet sprouted wings as I fairly flew off the porch to help her. Unaware of the trouble his actions had caused, Sport stood at the bottom of the pecan tree nearest the porch and barked at the squirrel that was now climbing around its branches, taunting him.

I scooped up Jewel, cradled her in my arms, and then put my cheek to her nose to see whether she was still breathing. A faint puff of infant breath reached my cheek and brought some relief, but not enough to counteract the worst terror I'd ever felt.

"Wake up, baby Jewel. Wake up, honey. Sport won't bother you anymore. He's busy with that squirrel."

Ruby came running outside, wearing her striped pedal pushers, white blouse, and holey Keds tennis shoes. "Lord in heaven," she exclaimed when she saw Jewel's motionless face and closed eyes.

One thing I'll say for sure is that my grandmother had a special talent for reacting quickly when disaster was in the making. She had the instincts and reactions of an ambulance driver and was naturally good at knowing what to do. She grabbed her patent-leather purse off the kitchen counter, and before I could even think good, we were in her Thunderbird on the way to the Fireside Hospital.

Ruby turned on her car's flashers and broke every speed limit along the way. I held little Jewel and prayed my head off that she would live. Furthermore, I begged God's forgiveness for having taken her on the porch in the first place. The thought that anything so terrible had happened to such a sweet baby broke my heart to pieces. I cried nonstop and began to hate myself for not protecting her better. I thought the Maitlin County judge might sentence me to hang just like they did in western movies like *Cat Ballou*, starring Jane Fonda, Michael Callan, and Lee

Marvin. You remember Nat King Cole and Stubby Kaye singing the ballad by Mack David and Jerry Livingston, don't you?

That would be just what I deserved, I decided. Furthermore, I didn't know how I could face Pearl, who had trusted me with her precious daughter.

As soon as we arrived at the hospital, they rushed Jewel through some swinging steel doors, and I lost sight of her. Ruby went back with her and told me to ask someone to call Diamond's Dance Hall and notify Pearl about Jewel.

Dixie Flagg, who had become a junior candy striper and tagged along with a full-fledged candy striper named Miriam Healy, walked past me in the waiting room. Being a junior candy striper wasn't a real job in my book—I felt quite certain that it was an activity created by her folks to keep her out of mischief.

She didn't notice me until I grabbed her arm. "Dixie, there's been a terrible accident I need to call my aunt Pearl about. I don't have a dime to use the pay phone. Can you get Miriam to take me to the office and help me make a call?"

"I will," she said, and sniffed, "if you call me Nurse Flagg."

"All right, then, Nurse Flagg, will you please help me?"

"Ok, but you owe me a batch of brownies with lots of nuts in them," she said and went to fetch Miriam.

I had never liked Miriam all that much. Although Evangeline and I were in the Fireside Elementary School and she was a freshman in Fireside High which was located just a block away from the playground, we shared a common gymnasium. Every Tuesday and Thursday afternoon, she spent a long time hogging the mirror after gym class while putting on her uniform and headband. While her class had just ended, mine was beginning, and I needed to change from my school dress into my navy-blue gym suit in the same locker room. She kept a can of Aqua Net in her locker and sprayed enough to form a cloud over several onlookers. Finally, after each hair had been cemented into place, she turned this way and that, admiring herself in her outfit. She had spent every summer watching *General Hospital*, which everyone in Fireside knew because that was all she could talk about. Sure enough, just as soon as she'd turned fourteen, she'd gotten herself installed as a candy striper. To top it all off with whipped cream and a Butterfinger bar, she sometimes rode our school bus when her parents wouldn't drive her to town. Whenever this happened, she always made a beeline for the back seat in the bus so she could smooch with the high school quarterback. There were two strikes against her in my book: she was a thoughtless hairspray queen and low-down seat stealer.

"Go away, kid," said Miriam, as soon as I asked her for help. "You're interfering with my schedule. I've got toys to pass out to twins in room one-twelve."

I could tell straight away that she was having a bad influence on Dixie, who was always so impressionable, due to the smirk that was now on Dixie's face.

"Please help me make a phone call to my aunt Pearl."

"Get away from my cart; you're blocking my path," said Miriam.

I raised my voice and clenched my fists. "Miriam, help me call my aunt Pearl, or I'll tell everyone I saw you kissing Danny Bush in the back of the school bus." Shock registered on Miriam's face as she reached up to pat her hair.

"Oh fine," she said, wrinkling up her perfect nose. "I'll get your stinkin' color-blind aunt Pearl on the stupid phone."

"You need an attitude adjustment. Lucky for you, Evangeline isn't with me. She'd have punched you in the nose for that comment. As for me, as my good friend William says, 'I don't get mad. I just get even.'"

When I finally got to talk to Pearl, I started crying so hard she couldn't quite understand what I was saying. She did get the words *hospital* and *Jewel*, and they were enough to bring her to us in no time flat. Along with her came Charles Wesley and Selma and Norman Densesky.

Pearl burst through the double steel doors and ran toward the emergency bay, hollering, "Where is she? Where is she?" The doors swung shut, and I couldn't see a thing afterward. I about worried myself into exhaustion until Ruby emerged to give us an update.

"She has a concussion, and they're still examining her spine for fractures. She's awake and crying her head off. That's a good sign at this point."

"Oh, Mamaw, I'm so sorry. I know Sport is too. He didn't mean to slide into her on account of that squirrel. It's all my fault. I shouldn't have taken her onto the porch like I did."

"It wasn't your fault, and that's all there is to it. Juliet, nobody thinks you meant for any harm to come to that baby. Everybody knows how much you love her. With the good Lord's help, she'll be all right by and by."

"I shouldn't have been practicing my guitar. I'm no good at it anyway."

"It's too early to tell whether you are or aren't." Ruby put her hand on my cheek. "If you make a habit of thinking like that, you'll just be shooting yourself in the foot."

On Friday morning, I had a tough time getting myself out of bed. I had cried myself to sleep, then stayed awake most of the rest of the night, staring up at the ceiling. Evangeline, however, slept much like Sport, turning this way and that, taking up both sides of the bed more than once. Whenever she did that, I'd just roll her back to her side and try not to awaken her. You know what they say: it's best not to awaken sleeping babies and dogs, even though, in my book, she was a full-blooded orangutan.

Ruby and Walt felt sorry for me, so they didn't make me get up early to ride the bus that day but drove us to school in the Thunderbird. William was waiting for me in the parking lot, expecting me to get off the bus. He carried two books covered in brown paper bags upon which his name was neatly stenciled on each cover, surrounded by floor-plan doodles and the names of his favorite musicians in his inwardly curved, left-handed script. When he spotted us, he walked to the car and opened my door lickety-split.

"We still on for roller-skating tomorrow?" he asked. His *Leave It To Beaver* haircut was interrupted by one strong rooster tail that stood straight up in the back. He wore his Fireside FFA navy-blue jacket with the name *Bartlett* written across the back, along with patches of the FFA shield and a chicken representing his personal animal project. I thought it took courage for a boy to walk around wearing a chicken on his jacket, a quality I admired.

"Roller-skating?" asked Ruby, as she rolled down her window and looked over her green sunglasses at him.

"Yes, ma'am," I said as I climbed out of the back seat. "Guess I forgot to ask permission with all the craziness that's been going on."

"Well, you have it," said Ruby.

"And mine," said Walt, "if you need a second vote. You clean up well, William." He pointed at William's jacket and smiled broadly. "I like your chicken."

William blushed. "It's all I can raise here in town in our backyard. I have ten Rhode Island Reds. Did you know each hen can lay somewhere around two hundred forty-five or two hundred fifty eggs a year?"

"What do you do with all those eggs?" asked Ruby. "As if I didn't know."

"I sell them," said William.

"Looks like I'm up against a savvy competitor, but I guess the market can bear both of us. Your hens' eggs have those pretty brown shells with freckles on them, don't they?" She smiled and winked at William, which made me realize she liked him for sure. Ruby didn't smile that way at all the kids in my class, especially the ones who were up to no good.

"Yes, ma'am," he said. "I've got my regular customers: Mrs. Walker at the bank, Shirl at the beauty shop, Leroy Elmore at the hardware store, and sometimes even Densesky's when they're hard up for eggs."

"And what does a young'un like you do with all that spending money?" asked Walt.

"I'm saving for college, 'cause I want to be an architect. I built my own chicken coop when I was only in the fourth grade. And. . . I do buy a lot of ice cream at Densesky's. I like their strawberry chocolate double dip quite a bit."

"Squirrel, do you want to go roller-skating with this boy or not?" asked Walt.

"Yessir, but maybe I could skip doing the broadcast tomorrow. I'm not sure my spirits are up to talking much."

"Whether you feel up to it or not, the show must go on," said Ruby. "But don't worry, I'll be right beside you if you get into a bind."

"Hey, what about me?" said Evangeline. "I'm not just fluff. I can entertain everyone with my stories. Like Yogi Bear says, 'I'm smarter than the average bear.'"

When I got to station KOFF the following afternoon, I stared at the microphone, unnerved. Still shaken over Jewel's fall, I felt my confidence level slide down the slippery slope of despair and anxiety. If I could make that terrible mistake with her, there was no telling what else I might misjudge.

My breathing was off, and my hands shook. I was also supposed to play "Sakura Sakura" today, but I couldn't even look at my guitar, and thankfully, Ruby and Walt didn't make me.

"Take a deep breath, sugar. You'll be all right. Don't let your nerves get the best of you. You can do it," said Ruby.

"No, she can't!" said Evangeline. "She's a pitiful mess. Anyone can see that."

"Hush that nonsense," said Ruby, frowning at my sister. "She's no mess, and besides that, no one can see her because she's on the radio."

"Are you watching the clock?" asked Evangeline. "It's time for me to hit the red button. One. Two. Three. You're live."

"Welcome to Fireside, Texas, home of the free and the brave and the everlasting polite persons. . ." My mind went blank. Ruby just calmly pointed to the copy in front of me. "Today's *Variety Hour* is sponsored by Horble's Sandstone Toadstools. Have you got a bare spot on your mantel that needs adornment? Does your dining table seem boring and humdrum? You can use any of our brightly colored works of art to enhance your home and bring exciting conversations to ho-hum mealtimes. Whether your decorating needs a whisper of powder blue or a shout out of fluorescent orange, we can fill your every whim with pride. Each toadstool takes only twenty-four hours to be carved by our nifty-jiffy cutter. Our motto is 'A day without a Horble toadstool is a day caught in the rain of monotony. Let a Horble toadstool be your umbrella.' Buy one toadstool today before five o'clock and you'll get the second one free if you mention you heard it first on station KOFF.

"Before we play Hank Williams's 'Moanin' the Blues,' I'm gonna ask all the KOFF listeners to join me in a prayer for little Jewel Gemburree, who's in the hospital recovering from a terrible fall the day before yesterday. She's under the weather, but she's a plucky little gal at heart." I started blubbering like a baby on the air, but Ruby just came up to my side and took over the mic and hugged me as she spoke.

"Heavenly Father, we ask you to perform a healing miracle for our little punkin, Jewel. There's no sweeter baby on this earth, and she needs Your divine touch today. While we know all your children are created equal, she is extra special to our family. You gave her to us to love for eternity. Now we ask for Your mighty power in healing anything that might be broken in her tiny body. In Your name we pray. Amen.

"Now, back to our regularly scheduled variety of musical offerings. Take it away, Hank Williams."

As "Moanin' the Blues" played, Ruby held me tight and let me blubber until the song was over. Before long, listener calls started rolling in. Some wanted to know what on earth had happened to little Jewel. Some called to say they and their families could be counted on to be on their knees praying. One old prune called in to say that God had smote Pearl for her sinful behavior, that this accident was no accident but justice in the making.

"Don't pay her any mind, Juliet," said Ruby. "I recognize her voice. That's old Stella. All her marbles don't roll in the right direction, I can tell you that for sure."

"What a mean thing for her to come up with," I said.

"How about we just say a prayer for Stella and let it go? Let Stella's attitude be addressed by the good Lord. We've got enough worries without taking her on too," said Ruby.

It wasn't long before William roller-skated up to the station KOFF front door. "Ready?" he asked, beaming broadly as we walked outside.

Just to show off, he made sure Ruby, Evangeline, and I saw him skate fancy circles around the driveway while I popped the trunk of the Thunderbird. As I lifted out my skates and sat on the curb to put them on, William lost control and wound up in a bush. He quickly pulled himself together and brushed off the twigs from his FFA jacket and out of his usually well-groomed hair.

"Don't worry," he said. "I'm OK. Accidents do happen."

"We can all see that," said Evangeline.

Ruby took Evangeline by the hand and left in a hurry. There was simply no telling what my sister would say next.

William and I skated to the city park and took a competitive stance toward roller-skating, both of us trying to outdo the other. We pretended we were ice-skating at the 1968 Olympics in Grenoble, just a little over a year earlier.

"You can call me Wolfgang Schwarz," said William.

"You're on roller skates, not ice skates," I said, taking him down a peg.

"Aw, come on," said William. "Use your imagination. I'm Wolfgang, and you're Peggy Fleming, and we're in Grenoble, France. Forget this is concrete rather than ice. You do your routine, and then I'll do mine."

"Where's the music?" I asked coyly.

"Just think of Tchaikovsky's *1812 Overture* with cannons in your head."

"What on earth?"

"The Fourth of July music."

"This is March, William."

"C'mon, Juliet. Quit worrying about the details. You can get stuck in your head that way."

William went on to skate around the water fountain and create a routine as he went along, clearly hearing the *Overture* in his head. After five minutes or so, he came to a stop in the front and gave an exaggerated bow.

"Bravo!" I shouted. "Good going, Willy Billy."

"Don't call me that," he said, perturbed. "Sounds like the name of a goat. Now it's your turn to perform, Juliet."

I skated around the fountain twice, smiled, extended my arms, and then tried to pirouette. Let me just say, it takes nothing for me to get drunk dizzy. When I saw loony candy striper Miriam pass by in her father's car, I accidentally reached out to stabilize myself on a rose bush. She was sitting on the passenger side of a blue Buick Skylark with the vinyl top down. A matching blue scarf held her perfectly teased and sprayed hair in place, but her father's toupee fluttered slightly in the breeze. It made me boiling mad to even look at her after the way she'd behaved at the hospital. "Ouch!" I cried, as the thorns stuck in my palm.

William was soon examining my hand and trying to pluck out thorns. "Good golly," he said. "You sure goobered up your hand. Didn't you see what you were grabbing for?"

"I don't know what happened," I said. "I was doing just fine and then lost it."

"It's a matter of mind control," said William. "Think on the sunny side and hold that thought. The minute you think about losing control, you're a goner."

"I'll keep that in mind," I said, plucking a thorn out of my palm. "Same way you did back at the radio station."

William just smiled and cocked his head. "Ready to go to Densesky's for ice cream?"

"Now you're talking my language."

It took ten minutes filled with giggles and playing tag on skates to get to Densesky's. We started to remove our skates, but Norman, who had stepped outside to smoke his cigar, said, "No, it's not necessary. I've been watching you, and I think you and our store will survive if you keep them on. Selma is restocking the napkin dispensers behind the soda fountain counter. She'll be glad to give you each a special on the house. By the way Juliet, you did a great job at our wedding, and we want you to know we appreciate your help."

"Thank you, Mr. Densesky."

Soon we were inside the store and skating across black-and-white tiles to the red vinyl–covered barstools that lined the soda fountain counter. Selma snapped shut several napkin containers and said, "Hey, kids, how about today's special? Three scoops of ice cream, vanilla, chocolate, and strawberry, topped with chocolate syrup, Reddi-wip, chopped pecans, and a cherry on top. How does that sound?"

"Like the dessert of my dreams," I said. "Quick, what did you have to eat on March seventh, 1948?"

"Let me think. . . Oh yes, I had two fat pieces of lemon pie with meringue and coconut. I ate them before my dinner, which was liver in fried onions and peas and carrots. That dessert was a chaser because I don't care for liver in the least; it was half-price on the menu at the truck stop where I worked, and I didn't have much money. The pie was four days old and was about to be tossed out, so I got it for free."

I nudged William as we ate our specials. "See, I told you she has an incredible memory." I turned to Selma and said, "I hate liver. It's so greasy and tastes half-rotten. Makes me sick to think about it. I guess they cook it with onions to hide the taste."

Selma turned green and said, "Oh, me too. I suddenly feel awful." She left the room in a dead run and headed straight for the restroom. When she finally returned several minutes later, she pulled some napkins out of a dispenser and ran them under water. She crawled up on a soda fountain stool next to me and dabbed her face and neck with the cloth. "Oh dear," she said. "I'm not myself."

"Miss Selma, should I go fetch Mr. Densesky?"

"He'll come back in the store directly. No need to trouble him. I'm sure it's just something I ate or at least thought about eating," she said. Pale, Selma folded her arms on the counter and rested her head on them, concerning me further.

"Don't fret, Miss Selma," I said. "Like my mamaw always says, 'You'll get to feeling better by and by.'" I reached over and put my cheek up next to hers. "Don't you worry. I'll look after you."

I fetched a cool rag for her and pressed it gently against her forehead. It was then that I realized I didn't need a fancy candy-striper uniform like mean Miriam had to make someone feel better; I just needed to share a piece of my heart.

Seventeen

The next day was Sunday, and Ruby and Walt awakened us at daybreak and told us to get up and get dressed. Soon as Ruby had milked Wynona and we'd been sent to let the chickens out of the coop, we ate a quick breakfast of scrambled eggs, bacon, and toast. Toast, as opposed to homemade biscuits, was Ruby's idea of a shortcut.

It wasn't long before we were off in the Thunderbird, heading to town to visit little Jewel and Pearl at the Fireside Hospital before church. All the while, I worried myself into a bothered mess.

I can't even begin to tell you how much Jewel's fall off the porch changed the trajectory of my life. I carried a heavy load of guilt that felt like a bag of boulders on my back. Please believe me when I say I didn't mean to turn away from my responsibility of caring for Jewel, even for a split-haired second.

That morning, we found Charles and Pearl leaning back in their chairs by Jewel's bedside. They were holding hands, his dark, large hand surrounding her slim one, callused from years of playing percussion. They were both about half-asleep. Daylight was streaming in through the blinds, ribbons of light cutting through darkness. At that moment, I had reason to believe their relationship had blossomed into something far more meaningful than an ordinary friendship. He had been there for her during tough times, and I felt he would be there for whatever might come in the future.

Jewel would remain in the hospital for some time to come. She had a hairline spinal fracture and a terrible concussion. I guess if there was anything good to come out of it, it was that the relationship between Pearl and Charles grew even stronger. He stayed by Pearl and Jewel's side every evening, spending nights sitting up in a hard-backed chair while Pearl slept in a recliner next to Jewel's bed. Then he worked all day, cooking and selling barbeque. Next, after long hours spent standing on his feet, tired to the bone, he packed a dinner and took it to the hospital. I decided if that wasn't love, I didn't know what love was. At the very least, it was love between good friends. At best, would they marry someday? Wouldn't that be the ideal situation for Jewel?

After we left the hospital, attended the Fireside Methodist Church, and went home to the ranch, I helped Ruby panfry chicken and make mashed potatoes with fresh butter and evaporated milk and salad. This can of milk was the last one that had been relieved of its wrapper due to Evangeline's collection. It appeared that cooking was getting back to normal, which was generally a good idea, although it brought less adventure and drama to meal preparation.

As Walt switched on the radio to listen to the noon broadcast, Carl Perkins's music came on. He sang "I'm Sorry I'm Not Sorry" and accompanied himself on the guitar.

As we sat down at the table to say grace, all sorts of feelings about Jewel's accident welled up inside me. I propped my elbows on the table and rested my head on my palms.

"Our Father, give us hearts of gratitude for these and other blessings. Forgive us for what we have done and left undone. Let us remember those people for whom we are truly grateful and make us vessels of everlasting kindness and examples of perpetual brotherly love. Amen," said Walt.

Ruby picked up her fork, the signal that we were now allowed to begin eating. I started to take my first bite of mashed potatoes, but a huge knot welled up in my throat. I put down my fork on my plate and folded my hands in my lap. Tears rolled down my cheeks.

"For heaven's sake, Juliet. What's wrong?" asked Ruby, puzzled.

"Mr. Perkins may not be sorry in his song, but *I'm* sorry. I'm truly sorry for what I've done that caused baby Jewel so much suffering."

Walt patted me on the back and said, "Squirrel, don't take the blame on yourself. Accidents happen to us all."

"I don't want to play the guitar anymore. I want to give it to Rabbit. She can have it."

Ruby's eyebrows drew together, and Walt stared down at his plate.

Evangeline looked perplexed for a moment, and then sadness spread across her face. She slowly got up from her chair, walked around to my side of the table, and draped her arms around my neck and shoulders. As she pressed her cheek to mine, I could detect the scents of sweat, Sport, and bubble gum.

"I'm sorry you're sad, Squirrel," she said. "Thanks for giving me your guitar. I'll play you a song on it when I learn one."

"You're welcome," I said. "But thank Mamaw and Popo. They're the ones who gave it to me." I looked at Ruby and Walt's faces, which were filled with sadness. "I'm sorry, but I can't even look at the guitar without seeing little Jewel lying on the ground."

"It's OK, Squirrel," said Walt. "We understand."

Thinking it would help me feel less of a wretch if I helped someone, I talked Walt into taking me to visit Seymour. I'd drawn a picture of our dog, Sport, on a piece of construction paper and thought if he taped it up on the wall in his cell, it would cheer up the place.

When I passed it through the bars, he looked at it, smiled, and looked away, like he was ashamed to hold eye contact.

"Thanks much, Sister Juliet. I'll enjoy looking at your artwork." His hair was combed and the dazed look he'd previously had was gone. He almost looked like anybody else in Fireside might, given the circumstances.

"Been sober now a good while," he said when he caught me staring. "I can feel again. Ain't easy, but I'm getting by."

"I guess you have a lot of time to think. How long will you be in here?" I asked.

"Till I go to trial and the judge sends me somewhere else."

I didn't know what the right thing to say was, so I fidgeted for a bit and finally came out with "Well, I hope they send you to a place that has good food."

"I doubt that," he said sadly, but then his face brightened. "When I get to heaven, I think the food will be real tasty. You can just pick fruit in the garden and lie down in green pastures and look at the sky and be free as a bird."

"I guess we all have that to look forward to someday," I said. "I've been thinking about what you said on the school bus."

"What was that?" he asked.

"About your daddy passing when you were five. Do you miss him?"

"I reckon I do."

"I miss mine too."

"Yeah, but if you believe in what the Good Book says, we'll see 'em again someday."

Days passed, calves were born in the north pasture, and bluebonnets bloomed everywhere. Sport roamed about the yard and surrounding acreage in search of rodents, low-flying birds, rabbits, and more squirrels. He had the habit of sticking his nose in holes and trying to get at whatever was hiding from him. He trotted out past the garden and started trying to get at whatever was hidden inside a dense area covered by prickly pear cacti. I'd been out in the yard helping Ruby weed her flower bed when I heard him yelping.

"Sport, what's the matter?" I called out and went out looking for him.

When I found him, the rattler was still coiled and rattling his tail. Afraid to walk any closer, I whistled at him, and Sport slowly made his way to me. "Stay away from rattlers. They're mean." As I reached out to grab his collar so I could lead him back to the house, I saw two fang marks just above his nose.

"Oh no. What have you gotten yourself into? You poor dog." I managed to pick him up, and as I started to turn away from the cacti, I saw the rattler sliding back into his hiding place.

We brought Sport inside the house and took turns waiting on him hand and foot. If he looked uncomfortable, we'd put ice on his wound. If he looked hungry, we'd sit by his side and hand-feed him.

"Will he live?" asked Evangeline.

Walt had examined him thoroughly. "Not much we can do for him. It's a head bite, and that works in Sport's favor. If that rattler had struck anyplace else on his body, he'd be a goner. But he just might make it. Time will tell."

Evangeline and I slept by Sport's side for the whole night. Walt sat up in his office chair in the living room, overseeing his care. Ruby kept the food coming, covered Sport's wound with Mercurochrome, and dried our tears.

When the sun came up in the morning, Sport was still with us. He'd suffer some for the next few weeks, but eventually, he returned to his old squirrel-chasing self. It took a while, though, for his brown fur to grow back over the spot where the fangs had gone in. We just loved on him and said lots of prayers on his behalf. I do think that the Good Lord smiled down on Sport, don't you?

It seemed as though we shifted from one challenge to another in the time it took to blink. If it wasn't a problem with Sport, cattle, sheep or goats, then it was a predicament caused by two rambunctious girls. The next day, our attention became necessarily focused on Evangeline. It seemed she had developed great disdain for her teacher, Mrs. Harvey Winslow, better known as Madge Winslow the child-hating, mud-wrestling ogre from the Midwest, who had recently come to Fireside and taken the place of Evangeline's previous teacher, Mrs. Whitley, on account of her advanced pregnancy.

I'm just going to tell it to you like Evangeline told me. We were standing outside the back steps of Ruby and Walt's house, while my sister gave a dramatic recounting of an unfortunate incident. Apparently, the whole situation went upside down when Mrs. Winslow didn't like the way Evangeline responded to the question "Who discovered the Canary Islands?"

"Sylvester the Cat," she said, putting her hands on her narrow hips and cocking her head to one side. "'Cause that's where he discovered Tweety Bird, Speedy Gonzales, and that smart little Hippety Hopper. Everybody knows that!"

Mrs. Winslow hadn't been amused. "I'll give you one more chance to give a real answer," she'd told Evangeline. "Otherwise, I'll send you to the principal's office."

"Oh, she didn't," I said.

"Yes, Squirrel, she's a toad in disguise. Bet she has warts all over her body."

"What happened next?"

"I told her the truth—that I didn't know where on earth the Canary Islands were and didn't much care if Sylvester, Tweety, Speedy, and Hippety weren't there."

"Evangeline, you've got to pull back the reins on that mouth. You were flat-out lucky she didn't whack you with the paddle for that."

"I'm not scared of a paddle. I'm tough. You know that."

I did know it. Evangeline had been born tough. She was mostly fearless and had become even more so since our father died and our mother had taken off. "What did she do to you?" I asked.

"Sent me down to Mr. Franklin's office. He made me eat my lunch across from his desk and not say a word. Said if I even opened my mouth, he was calling Walt to have a man-to-man talk with him about my rearing."

"So did you keep your lips buttoned?"

"I held in as long as I could. How was I to know he wore false teeth? After he finished eating his hamburger, his choppers fell out of his mouth and onto his desk. When he stuck the whole shebang back in, I couldn't help but say, 'Good gravy, you ought to use Fixodent. You know what they say in the commercials: 'Fixodent helps to fix loose spots.'"

"Did he call Popo in to visit?"

"Yup, and when he put me in his truck, he just said I'd have to pull weeds out of the yard on Saturday morning instead of watching *The Flintstones* and eating Frosted Flakes with Tony the Tiger. Then he just winked, clicked his teeth, and pretended they jumped out of his mouth."

To say that Evangeline was a tad stubborn in addition to being tough was an understatement. In my opinion, she had come out on top of the whole ordeal. Was she destined to one day become a politician? I wondered. Or was she headed straight to the penitentiary before she even got to junior high? Seemed to me, Evangeline was a lot like those new Teflon pans I'd seen on the TV. Nothing stuck to her when she got into trouble.

I was so concerned about her that I went into the living room that night to discuss her case with Walt. I found him studying pictures in the *Guide to the Universe* book so he could see exactly where the Andromeda constellation was.

"Popo, aren't you worried that Evangeline will someday get herself into trouble she can't dig herself out of? Shouldn't you give her more punishment than just pulling weeds Saturday morning?"

"I think I have a pretty good handle on the situation, Juliet."

"Are you certain? 'Cause I've got my worry face on."

"Squirrel, just take a deep breath. There's a new tune the Statler Brothers recorded, called 'Walkin' in the Sunshine.' Listen to it and see if it don't help you feel better. You ought not worry so much because you'll age before your time. Whoever heard of a fifth grader with wrinkles?" Then Walt just reached over and tousled my hair, curling it up into a squirrel's nest. "Say, you've got a birthday coming up in a few weeks."

"I do," I replied.

"Do you know what you want?" he asked.

"No, sir," I said.

"In that case, we'll just play it by ear," said Walt.

"OK, that's fine by me."

"All right, then." Walt stood up, walked over to the TV, and turned on the news. A picture of Martin Luther King, Jr. flashed across the screen. "This is changing the subject, but you know what I heard at the hardware store today when I went?"

"No, Popo."

"I missed this news on Monday due to calving season. What I heard was that James Earl Ray, that old boy who shot Martin Luther King, Jr., has pled guilty. Thank heavens. Justice does come, even if it comes slowly. Furthermore, Golda Meir has become the fourth prime minister of Israel. She's a smart, strong woman. No telling what she'll do for her country. Mark my words, these events will be remembered in history for a long time to come. Write these events down on your calendar, and don't say I never taught you anything when you're grown."

"Oh, I would never think that, Popo. "

And don't you worry about Rabbit. She'll be OK."

When Evangeline went back to school, she had drawn a poster-size version of the Canary Islands with colored pencils, listed their coordinates and demographics, and buried tiny pictures of Sylvester, Tweety Bird, Speedy Gonzales, and Hippety Hopper in the midst of palm trees, high grasses, and mountains and in the seal of the Canary Islands flag. I doubted seriously that Mrs. Winslow would even notice the characters lurking there and that Evangeline was possibly having a good laugh at her expense.

Evangeline's strong will was ever present, but it had a flip side that was gentle and kind. No one really understood that until Davy Ottmers started having a grand mal seizure by the playground slide.

I had just gone outside to walk past the area to join my class members in the school cafeteria for lunch. Evangeline's class had already moved outside to play, and I saw her seated at the top of the slide. Her red shorts peeped out from underneath her orange dress that had a plastic belt covered with daisies at the waist. Her socks were rolled down to her ankles, and a Band-Aid covered a fresh wound on her knee, the second of the week.

Poor Davy lay in the dirt struggling, but Evangeline slid down and was soon at his side. "Oh, Davy," she said, "I've got your back. Don't worry; I know what to do." She took off her corduroy jacket and stuffed it under his head as he banged it repeatedly against the ground. Then, although it was difficult, she rolled him on his side. The seizure lasted for several minutes, and when it was over, Evangeline patted him on the head.

"I'm sore all over," said Davy eventually.

"Anyone would be," said Evangeline. "I'm just glad your mother told me what to look out for."

Davy just sat there for a while, looking a little stunned, but eventually, his old quirky smiled returned. "Want me to play 'America the Beautiful' in my armpit, Evangeline?"

"Thanks, Davy, but I've heard you play that a thousand times. How about 'Turkey in the Straw'? Do you know that tune?"

"Of course I know it. Everybody knows that song."

While Davy began entertaining himself and the concerned crowd who'd gathered around him, Mrs. Winslow said, "So glad you're feeling

162

better, Davy." Then she turned to Evangeline and said, "You did well, Evangeline, and kept a cool head during a tough situation. That ought to make you feel good, and I know it does me. Perhaps you'd like to help me put together a first-aid lesson for your fellow classmates."

Evangeline flushed and looked flustered. "Sure, Mrs. Winslow. I was glad to help." She started to walk away but stopped and looked at her teacher. She smiled slyly and said, "I'll do that if you'll give me my poster of the Canary Islands back. I feel like I need to touch up a few things on it."

"Would that involve using an eraser on Sylvester, Tweety Bird, and the others who are hidden?" she asked.

"Yes, ma'am. A good poster is never finished."

"Like a piece of art," said Mrs. Winslow. "Like you, Evangeline."

"Thank you. Thank you very much," said Evangeline, as she gave an Elvis wiggle.

For the first time in a long while, I saw my sister as something besides an annoyance. Tears of joy welled up in my eyes; I felt so glad for her. That she'd risen to truly help someone. That her friend could depend on her when things were tough. That she could lead with her heart and not her fist.

When I turned eleven on Tuesday, Ruby baked my favorite angel food cake and covered it with fresh strawberries soaked in sugar and home-made whipped cream. She had put eleven white candles together on one side of the cake in the shape of a squirrel and one to grow on by itself.

We waited until the *CBS Evening News* with Walter Cronkite was over for me to blow out the candles because we were all so excited about Israel's new prime minister.

"Just think, Squirrel. Golda Meir wants to be an instrument of peace. You can be one too. They call her the Iron Lady. There's a look in her eye, a tone in her voice, and a determination in her walk that make me believe she can do most anything she sets her mind to. She went to the University of Wisconsin in Milwaukee. Maybe you could go to school there someday," said Ruby.

"Maybe," I said. "On the other hand, I want to keep my options open. It's cold up there."

"That's true," said Ruby.

At age eleven, I was nearly her height of five feet, so I wrapped my arm around her shoulder and looked her in the eye. "You're getting so big, Juliet. Growing up right before my very eyes. Just popping up like a flower in my garden. Happy birthday to you, sugar foot. Better blow out those candles before they melt into the whipped cream."

"I wish Jewel, Pearl, and Sapphire could be here," I said, my eyes filling with tears.

"Don't you fret," said Ruby. "The Easter Bunny told me you'll see them again soon."

When baby Jewel got released from the hospital, I was on the air at station KOFF on Saturday, April fifth. Evangeline was playing tiddlywinks on the station floor, but yawned, stretched, and eventually jumped up to hit the red button when I said, "Last person to hit the red button is a rotten egg." She always did move faster whenever she thought I might take her turn, but that wasn't the only thing that got the lead out of her drawers. The fact that Ruby was on the other side of the glass tapping it with her fiddle bow and giving her the eye made her speed things up even more.

"Thank you for joining us on this windy April afternoon. As you know, yesterday was Good Friday, and tomorrow is Easter Sunday. Remember that as soon as this broadcast is over, the annual Maitlin County Easter Eggstravaganza is happening right across the street from station KOFF on the courthouse lawn. Word has it that our very own Fireside Easter Bunny has finished boiling and painting the eggs and has a special treat for each child who attends. There'll be a cookie-decorating booth, deviled egg competition, tow sack racing, balloon painting, mustache waxing, and a pipe-cleaner-chick-and-bunny-folding contest. Don't be square. Be there!"

It was at that moment that Pearl walked in carrying baby Jewel. Charles Wesley accompanied her, carrying a diaper bag. They stood just on the other side of the studio's soundproof glass. I passed through the door and hugged Pearl's neck right away. Then I looked down at little Jewel and kissed her chubby cheek. "Oh, little Jewel Bug, how's my sweet cousin?"

"Just peachy keen," said Pearl.

"Yes, she's jim-dandy," agreed Charles Wesley.

Ruby said, "Time's up, Juliet. The record is almost over. Remember what Miss Alma Webster always says: 'No dead air. . .'"

I walked back into the booth, smiling through tears of joy. "I have a special announcement for all station KOFF listeners: the Easter Bunny has just dropped by with little Jewel Gemburree, who was released from the Fireside Hospital this afternoon. By all appearances, she looks full of vim and vigor and ready for Easter. As a special note, I want to thank all our listeners for their prayers. They made a difference in Jewel's life and in those of all of us who love her. Happy Easter, everyone. See you shortly at the Maitlin County Courthouse at the Easter Eggstravaganza!"

Pearl and Charles Wesley briefly brought Jewel by the event so she could see the Easter Bunny, who was really Mayor Bruce Healy. Mayor Healy was five feet tall and just as wide, so his wife had had a whale of a time sewing a costume to fit. He wasn't doing a very good job of hopping around, handing out eggs to the children, and instead spent most of his time mopping his forehead with his handkerchief, saying, "Lord, it's hot in here. Whose idea was it to make April so hot anyhow?" The rest of the time, he was eating Jordan almonds in various pastels and marshmallow PEEPS he'd stashed inside his enormous Easter basket.

Because he was running for reelection again, Mayor Healy made sure he would have his moment at the podium. "Jeepers, I love our town. Don't y'all? Let's give it up for Fireside, Texas!" I thought he'd done a good job of whipping up the crowd right off the bat because naturally, everybody clapped enthusiastically. "I've never been the Easter Bunny before, but I've always loved me some bunnies. Speaking of which, let me recognize my wife, Louise, who made my costume, and my precious only daughter, Miriam, who has come here today with a message from the Fireside Hospital Chapter of Candy Stripers."

That's when I saw that mean devil. She wore a plastic smile and said, "Thank you, Mayor Daddy. Yes, I'm here with a very important word from the candy stripers. We have a kissing booth over yonder on the far side of the courthouse lawn. All kisses last thirty seconds and cost a dollar. The money goes to buy books and stuffed animals for hospitalized children and old people." Then she looked directly at me and smiled smugly. "And the first kiss I'll accept will be from William Bartlett, whose hens provided many of today's eggs. Pucker up, William, is all I have to say about that."

Let me just mention, I saw red for a split second before I took a deep breath and calmed myself down. It didn't take me long to peg her as the lowlife scumbag of Fireside High. She knew he was my special friend; she'd seen us skating together in the city park. Oh, William was cute all right. Smart. Kind. Friendly. But he was eleven years old. Why on earth was a fourteen-year-old girl throwing herself at a boy years her junior? Clearly, she was trying to get under my skin.

William stood near the podium, but his face was bright red. He looked down at his tennis shoes and tried not to make eye contact with anyone. I felt sorry for him and mad at her at the same time.

I can't say what came over me next; I just walked right to the front and planted a big kiss on his lips. Shocked silence swept the crowd. I leaned over and whispered in his ear, "Now give me a dollar and make sure everyone in the crowd sees you doing it."

To his credit, William didn't argue a bit about digging into his pocket and pulling out a folded dollar bill. He smiled, waved it around so the crowd could see it, and then made a great show of handing it to me.

"Thank you, William," I said. Then I walked over to Miriam, who was fuming. I leaned over the microphone and said, "Miriam, here's the first dollar donation for the candy stripers' fund drive. I took the first kiss, so you didn't even have to pucker. Although everyone in Fireside knows you're an old hand at kissing boys on the back seat of the school bus." The crowd roared with laughter.

"Hopefully, you'll have some takers in this crowd and can still talk somebody into giving you a dollar. OK, all you guys out there in the audience, just follow her over to the kissing booth. Try not to trip over yourselves getting to the front of the line. Remember, this is for a good cause. Don't be shy, now. Hold your nose if you have to."

I left the podium feeling justified in having called Miriam down. As William had taught me, I didn't get mad, I just got even. Right or wrong, I felt somewhat victorious.

It was then that Selma and Norman Densesky walked up to the podium. He was carrying an enormous box that seemed rather heavy but soon rested it on the podium, pushed back his fedora, and leaned into the microphone. He had the broadest grin I'd ever seen on him. In short, Norman had never looked so happy.

"Hello, everyone. I'd like to say a few words, if I might. Everybody knows this has been the best year of my life. First, I got to make the most beautiful woman in the world my wife on Valentine's Day. Well, you already know that because so many of you were at our wedding and reception. Secondly, we've just learned the rabbit has died, and there'll be a new little Densesky this coming November. And to celebrate, I'd like to give everyone a bubblegum cigar, compliments of Densesky's Groceries and Dry Goods." Norman reached into the large box and lifted out the first handful of pastel Dubble Bubble cigars. Many members of the Fireside audience clapped and cheered, but not all.

Selma gently ushered Norman to the side. Dressed in lemon yellow, with a matching yellow headband and white Easter sandals, she'd never looked lovelier. Smiling, Selma quipped, "Norman always did like to count his chickens before they hatched. But in this case, I'm the chick that's doing the hatching. So I guess it's all right."

It wasn't long before I heard Shirl the beautician remark to Sapphire, "Goodness to gracious, how old are they anyway?"

"Apparently, not too old," said Sapphire.

"I'm just saying, they'll be a hundred years old before the kid goes to college. What a lot of fool nonsense." Shirl popped her gum incessantly. "I'm still trying to raise the two I've got."

"Sounds like you've got a string of firecrackers in your mouth," said Sapphire. "Aren't your boys in their thirties?"

"Some just stay in the pouch longer," admitted Shirl. "I'm about ready for those little joeys to leave home."

"Each to his own," said Sapphire. "I know you've been down some rough roads with all your husbands and whatnot. I guess you haven't had it easy."

"That's what I know. . ." said Shirl. "That's what I know. . ."

Late that night, as Ruby, Walt, Evangeline, and I sat in lawn chairs, star-gazing and listening to station KOFF through the screen door, I thought about what Walt always said about paying attention so we don't miss what's important in this life. What was the big picture anyway?

Deep down, I knew Sapphire had hit the nail on the head. Shirl hadn't had it easy; everyone knew that. Neither did anyone else, in the scheme of things, no matter how it looked from the outside. Not Mr. Roper, our school bus driver, or even Seymour, who'd suffered in old Vietnam and was still awaiting trial in the county jail.

Walt and Ruby had been taking care of us when they could have just ditched us and basked in the easy life—sitting around eating ice cream bars or sunflower seeds, watching endless hours of *Gunsmoke*, and having themselves a ball. But they couldn't do that with us taking so much of their air space and time.

Sapphire had to work hard for a living, and her best friend, Violet, lived hours away in San Angelo. She must have felt so lonely at times and as if there was no one in the town of Fireside who completely understood her.

Pearl had it tough, trying to raise baby Jewel. Charles Wesley had lived a solitary life, his hours filled with endless cooking for and clean-ing up after his customers since his days as a fighter pilot had ended. But the sunny side of that story was that now Pearl, Charles, and Jewel had recently connected the dots in what I hoped would become a complete family picture.

And there was Selma, who'd finally found happiness with Norman and had a baby to look forward to, but there were always folks ready to shoot down happiness if they didn't have any in their own lives. Like sticks of Fruit Stripe gum, bitterness came in many flavors.

Why couldn't folks just be joyful for the happiness of others?

Eighteen

Not long after Pearl and little Jewel went home from the hospital, Ruby drove me out to their house so I could see for myself how she was getting along. Jewel seemed as happy as ever to see me. She waved her arms and smiled, exposing two new front teeth. She wore a pink calico outfit and a drool bib that was damp from the saliva that dripped from her chin as she cooed.

"Be careful," said Aunt Pearl. "Jewel has a new talent."

"What is that?" I asked. I noticed Pearl was wearing a new pink-and-green paisley dress with a pointed collar accented with white zigzag trim. Her blonde hair had been pinned up beneath a big floppy hat that had a band around its crown covered in the same paisley material as her dress. She was a fabulous seamstress, so I was sure she'd bought a McCall's pattern at Densesky's and made the outfit herself. I wondered whether I could learn to do that as well.

"She's a champion biter. I guess her gums are bothering her. See, the bottom middle two are about to come through her gums."

"How's her spine?" asked Ruby. She was wearing her green calico dress and matching green beads and earrings. I saw a few new crow's feet around her eyes and two slight wrinkles on her neck. Like always, she smelled of Noxzema, talcum powder, and faintly of the pecan cookies she'd baked that morning.

"She's so young, she'll be all right. I've been putting her on the pallet to see if she feels like crawling, but she seems to have been set back some by the accident. I'm not sure why, but her muscles don't seem to have the strength they did before."

169

"Well, don't worry," said Ruby. "Before you know it, she'll be up and running."

"I'm so sorry, Aunt Pearl, that I took her out on the porch. I should have put Sport in my room beforehand or at least thrown a ball to get him away," I said.

"This wasn't your fault, Juliet. Don't you know you can't keep a dog from his squirrel or rabbit? No pun intended," said Pearl, and she smiled.

"If you can ever trust me again, I'd love to babysit her. This time, I won't take her to the porch."

"Of course I trust you, nutty Squirrel. You're my favorite oldest niece."

"Are you about to go on a date?" I asked hopefully.

"Not exactly," said Pearl. "I'm taking Jewel to have a family picture made in the bluebonnets this side of Fredericksburg."

"Will Mr. Wesley be in the picture?"

"He should be, on account of all he's done for us. But no, just Jewel, Sapphire, and me."

"Oh," I said, disappointed. "Maybe he can be in one next time."

"He has to take care of business today," said Pearl. "He spent so much time at the hospital, he didn't have time to take care of a few details. Now, April fifteenth is nearly upon us, and tax day is looming large."

"He would make you a real good husband," I said, trying to drive my point home.

"Charles Wesley would make any lucky woman a good husband," said Pearl. "No doubt about that."

After Ruby and I left Pearl and Jewel at their house, we went straightaway to Densesky's, which was only two blocks away. Selma and Norman stood outside the front door of the store while he snapped her picture as she turned sideways and cupped her hands around her abdomen. The sun was bright and glared in her eyes, causing her to squint.

"I can't tell anything yet," said Norman. "It's too early. But we don't want to miss capturing every month on film until Norman Jr. is born. We'll want to remember how much you changed from month to month."

"Excuse us," said Selma when Ruby and I walked up beside Norman. "We're just excited. Who knew people our age would ever get a chance at becoming parents? The Lord is good."

"He's good indeed," said Ruby. "Why do you think it's a boy?"

"Oh, that's Norman's idea. His name goes back five generations, and they've all had nothing but boys in each one. He says it will be a boy, and the name has to be Norman."

"Can you blame me?" asked Norman.

"No," said Ruby. "But what if you wind up surprised with a girl?"

"Then we'll call her Norma. It's as simple as that." Norman moved the cigar he chewed around in his mouth and fairly giggled. "I can't wait until November. We'll have a Thanksgiving to remember, with a new baby to pass around while we're having turkey and dressing."

"Norman, you'll be cooking this one," said Selma. "I'll likely be busy."

"That's no trouble for me. Being the oldest in a family of eleven boys, I had to learn to cook or starve. Comes with the territory, I guess."

Once everyone went inside the store, Ruby bought patterns, three yards of purple gingham, three spools of red thread and zippers to match. After she'd paid for them, we walked outside Densesky's toward her Thunderbird.

"I'm going to teach you girls how to sew a simple dress pattern. It's a skill that will serve you well, and you'll have something useful to show for your work."

"On your old treadle Singer sewing machine?" I asked.

"The very one."

"How much fun! I can guide the stitches, and Evangeline can work the pedal."

"Oh, my stars," chuckled Ruby. "I can just imagine how this will go. Maybe it would be better if I work with you one at a time so there'll be no fighting."

I smiled over the car at Ruby as I opened my door. "You know us well."

It was at that moment that I saw *her* again. She was walking into Densesky's, away from us. Away from me. Away from the life we'd shared.

"Mamaw, it's her!"

"Who are you talking about?" asked Ruby, turning to see where I was pointing.

"Mama!" I ran straight back into Densesky's. She was dressed in a pair of blue jeans and an orange blouse. Gigantic hoop earrings swung from her earlobes. Brunette hair teased up high and cut short over her ears and straight across at the neck was the dead giveaway.

"Mama! Marguerite!" I called, but she ignored me and kept on moving. So I just reached out and grabbed her by the back of the arm. "No, you don't. Don't walk away from me again."

When she turned around, I realized my mistake. It wasn't my mother after all. The poor woman turned and looked at me, startled. "I beg your pardon?" she said.

"You're not her," I said. "You have to be her."

"I'm sorry. . ."

I felt Ruby's hand on my shoulder, pulling me back. "It's OK, Juliet. It was just a mistake. Your mama's in New York."

I turned to the puzzled woman, who was adjusting her glasses to get a better look at the spectacle I was still making of myself as I crumpled to the floor, crying. She shifted her straw handbag from one arm to the other and then put her hand out to help me up.

"It's OK, young lady. I hope you find the person you're looking for."

"I don't know if I ever will." I said, still undone.

"Squirrel baby, let's go home," said Ruby.

I let her pull me up, and then I wrapped my arms around her and wept some more. She led me out to the Thunderbird. By the time we backed out of the parking lot in front of Densesky's, I had mostly gotten a hold of myself.

"You're always there when I need you most, Mamaw."

Ruby kissed my cheek and said, "This is a tough old world. I promise, if I know your mother is anywhere in the area, you'll be the first to know."

I supposed the woman I'd seen on Groundhog Day hadn't been her either. What a crazy fool I must have been to think she would come back at all. I wouldn't let myself be so disappointed ever again. My heart couldn't take getting my hopes up and then having them dashed.

"Sometimes, it is hard to fathom the reason behind the loss of a loved one," said Ruby. "Only the Good Lord can see the big picture when he looks down from heaven above. Who knows why we lose the people closest to us every now and then?"

"Like your boy, my daddy?"

"Exactly. And like your mother. What do you say we go home and press a few wildflowers into the family Bible? One for each person we've lost."

"That will take a whole garden of flowers, won't it?" I said sadly, blowing my nose on the handkerchief Ruby offered me.

"I guess it will take a small bouquet, anyway."

When we arrived back at the ranch, Sport was waiting by the garage, panting like he'd just returned from chasing something. "Oh, Sport, you're always on a mission, aren't you?"

He looked up at me, peering through shaggy, furry bangs. "I think Evangeline and I need to give you a haircut."

"That's a good idea," said Ruby. "I think I've got an old pair of scissors around here somewhere. Sport needs to see what the world truly looks like. Who knows? Maybe he thinks he's chasing a cute female dog when he hauls out after those squirrels and rabbits. Perhaps if he could see better, he wouldn't get into so much mischief."

"Sort of like Rabbit and me. If we could always really see what we were looking at, we wouldn't get into so much trouble."

"There's more truth in that than you know," said Ruby.

After Evangeline and I got the scissors after Sport, he looked rather raggedy but seemed appreciative, if you judged him by the number of times he licked us.

Ruby called us inside and told us to wash our hands. She then directed us to the Singer treadle sewing machine that was pushed up against one wall of our bedroom. After showing us how to thread it and wind the bobbin, she showed us how to place the Simplicity pattern pieces on the calico yardage she'd bought each of us. After she helped us pin the paper into place, she sent me to the kitchen table to cut mine out and remained behind to assist Evangeline with hers. Clearly, Evangeline needed help the most. It was then that I spied Hadley King out on our back porch. She was hoisting up two small boxes on a rigged rope pulley and tightening it so it stayed in place on the outside of our screen door.

I ran to the door and peered at Hadley through the metal mesh. "What on earth are you doing?"

Hadley looked perplexed and put her hands on her hips. "What does it look like I'm doing? I'm leaving you two boxes of Girl Scout cookies."

"How nice. But why?"

"I'm your secret pal. Like they have in those women's groups at the Methodist church."

"I didn't sign up for that."

"I signed up to be *your* pal," said Hadley with a grin.

"But I have nothing to give you back," I said, folding my arms across my chest.

"You're missing the point. It's something I wanted to do for you, without expecting anything in return."

"You're such a groovy friend," I said and smiled.

"What can I say? I was born that way." Hadley released the pulley and let down the boxes. Then she opened the door and handed them to me.

"Thanks for being my pal, Hadley."

"It's fun. I dig doing good deeds on the q.t."

My thoughts went back to the day when I'd found the bag of cinnamon Red Hots tied up on the door, which I'd previously believed my mother had left. "Did you leave the Red Hots here a couple of months ago?"

"Yup, that was me."

I'd let my imagination get away from me so many times, believing our mother was thinking of us. Apparently, I'd been the only one doing much thinking. There'd been that one letter and package with two T-shirts that were too small and couldn't do either of us any good.

174

Ruby, upon seeing our disappointment, had made pillows from them to go on our gingham bedspread. That had taken some of the sting out of things.

After Hadley was driven back to town by her mother, I went straightaway into our bedroom, picked up the T-shirt pillows off the bed, stuck them in a brown paper bag, and shoved them into the top of our closet. Even though Ruby had meant well, one thing I knew for sure was that what I really didn't need was one more constant reminder of our mother's absence.

Over the next few days, my spirits took a turn for the better. It wasn't long before Charles Wesley called Walt and asked for us all to join him in the private gathering room of Wesley's Barbecue Heaven in a week. He said he was having a get-together with family and friends and that he thought of us in both categories. We could hear his velvety voice coming through the receiver as we gathered in the kitchen around the wall phone. Ruby gently took the phone from Walt and started talking.

"Say, Charles, why don't you let the Gemburree Sisters come play a few tunes for your party? It'd be an honor for us to do that." Ruby smiled big as you please.

"Good deal. Sounds like fun. See you then."

Ruby hung up the phone, gave us the thumbs up, and raised her eyebrows. "This is going to be so much fun, y'all," she said. "Best people in the world, barbeque sauce that can't be beat, and some music on the side."

Evangeline and I were beside ourselves with excitement to be invited to Charles Wesley's for any reason. After all, he was one of the nicest people we'd ever met and was beloved by all who truly knew him.

The day of Charles Wesley's gathering was upon us in no time. When we arrived, we noticed fifty papier-mâché flying pigs suspended with wires from the ceiling, giving the place a downright festive feel. All the tables were covered in white butcher paper taped down tight underneath. In the center of each one was a pink papier-mâché pig decorated with multicolored flower-power cutouts and golden wings.

Ruby walked inside, put her violin case on the table, and then looked around the room. "Interesting décor. I guess you've redecorated.

"A bit," said Charles sheepishly.

Where's everybody else?" she asked.

"Some of my folks are coming in a while," he said. "From Amarillo. Thanks, Ruby, for agreeing to warm up the place with a little music."

I looked around the room and noticed that Pearl's percussion instruments were already set up on the ministage in the back center of the room. On the far left was a pool table and thirty or so dining tables with chairs. While Wesley's wasn't a bar or nightclub, it did have the setup for special events. Tonight felt special indeed.

It quickly became clear to me that he'd invited all us Cranbournes, plus Pearl, Jewel, and Sapphire, on account of some undefined celebration. Straightaway, I stood closer to Charles Wesley, words pouring out. "Is this a party on account of having filed your income tax with the IRS?"

Ruby laughed and said, "Anything that points to getting income tax behind you is worth celebrating."

Charles laughed and said, "No, but I might give a party just for that reason. Regarding tonight, well, to tell you the truth, I just realized life is getting away from me. I'll soon turn fifty, and likely there's more years in my rearview mirror than ahead. One morning, I woke up and realized I wasn't spending enough time with those folks that count."

He looked more handsome and distinguished than he ever had in his perfectly pressed Levi's, crisp white shirt, Navajo silver bolo tie depicting a longhorn, and Tony Lama boots. His barbecue apron was nowhere to be seen. I hardly recognized our friend without one.

A sweaty Evangeline ran up to Charles and stuck to him like Velcro. She'd been running around the room, trying to reach up and grab low-hanging papier-mâché pigs from the ceiling, certain they were piñatas filled with her favorite candies.

"Howdy, Mr. Wesley," she said breathlessly. "Got any candy for us sweet children?" She batted her eyes and looked up at him so appealingly, he couldn't help but chuckle and pat her on the back.

"Well, let me see," he said. "We've got some nice liver-flavored jujubes; some brussels-sprout brownies with creamy beet icing, because green and pink go nicely together; and some crunchy asparagus tips dipped in marmalade. How does that sound?"

"Like you won't be in business long," said Evangeline. She wrinkled up her nose, let her arms fall from around Charles, and gave him the stink eye, but she was just fooling. She knew all along he was pulling her leg.

Walt came to steer Evangeline away from Charles, just in case he'd already had enough togetherness with her, and showed her how to shoot pool on the table in the corner of the large room. Ruby followed them and watched for a while.

"Walt, honey, you teaching our Rabbit how to shoot pool?"

"I am indeed. Rabbit needs to stay occupied and out of trouble."

"Well, then, while you're teaching her, make her a shark. That way she can whup the boys when she gets older," Ruby teased.

Walt showed Evangeline how to hold the cue stick and let her practice a minute. Her third try landed a ball in the corner pocket.

"My money is on Rabbit," said Ruby. "Walt, something tells me you don't stand a chance. Remember that movie *The Hustler*? I'm willing to bet she can beat both Fast Eddie Felsen and Minnesota Fats when she gets a little more practice under her belt."

"How 'bout we make a bet I'll have her playing like a pro before we leave tonight?"

"Well, I think it might take more than one night to make her that good."

"I'll bet you a trip to San Antone to see the Fiesta Parade next week if I'm wrong. And if you lose, I want you to make me banana pie with that mile-high meringue I love so much." Walt was leaning close to Ruby now. He drew her up in his arms and kissed her square on her lips.

Evangeline looked up from the pool table just long enough to say, "Ew, gross," before she went back to playing her game.

"You drive a tough bargain," said Ruby. "But I'm in."

Sapphire arrived, bringing her friend Violet from San Angelo. Sapphire wore her long dark hair back in a braid, but it was fuzzy and as wild looking as Evangeline's. She was carrying her guitar case and set it down on the table. Violet, who sported a very short haircut, khaki pants, and a yoked western shirt, put a harmonica down on the table next to the guitar.

"Hey, Miss Violet," I said. "How're you getting along?"

She folded her arms and scratched at one elbow. "Fine," she said, "now that the poison ivy has nearly quit itching me. It doesn't pay to trim trees in short sleeves. Remember that."

"I will."

Before long, Charles Wesley's family arrived from Amarillo. A sea of women with molasses-colored skin wearing church clothes and beautiful hats arrived. Two men in dark suits and black shoes that had been polished to a fine sheen escorted some eight ladies. One woman in a bright pink dress put a cake box down on one table and then rushed over to meet Ruby, Walt, and the rest of us.

"Hello," she said. "I'm Mary Joe, Charles's oldest sister. And this one on my left is Betty Lou, the second child, and here on my right is Nancy Beth, the baby of the family."

Mary Joe looked at me, winked, and said, "I bet you're a good horsewoman if you live out there on a big ranch and all."

"Not really," I said. "Whenever I mount a horse, it generally acts up and heads straight to the barn."

"Can you pick a horse?"

"No, I'm sorry."

"Well, I'm gonna give you a tip: Majestic Prince is gonna take this Kentucky Derby. I've been watching him all season, and there's no doubt about it. I can tell by the way he knows he's king when he starts out of the gate. Last year, I bet on Dancer to win, but that horse was disqualified on account of drugs. I lost five dollars when his title was stripped. Now that was a crying shame."

"I see. . ."

"In sixty-seven, I won twenty dollars on Proud Clarion and used it to buy a Lady Schick hair dryer."

"Neato," I said. "I guess that means you don't have to sit in front of the fireplace till your hair dries like we do sometimes."

"That's a fact. It's the only one of its kind in the neighborhood. My friends like to come over and borrow it sometimes. I bring 'em a cup of coffee, and we look at magazines until they're done. I shoulda gone to beauty school is what I shoulda done. Guess it's too late for that, and I'll have to settle for being a bookie instead. Anyway, I can pick a good horse. Today, I'm picking your aunt Pearl to come in first at this party."

"OK. . ." I said, not sure what on earth she was talking about.

Charles came walking up with the two men, saying, "Allow me to introduce you to my cousins, David Lee and Elmer Lee, from my mother Esta's side. The five ladies behind us are their sisters; we're all so tight-knit. Grew up next door to one another. As kids, we slept in each other's houses so often, our parents could hardly tell which kids belonged to who."

"Pleased to meet you," said Walt. He and Ruby stood next to each other. He had his arm wrapped around her waist. She leaned slightly into him as she reached out to shake hands and exchange further greetings.

Next to arrive were Pearl and Jewel. Pearl was sporting an orange Dreamsicle-colored dress with a cream-colored belt. Jewel was wearing a smocked dress in the same color, with a matching eyelet lace–trimmed diaper cover.

"Don't you both look beautiful tonight," said Charles.

"Thank you so much," Pearl said, seeming uncharacteristically nervous. Then she handed Jewel and a thin quilt to me and said, "Do you mind?"

"No, Aunt Pearl. I surely don't ever mind holding this sweet girl." I carried her over to a corner of the room, spread the quilt down on the floor so she could do that horned-toad squat she normally did. But Jewel just lay down on her belly and went to sucking two fingers.

"Don't you want to crawl?" I asked her. She smiled at me and pushed up a little but then lay back flat and tuned out.

"You still not feeling good, punkin?" I asked as I stroked her chubby cheek. After a few minutes, I gathered her up in my arms and took her back to the center of activity, thinking it might give her something to capture her attention. Maybe cheer her up.

Soon, the room began filling with Fireside folks, including Selma, Norman, Alma Webster, and at least a hundred other friends. Everyone picked up a glass of iced tea or lemonade and began visiting as though they were all part of a larger reunion of family and friends. Many had come out of their respect and love for Charles Wesley, whereas others came mostly to hear the Gemburree Sisters play their favorite music.

After Pearl met Charles's family, she told Ruby and Sapphire to follow her up to the small stage. Ruby started tuning her fiddle while the others warmed up on their instruments.

Sapphire stood up and said, "Violet, why don't you bring your harmonica and join us?"

"I was hoping you'd ask."

Pearl played a quick drum solo to get everyone's attention so they'd quit talking. Baby Jewel's eyes followed the sound of her mother's music and voice. She smiled brilliantly and cooed.

"Let's get this party going, shall we? How about everyone join in the fun while we have a sing-along? Ruby will cue you in. First song up is 'To Know Him Is to Love Him,' first recorded by the Teddy Bears. And Charles, why don't you come up onstage? We need to have the host up here with us so we can thank you for having us."

At that moment David Lee, Charles's cousin, came up onstage and took over Pearl's spot behind percussion. Charles, smiling from ear to ear, quickly made his way up onstage and stood next to Pearl and Ruby.

"One. Two. Three." After the intro, Ruby pointed her bow briefly at the audience as everyone began singing along. All the Gemburree Sisters sang "To Know Him Is to Love Him," but I thought that Pearl sang it from the depths of her heart.

Charles was treated as though he were Elvis the King, not just Charles the Barbecue King. I can't even begin to tell you how happy it made him. It felt good to make this beautiful man feel loved, just the way he'd made so many others.

After the song ended, Charles raised his hand to quiet everyone down. "I'd like to say a few words to thank you all for coming to bless me with your friendship and love. In just a few minutes, we'll be serving barbecue and all the fixin's. But right now, how about if I sing you a song?"

Everyone cheered as though we had good sense. Actually, none of us had ever heard Charles sing and didn't know whether he could. He continued, "And Pearl, how about you help me sing 'The Twelfth of Never,' written by Jerry Livingston and Paul Webster? You've all probably heard Johnny Mathis sing it, but I can't compete with him, that's for sure." He laughed.

"You bet," said Pearl. "I've sung it a million times."

Charles put forward his best Mathis moves and sang fearlessly, with a voice of pure velvet. I have to say, until that moment, I had no idea what we'd been missing. Charles looked right into Pearl's eyes the whole time. After he sang the last few phrases, he reached out for her hand and started talking.

"Pearl, when we first met, I said, 'Someday I'm gonna marry you.' And you said. . ."

"'When pigs fly. I'm not cut out for marriage.'"

Charles smiled again and looked at Pearl and then around at the guests who filled the room. "Did anyone notice any flying pigs in this room when you arrived?"

"Yes!" shouted Walt and Norman.

"So, Pearl, I'm asking you again, this time with my whole heart. Will you marry me?"

Pearl's eyes teared up. She pulled a handkerchief out of her Dreamsicle dress pocket. It took a minute for her to pull herself together. Finally, she leaned into the mic and smiled at Charles. "I'm surprised to learn that pigs actually can fly. Yes, with my whole heart, I'll marry you, Charles."

I cheered, kissed Jewel on her forehead, and said, "Jewel, did you hear that? Your parents are going to get married. Maybe you can be the flower girl if I carry you down the aisle and help you throw rose petals out of a basket."

Jewel just looked at me and tried to pull my fingers into her mouth to teethe on. Then she smiled at me and started to coo. These were good signs, pointing to a better future for all involved, weren't they?

Nineteen

Just four weeks after Charles Wesley proposed to Pearl, our families gathered in the Mount Zion African Methodist Episcopal Church, ten miles outside Fireside on a hilltop to the east of Fredericksburg. The church was an old white frame building with a monster of a live oak tree in front, had no indoor plumbing, and a cemetery out back. On the side was a weathered outhouse that leaned near honeysuckle vines and had a hornet's nest waiting to be knocked down. Hanging from the live oak tree branches was a rope swing with a broad piece of pine for a seat. Weathered by years, it had been worn smooth by all the children who'd sat upon it during church picnics and swung to their hearts content.

It was Saturday, May tenth, the day before Mother's Day, which I thought Jewel would someday appreciate. We were inside a Sunday school classroom that was being used by Pearl as the bride's room. There were old wooden desks that had been pushed into one corner and were covered with students' carved initials, ink splotches, and scratches. I was helping watch Jewel and keeping both mother and daughter company. Selma was working on Pearl's makeup, applying liquid black eyeliner and lavender eye shadow to Pearl's dewy face. I stood close to them both, inspecting what was being done to help make my already-glamorous aunt become even more so.

I asked Pearl, "Why didn't you just go ahead and get married in the Fireside Methodist Church, just like Selma and Norman Densesky?"

"Well, I suppose Fireside isn't quite ready for that," said Pearl, "Squirrel girl." She tweaked my ear and tried to casually slough it off.

"Did you ask them?"

"Oh yes. But they were booked."

"For today?"

"For all days."

"Oh. Well," I said looking around, "this is a nice place. The Fireside Methodist Church doesn't have a swing like the one outside this window."

"Would you look at that?" said Selma in agreement. Then she studied my aunt's eyes. "Hold still, shug." She leaned forward and started applying mascara to Pearl's pale eyelashes. "Try not to blink."

Pearl hadn't gone to Shirl's Curls but had relied on Selma's expertise from top to bottom. For one thing, Shirl liked to smoke as she worked, and when she wasn't smoking she popped gum to steady her nerves. For another, Pearl said Shirl had a nasty habit of saying whatever came to her mind and not always for the good.

Ruby and Sapphire were setting up instruments in the front of the church while we got ready. I could hear them tuning up, along with Charles's cousin David, in the front of the sanctuary. I peeked out the door and watched them as Evangeline stood in the narthex next to Walt to greet the guests as they filed in. She was wearing a lavender dress exactly like mine. Her hair was pinned up over one ear by a large lavender bow that looked alien against her wild, bushy hair. She wore white anklets and white patent-leather shoes and had one scraped knee with a splash of dried red Mercurochrome, which was better known to us as monkey blood.

Beautiful large women in spectacular hats, small boys in starched white shirts and black pants, girls in ruffled organza or smocked gingham, old men in loosely hanging jackets and bow ties, and a myriad of other folks clad in their Sunday best were ushered in by Walt and Norman.

A Bible, hymnal, and fan donated by the Fireside Funeral Home were stationed in front of each pew. Mary Joe's voice carried across the small room. "Lord, it's hot already. And this ain't but May eleventh.

Temperature wise, 1969 is already a humdinger of a year. What poor folk gonna do to stand the heat come August?"

"Gonna have to fan mighty fast is what I guess," said Betty Lou. "But to me, it's not hot at all. I think it's your hot flashes giving you trouble.

"What I'm thinking is we'll use your winnings from the Preakness, if there are any, to donate electric fans to Charles's church come May seventeenth," Nancy Beth said and winked.

"What are you implying, sister? You think I can't pick the Preakness too? Of course I can. Then comes the Belmont. I'm not saying we're gonna have a Triple Crown winner this year. I'll pick the last race later on when the muse is on me."

"You mean the muse ain't on you today?" asked Betty Lou.

"Well, I'm distracted due to the shock that our brother is finally getting married. I thought he'd go to his grave a single man. Sure am glad I don't have to worry about that anymore. And I sure as shootin' never thought he was gonna be no daddy, but, look, he's getting himself a cute baby girl today."

"Sure is," said Nancy Beth. "Cute as the dickens."

My attention shifted back into the classroom where Pearl finished getting ready. Selma suddenly dropped the hairbrush on the floor and said, "I just feel so dizzy." She sat down on the oak plank floor in her pink dress, lay back, and covered her eyes with her hands.

"Miss Selma, are you all right?" I asked, dropping down by her side. Jewel looked up at us from her nearby quilt, smiled, and blew bubbles.

"I feel faint sometimes, but it passes quickly," said Selma. "I just generally lie down on the floor so I don't fall. Bringing a child into the world at the age of forty-five isn't as easy as I thought. But it'll be worth everything when Sugar Plum arrives in November."

"Maybe when it gets here, it can play with Jewel," I said hopefully.

"Wouldn't that be the cat's pajamas?" said Pearl. "Can I do anything for you, Selma?"

"I'm all right now. Just help me up," said Selma, lifting up one hand.

"Are Charles and Pastor Ardelle here?" asked Pearl. She looked like a picture, dressed in a strapless gown covered with handmade rose petals and white tulle.

"Where'd you get your dress?" I asked, studying the white petals with curiosity.

"Well, Selma made the dress itself, but all the roses were hand-made by Patsy's Hose Recycling Factory. Every petal is made from used stockings."

"No kidding. By the business we advertise on station KOFF?"

"The one and only," said Pearl. "And Patsy attached them one by one. All four thousand and seventy-three."

"Your dress reminds me of a Rose Bowl parade float," I said, meaning it as a compliment.

"Careful," said Pearl, putting her hands on her hips and raising one eyebrow. "Charles and I keep a watchful eye on the environment. Nothing goes to waste if we have anything to do with it."

"Aren't you two just like biscuits and honey," said Selma, winking at me.

"Quick, Selma, what did you have to eat on May tenth, 1950?"

"Meatloaf smothered in tomato sauce, brown sugar, and onions; mashed potatoes; and spinach casserole."

"I'm surprised you can remember that far back," I said.

"What, do you think I'm slipping?"

"No, but forty-five. That's kind of old."

"Honey, I'm just getting started in life."

Pearl said, "Squirrel, how about you go be my spy and check on how things are coming?"

I slipped back into the sanctuary to see whether the pastor and Charles had arrived. Since there was no other room for them to wait, they were just standing around talking to the guests. Charles was wearing a white suit, shoes to match, and a beautiful lavender shirt and tie. After spotting them, I hightailed it back to Pearl and Selma.

"Don't worry, Aunt Pearl. He didn't stand you up. They're in there waiting on you."

Pearl laughed so hard, I was worried she'd split her dress. "Well, then, go tell your mamaw to start the music. I'm as ready as I'll ever be."

I scooped Jewel up off her pallet and smoothed down the front of her smocked dress to make certain her diaper was covered and she looked her most beautiful. I picked up the little Easter basket that had been spray-painted white, covered in fresh lavender, and filled with white rose petals and positioned it over my arm. William Bartlett waved at me from the back of the church. He was perfectly groomed, as always, and had apparently put something on his cowlick to make it behave. I waved back and smiled. Next to him were a few other students and my good friend Hadley King. How wonderful it was that they'd come to cheer Pearl and Charles onward.

After I told Ruby it was time to start the processional, Evangeline, Jewel, and I got in line. I had to pinch myself, thinking how lucky I was to be walking down the aisle just ahead of my beloved aunt while holding her precious daughter. This time, I didn't hurry but took my own sweet time down the aisle, helping Jewel throw rose petals out of the basket. I wanted to bask in the moment, so I could preserve and record the memories in my heart. After Ruby, Sapphire, and David Lee played a jazz version of "Here Comes the Bride," Pastor Ardelle began the service.

"On behalf of Pearl Gemburree and Charles Wesley, I'd like to welcome you to Mount Zion this afternoon and to the blessed union of these two beloved children of God. I can think of no finer occasion than this. I'd like to make one comment about their marriage and what the journey ahead may become. As I look out the windows of Mount Zion, our little church on a hilltop, I cannot help but think that God's view is perfect. And yet while we may be able to see a great distance from our little perch, humans cannot see everything.

"Not everyone can see the barriers Charles and Pearl will have to face: the barriers of skin color, of doors that may close just as others open, of prejudice and injustice. But He reminds us to count our blessings and to remember that wherever Pearl and Charles's lives may lead, there shall He be also. God is great, and His blessings will fall upon them, no matter the struggle. Turn in your Bibles to Matthew five-one. We'll skip around a little, but you'll get His meaning:

"'Blessed are ye, when men shall revile you, and persecute you, and shall say all manner of evil against you falsely, for my sake.'

"'Troubled waters will come your way, but do not despair.'

"Matthew five-fourteen: 'Ye are the light of the world. A city (like this church) that is set on a(n) hill cannot be hid.'

"'Neither do men light a candle, and put it under a bushel, but on a candlestick; and it giveth light unto all that are in the house.'

"'Let your light so shine before men, that they may see your good works, and glorify your Father which is in heaven.'

"Do not be afraid to let the world see your love for one another as husband and wife, Pearl and Charles. Instead, let your union serve as an example of the good that love, devotion, and kindness can bring to this harsh world. Remember what Scripture says:

"'Blessed are the pure in heart; for they shall see God.'

"I know of no other couple who has purer motives than the two of you. May the Good Lord bless and keep you all the days of your lives."

Pastor Ardelle took a white handkerchief out of his pocket and mopped his brow. "After a moment of silent prayer, please join the Gemburree Sisters in singing 'What a Wonderful World.' Oh yeah, Satchmo, eat your heart out."

Everyone laughed, women's hats bobbed, and fans fluttered before smiling faces. When the wedding drew to a close and Pearl and Charles were pronounced man and wife, I leaned over Jewel and kissed her on her forehead. "Now, isn't just everything perfect?"

But it wasn't. My mother was still missing. There had never been or would be a neat resolution that somehow made our lives perfect.

Though she was still gone and our father dead, Evangeline and I needed to keep having faith that good things lay ahead. That our lives, even at the ripe old ages of nine and eleven, would keep unfolding for the good.

What I didn't understand was why the pastor spoke of barriers and trouble ahead.

Ruby said that just because Pearl and Charles had gotten married that day didn't mean we could forgo our commitment to station KOFF. So just as soon as the reception luncheon was over, we hightailed it back to Fireside.

Ruby screeched the Thunderbird to a halt in front of the station's yellow building, and we ran down the sidewalk, up the steps, and inside. Barely into position on time, I took a deep breath to center myself and then started talking into the mic.

"Welcome to Fireside, Texas, home of the free and the brave and the everlasting polite persons. In local news, we celebrate today's wedding of Pearl Gemburree and Charles Wesley. Congratulations, Mr. and Mrs. Wesley, from all of us here at station KOFF."

Ruby played a few phrases from "Here Comes the Bride" on her fiddle while Evangeline chased a fly around the studio with a yellow plastic swatter. She nailed it on the turntable and then used Ruby's fine handkerchief to wipe up the mess. After she finished playing the tune, Ruby waggled her bow at Evangeline and frowned.

"In national news, in Vietnam, American forces are waging Operation Apache Snow in the A Shau Valley. I don't think this is a good idea because more daddies or mommies might be killed out there. All Rabbit and I have to say about that is, for the sake of all kids, let's get our troops outa there. 'No more Nam!'"

"In other news, the Monkees will perform in Wichita, Kansas, today. The 'Last Train to Clarksville' is a song you have heard us play here on station KOFF many times. We've watched quite a few episodes of their show, also called *The Monkees*, on TV over the past couple of years and are sad they quit making any new ones. Every time their theme song, 'Hey, Hey, We're the Monkees' came on, it practically turned my sister into an ape. As you know, most monkeys are related to Evangeline, especially the orangutans.

"Now for a word from our sponsor, Lucy's Float Your Boat Chips. Come visit our kitchen off Main and Peach Tree Avenue and taste the many flavors our tantalizing toddler biscuit chips come in. There's Space Snack Jack, which is a combination of bubble gum and watermelon for a little lift, or bayberry chamomile, frosted banana licorice, and peach tangerine. Deliciously fruity cream cheese dip comes with every bag of chips in a hermetically sealed container. Each specialty flavor has been specially formulated to ignite a two-year-old's taste buds. Lucy's Float Your Boat Chips never go stale. Each chip has a locked-in humidity guard that protects its freshness. Remember, if our specialty flavors don't float your tot's boat, they can be turned into actual marine vehicles in the family tub; they're that waterproof. You just can't lose with Lucy's Float Your Boat Chips.

"Densesky's Groceries and Dry Goods is having a sale on baby clothes and maternity items. They've got bibs and diaper shirts galore; all can be monogrammed and gift wrapped for that special infant in your life. Densesky's maternity clothes are stylishly designed with the latest zigzag, pom-pom, and fringe trims available on today's market. Don't hide your expanding waist under a sloppy dress; wear hot numbers from Densesky's."

Sapphire and her friend Violet had watched Jewel for the rest of Pearl and Charles's wedding day so they could relish every moment and enjoy a romantic dinner in Fredericksburg. The newlyweds had decided to spend the following day, which was Mother's Day, with Jewel before going on a short trip to South Padre Island to relax in the May sunshine and get their fill of deep-fried shrimp, hush puppies, and beer-battered jalapeños. We had promised to keep Jewel for their four-day honeymoon, and I was determined to do the best job anyone could.

Mother's Day had been a painful day since our mother had left for New York. This year, I decided it didn't help us girls one whit to mope around all day but that we should focus our intentions instead on Ruby.

"Let's make her breakfast in bed," I said when we woke up on Sunday morning.

"Now how can we do that? She's already been up milking the cow," said Evangeline with a put-out expression on her face.

"We'll tell her to get back in bed. Maybe Popo can drive into town and buy her a copy of *The Fireside Telegraph* or *The Austin American-Statesman*, and she can lie back in bed and drink coffee like a queen."

"Well, I'd rather she get going and make us a batch of icebox cookies," said Evangeline. "Isn't that what mothers do?"

"Come on, Rabbit. Get in the Mother's Day spirit. It's not about her waiting on us; it's the other way around."

"Well, all right. I suppose we can spoil her a little bit."

"You go talk her into getting back in bed. I'll talk Walt into getting her a newspaper. Then we'll make her waffles, sausage, and eggs. I'll put on the coffee to percolate."

"We could put Hershey's Chocolate Kisses in the batter to make her feel extra special."

"Good idea."

While Evangeline was coaxing Ruby to get back into bed, I could tell from the sound of our grandmother's voice that she was a tad anxious about our "gift" of breakfast.

"Just don't burn yourselves," she called out from the bedroom. Walt came into the kitchen, washed his face, and took his pickup truck keys from the counter.

"I'm off to get Mamaw a newspaper," he said and smiled. "You monkeys need anything from town?"

"Not especially. Just bring extra newspapers. Making breakfast might take us a while."

As Walt walked out the kitchen door, I picked up the percolator from the electric stove burner. As always, it was clean and ready to go.

I filled it up with water to the level line and started spooning coffee into the basket. "How many scoops you think it will take?" I asked Evangeline.

"How should I know? I ain't a cook. Working outside is my area. This is yours."

I walked into Ruby and Walt's bedroom and found her propped up against her pillows, fully dressed in her milking clothes and looking frightfully uneasy.

"Mamaw, how many spoons of coffee to make a full pot?"

"Twelve. Want me to come help you girls?" she asked anxiously.

"No, thanks. We've got it covered."

"Just keep the burners turned low."

"Will do."

Next, I took two rings of venison sausage out of the refrigerator, cut them into chunks, and split each one in half as I'd seen Ruby do so many times. I put them in an iron skillet with the open side facedown, set down the heavy pan on the stove, and turned the burner on low. Pretty soon a delicious smell wafted up.

Evangeline agreed to break eight large eggs into a bowl to make scrambled eggs, but that wasn't a pretty sight. She accidentally dropped two on the kitchen counter, and they dripped down the cabinets onto Ruby's spotless linoleum floor. Whenever I looked into the jade-green bowl at the six eggs that had made it inside, I was dismayed to see seven or eight fragments of eggshell in the bottom. When I pointed them out, Evangeline used her fingers to try to fish them out. "They just scatter when I try to get 'em." She growled in frustration. "I just hate cooking. When I grow up, I'm going to have a chef live in my house. Or maybe I'll just stay here with Mamaw and Popo forever."

"Just take a piece of eggshell and fish the bits out with that."

Evangeline had no trouble removing the fragments by using the larger piece of shell. "Oh, that's magic. I need to teach this trick to Davy."

"After you beat those eggs, we'll add in a bit of cheese, salt, and pepper and set them aside to cook later."

"What about the waffles?"

192

"How about I make the batter, and you take the foil off the Kisses?" I plugged in the waffle iron to let it heat while I stirred the ingredients together.

Evangeline peeled a bag of Kisses willy-nilly and dumped them into the batter. They looked like turtle heads poking out of a batter swamp. "They're kinda big, aren't they?" she said, giggling.

"Yes. Maybe we should have chopped them up."

"No way. Mamaw will love this."

"I think *you'll* love this."

I peeled back the wrapper of a stick of Blue Bonnet margarine and ran it over the hot grill. When black smoke poured out, I said, "It's hot enough, all right." I poured the batter in the waffle iron and closed the lid. We tried to peek at them prematurely, but the lid seemed stuck. Eventually, it let go, and we stared at the waffle.

"Oh. It smells delicious, but look at those big round circles of melted chocolate. I think they look like cow patties in the pasture," said Evangeline.

"What a gooey mess," I said, unsuccessfully trying to get the waffle out of the maker. I finally scraped most of it out with a spoon and dumped the mess on a plate. "We can't feed Mamaw this." Tears welled up in my eyes.

"It's OK, Juliet. We can pick the rest of the chocolate out of the batter and make plain ones. I'll give Sport the bad waffle. He'll eat anything. I'll give him all the Kisses we dig out of the batter too. Even I won't eat them like this."

Evangeline squeezed me around the middle in the biggest bear hug she could muster. It was a rare occasion for her to do such a thing, which only made me want to tear up again.

Once we'd picked the rest of the chocolate out of the batter and placed it on the plate, she took the whole kit and caboodle outside and let Sport have at it. Meanwhile, I worked hard to clean the waffle iron, reheat it, reapply margarine, and put in the batter minus the big chunks of chocolate. Now, there were only swirls of it. When the waffle came out perfectly, I felt so relieved.

Walt came back from town carrying not only two newspapers but some wildflowers he'd picked from the pasture. By now, it was nine thirty in the morning, and we were all starving.

When Evangeline and I carried Ruby's breakfast tray into her room, her hands flew to her cheeks. "Oh my stars!" she said. "You sweet girls are the most wonderful, perfect granddaughters anyone could ever have."

But we weren't perfect. We were far from it. Sport could have vouched for that.

Twenty

When Pearl and Charles brought Jewel to Walt and Ruby's house, I made sure Sport was nowhere in sight, lest he jump up and knock her out of my arms by accident. He was such a sweet dog, but he had a lot of spunk and didn't always think ahead. He lived in the moment, just the way Evangeline always did, and if he saw something he wanted to do, he just went ahead and did it.

I could see him curled up in a shady spot beneath the cottonwood tree by the tank. He seemed sound asleep, probably due to the full belly he had after eating all the chocolate Kisses covered in batter Evangeline had put in his bowl.

I took Jewel from Pearl's arms and said, "There's my sweet cousin. I'm so glad you've come to stay for a few days. There's lots of fun ahead."

Pearl and Charles brought in bags of Jewel's clothes, favorite toys, jars of Gerber and Beech-Nut baby food, and even oatmeal. "Do I have to make her eat this?" I asked, holding up the box of Beech-Nut Oatmeal in our living room.

"What's wrong with it?" asked Pearl.

"Nothing, I guess. Our great-grandmother Itasca used to make us eat oatmeal every morning when she was living. She always scorched it, but I'm sure she meant no harm."

"God rest her soul," said Pearl.

"Amen," said Charles as he reached out to comb Jewel's wild hair with his fingers.

"She's got hair just like mine and Evangeline's," I said.

"And like mine," said Charles. "Poor child."

"Of course she does. She's your girl."

"She certainly is, at that. She's the crown jewel in Pearl's tiara and in my heart. I'm blessed, finally at this ripe old age, to have a family."

"Doesn't get much better than that," said Walt, who'd just come in, along with Evangeline, from checking on the cows.

Ruby was in the kitchen making dinner: meatloaf, creamed peas, mashed potatoes, and buttermilk biscuits. On the counter was apple pie with lattice that had been brushed with egg and was a shiny, golden monument to perfection. "Will y'all stay for dinner?" she called out to Pearl and Charles.

"No, thank you, Ruby. We need to get on the road if we're going to make South Padre before midnight." Pearl was smiling so big, I couldn't remember having seen her happier. She wore a turquoise dress that was belted at the waist with a matching choker necklace made of large beads.

"Aunt Pearl, you look like Wilma Flintstone, only with blonde hair," said Evangeline.

"I get that a lot," said Pearl and laughed.

Pearl had a confident air about her. I thought back to the day when I'd first asked her if she loved Charles Wesley and was she gonna marry him. She'd said no, that Fireside wasn't ready for a black-and-white marriage. I doubted Fireside had changed all that much in such a short period of time. Apparently, she'd fallen in love and decided, ready or not, Fireside, here they come. There was a lot to admire about a person who wasn't going to let her life be controlled by what other folks thought.

"We'll take good care of your baby girl," I said. "And I won't let Sport hurt her."

"You're a trustworthy person," said Pearl. "I don't doubt your word. What happened was an accident."

"Is she, you know. . .?"

"Is she what?"

"Back to normal?"

"Not quite back to her floor-scootin', boogie-woogie self. I can't quite put my finger on what's wrong," said Pearl. "She doesn't seem to want to crawl anymore."

"Oh, I'm so sorry."

"Maybe she just needs more time to heal."

"I'll try to help her mend," I said. "Evangeline and I can teach her to crawl."

"That'd be a good project for you girls," Ruby called out.

After Pearl and Charles kissed Jewel goodbye, they left for their honeymoon.

"Happy Mother's Day," I called out after them. "And have a great time on the coast. Bring us back some seashells."

"I want a rooty-toot conch shell," yelled Evangeline.

"Honey, you're the rootinest-tootinest girl I've ever known," said Pearl.

"I'd like a seahorse or a sand dollar, if that wouldn't be too much trouble," I said.

"I'll do my best," called Pearl. "Love all you girls."

She and Charles faced us as they let themselves through the yard gate. He had opened it for her to let her pass first and then put his hand gently on one shoulder as they waved goodbye. They remain that way in my memory even today, standing together, one lovingly supporting the other. Like lapis beads strung together, they were strong but beautiful.

When Sport didn't come to eat out of his bowl that early evening, I went outside looking for him.

"Sport, come on, boy! Time to eat," I called out, but he didn't appear.

Jewel had settled into an especially bony place on one of my skinny hips. She had put on weight, which I thought to be a good sign considering all she'd been through. She was content and fairly purred as I carried her around with me in the yard, looking high and low for our sweet but unruly dog.

He wasn't in his dog house or standing sentinel at the yard gate, waiting to dash out to chase Ruby's chickens. Neither was he sitting on the closed metal door to Ruby's cellar or near the leaky yard faucet where wild mint grew abundantly each spring and summer. He often liked to go there and lie down where it was damp and cool, but he must have had other plans that day.

As usual, Jewel was sucking on two fingers, and drool was running down her chubby arm and onto my bare arms. Her diaper was also wet, and I knew I'd shortly need to take her inside to change it.

I finally thought to head back to look underneath the cottonwood tree where I'd last seen Sport but didn't expect to find him. Yet he was curled in the same position as earlier. His head was down on his paws, and his eyes were closed.

"Sport, wake up, boy. Time to eat."

Sport didn't jump up and wag his tail like he always did, so I nudged him gently with my tennis shoe. When he still didn't move, I held on to Jewel cautiously as I leaned over to pet him. He was stiff as an old board, his spirit clearly departed.

What immediately came to my mind was the bag of chocolate we'd given Sport that morning. Had it made him sick? Had we accidentally killed the pet we loved so much, the dog who'd provided amazing comfort to us when we'd needed cheering up? Or had his life been taken by an unseen hand due to the damage he'd caused Jewel? Surely our precious dog wasn't taken out by God for chasing squirrels on a porch because he'd caused injury to a child. But did He punish children who ought to have known better and didn't? Could anyone be punished for blind ignorance?

I posed these questions to Ruby that night as we sat in the kitchen. We blubbered over Sport and planned his burial for the following morning just outside the chicken pen, where he'd loved to crouch, bark, and wait for a hen to flap against the chicken wire. I had just put Jewel to sleep in her playpen, which stood in the corner of our bedroom, for the night. Oblivious to Sport's sad demise, she had eaten enough jars of Gerber's sweet potatoes, dense chicken, and plums to pass into a deep sleep without a peep of protest.

"No, honey. I don't think God punishes children or pets. How would it behoove Him to do that? How would it make Him feel better? When you're sad, He's sad."

"I don't know about that, Mamaw," said Evangeline. "I feel a lot better if I punch a boy when he makes me mad."

"Now, Evangeline. Punching another child is no way to handle an issue. Later on, you'll have to live with that decision. You'll have hurt another person and have to live with the guilt in the bargain," said Ruby.

"Do dogs have spirits?" I asked her. I was hunched over the kitchen table, writing Sport's obituary, which we would read the following day at his funeral.

"I believe they do," she replied. "Anything that can help your spirits that much must have one himself. At this very moment, I suspect he's in heaven lying next to your great-grandmother Itasca's feet."

"And by our daddy?"

"Yes, he'd want to be close to him too."

"Well, I'm not gonna die," said Evangeline matter-of-factly. "I've got way better things to do. Waaaaay better."

"I see," said Walt, who'd just snapped off the TV and come into the kitchen. He never missed an episode of *Gunsmoke*; everyone knew that. I'd watched him dig Sport's grave earlier, and when he'd come into the house, he'd taken a shower and sat down in his chair. I suppose it was Evangeline's words that had brought him to his feet. "I'm afraid you'll have to take that one up with the Lord, Rabbit. Everything that has ever lived has had to die at some point."

"Not me," she said. "I choose not to."

"Choose or not, all humans and animals eventually pass away. Like Sport's heart, our tickers will wind down," said Walt.

The following morning, we ate breakfast, washed the dishes, and filed out to the spot where Walt had dug Sport's grave just outside the chicken house. He'd wrapped the dog in an old white chenille bedspread Ruby had pulled out of the linen closet. Walt bent down on his denim-covered knees and lowered poor Sport into his grave.

Evangeline and I stood quietly by, each holding a paper with words we wanted to say over him.

Walt stood up and took his position by Ruby while Evangeline reached out and held my hand. She was shaking.

"Lord, hear our prayers," said Walt. "We pray that our pal, Sport, is now in a land of everlasting peace filled with squirrels and rabbits. We pray he has a shady spot to rest under and beautiful stars to light his path when he needs them. He was a loyal friend to us, and we loved him. In our opinions, he was a pretty good pup." He stopped and looked over at me. "It's your turn, Squirrel."

I opened my sheet of paper, where I'd copied the verse I thought most like Sport. "Today's verse comes from second Timothy four-seven: 'I have fought the good fight, I have finished the race, I have kept the faith.'"

"Yes," said Evangeline. "Sport did like to race and kept the faith in chasing squirrels and rabbits. He liked to chase cars, too, but never caught one. Maybe he'll be luckier in heaven."

"We hope the chocolate we gave you didn't do you in. If that's what caused you to leave us, we're truly sorry," I said.

"Me, too, Sport. I'm so sorry," said Evangeline.

Ruby said, "I think he had a heart attack. This breed of dog is known for that. But I guess we'll never know for sure. There's just no telling."

"Anyway, we need to say goodbye, Sport. Take good care, sweet dog. We'll see you again someday." I picked up a handful of dirt and dropped it inside the open grave. "Ashes to ashes, dust to dust."

By the time the funeral was over, there were no dry eyes. Even Walt pulled out his handkerchief, blew his nose, and stared off toward the chicken house.

The next day, Ruby took me over to visit Seymour in the Maitlin County jail. His case was about to go to trial that afternoon, and I thought he might welcome a visitor. But when I asked Deputy Bill to take me back to his cell, he said, "Can't do that."

"Why not?" I asked, setting down a plate of brownies on the counter.

"Old Seymour has gone to meet his maker."

Ruby took hold of my hand straightaway and squeezed it. "Well, I'll say," she said.

I was so surprised, it took a moment for me to respond. "Was he sick?"

"No, he took his life," said Deputy Bill, shaking his head. "Used a sheet. . ."

"Oh," I said, trying to get my mind around what he'd said.

"But he left a note. Said he wanted to give you his watch, young lady. We locked it up here in the safe when we brought him in. Said Sister Juliet was to have it."

"Why would he leave it to me?" I asked, a tear slipping down my cheek.

"I imagine it was because you were kind to him and because you forgave him. Look, here's the note he left for you."

Dear Sister Juliet,

Sorry to leave so sudden, but I wanted to be free. My lawyer said I didn't have a prayer to ever see the light of day outside a jail cell. I decided I'd rather not go on to prison and to take my leave now. I hope you understand why I didn't tell you goodbye in person.

I'd like to thank you for being my friend, despite the rotten way I treated you and them other kiddos. My mind is clear now, and I'm clean as a whistle.

I don't own much to speak of except this wristwatch that was my father's. He was killed when I was a boy, but I hear he was a good man. You can keep it to remember me by, or you can sell it and have a party for all them kids I scared on the bus.

Tell them I said I'm sorry as I can be, and I hope they get over what I done someday.

By the time you read this, I'll be eating that fruit in heaven that I told you about. I asked the Good Lord to forgive me of my sins, so I'm thinking that Saint Peter will let me in the pearly gates. If I'm still waiting outside when you get there, I know I can count on you to be my friend and vouch for me.

Vaya con Dios, *Sister Juliet! Never take drugs. You won't like the results. . .*

Your pal,
Seymour

Those days of our lives were good, but they were also tough. We didn't understand exactly what would lie ahead. That all the people and animals we loved would eventually pass away. That time was bittersweet, that it wasn't a straightforward journey to getting there from a known beginning to an unseen end. We didn't understand that time bent back upon itself, making a pretzel out of all of us until we were so connected in every extraordinary moment of our lives that we couldn't be undone. Not in this life and possibly not in the next. Because what lies ahead is more than we ever understood it would be. Like braided dough, one life entwined with all the others, until finally finished and baked in the Master Baker's oven to golden perfection. Isn't that the way you understand it works?

Twenty-One

Toward the end of May, Evangeline and I were playing checkers in the living room while listening to Ruby tune her fiddle in the bedroom. We'd just finished watching *The Lawrence Welk Show*, washing and drying the dinner dishes, and now Walt was trying to keep our attention off fighting each other. He was sitting in his office chair, looking at Orion in a magazine. He peered through a magnifying glass.

"Crown me," demanded Evangeline, sticking out her tongue and sashaying back and forth on the ottoman, which she'd claimed as her rightful throne the minute we'd walked in the room. I, on the other hand, was sitting on my knees.

"All right, smarty-pants," I said grumpily. I didn't much like to play checkers in the first place, but Walt, in his sweet way, had talked me into it.

He reached over and tweaked my nose. "I got your nose, see here?" he asked, sticking his thumb up between two fingers.

"That's for babies," I said. "Evangeline might fall for it."

"You're the crybaby," she said, baring her teeth and smiling. I pointed to the spot where a button of her blouse had come undone, exposing her belly button.

"You've got an outie. Just more proof you're not my real sister. You're the only Cranbourne with an outie."

"Not so," she said. "Cousin Jewel has one."

"You rascals need to quit picking on each other," said Walt. "Pay attention to what's important. Squirrel, you need to focus on the game in front of you. Rabbit is about to whip you."

"It's all right. Wouldn't be the first time. I've been whipped before."

203

Ever since Sport had died, I'd had a hard time paying attention to anything. There were about three things on the horizon that could still perk me up. One was Jewel, of course; the second was my excitement over Selma's coming baby; and the third was that William had been sitting by me in the school cafeteria at noon. Everything else seemed joyless.

"I'll share my Spam sandwich with you, Juliet," said William the following day at lunch. "What are you having?"

"Leftover fried chicken, corn on the cob, peaches, and a butter-and-sugar sandwich," I said. "Mamaw made them." I cut the butter-and-sugar sandwich into two halves. "Here, you can have this and a drumstick. I'll break the corncob in half if you'd like that too."

As he reached for my food offerings, I noticed the gleam of a silver ID bracelet on his arm. "Is that new?"

"Yes. Do you have one, Juliet?"

"No, but I did see one at Densesky's I thought was nice. It was a silver color, and you can get your initials put on it for seventy-five cents."

"If you were to buy that and have it engraved, we could swap bracelets and go steady," he said. Sugar crystals lined his lips. He studied me with big eyes, waiting for my response.

"Would that mean I was your girl?"

"I reckon so."

"And you'd be my guy?"

"Guess it'd work both ways."

"All right," I said. "Let's shake on it."

"It's a deal," he said, smiling and shaking my hand. "How about we go to Densesky's after your radio show on Saturday? You can pick out a bracelet, and we'll have a root beer float or something."

On Saturday afternoon, I opened my broadcast with a huge smile on my face for the first time in a long while. Even when Evangeline spit a piece of chewed gum down on the middle of my sponsor sheet during my broadcast, I didn't let her get me down.

"Welcome to Fireside, Texas. This is Juliet, also known as Sunshine Cranbourne. . ."

"Or Squirrel the girl," chimed in Evangeline. She gave me the stink eye and spit a second piece of gum right in the first paragraph, so I couldn't read one very important word, so I just ignored her and winged it.

"Today's program is brought to you by Hank's Jiffy Appliance Art Service. Do you have a range that won't get hot, even in June? Do your biscuits burn, even when it's turned on low? Does it stink to high heaven from that sweet potato you let cook for two days too long? Just drop it by (splat) and we'll turn it into an artistic vision.

"Hmm, I think they must want you to drop it by station KOFF. Having a tough time reading the type on this one, folks. I'll just continue. . . We can make yard art out of any discarded range of any color, shape, or size. Our reconditioned yard-art ranges are functional too. They become conversation pieces and outdoor grills. No front or backyard is complete without a psychedelic, flower-power grill. This week's special is our fifty-percent-off, friend-referral system. Drop off your range, get a friend to drop his or hers off too, and we'll give you half off our artistic interpretation fee.

"On a sad note, a Memorial Day picnic will be held at Fireside Shores on the Pedernales in honor of all veterans and especially those who have died in service to our great nation. Michael Hubek, VFW District thirty-one commander in chief, will bring out his mobile barbecue unit and grill hamburgers and hot dogs for families honoring their loved ones.

"In conjunction with Memorial Day observances, a prayer service and candlelight vigil will be held beginning at nineteen-hundred. Bring a photograph of your lost loved one and place it on the mobile altar at Fireside Shores.

"Tens of thousands of lives have been lost so far during the Vietnam War, untold numbers are missing in action, and there are scores of prisoners of war held captive by the Vietcong. This month has been particularly tough due to the Battle of Hamburger Hill, which has meant the loss of more than four hundred troops.

"Bring your family members at nineteen-hundred hours this Friday, Memorial Day, to Fireside Shores. Rabbit and I will bring a picture of our father, Lieutenant James Cranbourne, to place on the altar. We hope to see you there."

Ruby played "The Battle Hymn of the Republic" on her violin, but I could see tears trickling down her cheeks. I knew she was thinking about her boy—our daddy. Although he'd been dead for nearly two years, there wasn't a day that went by when she didn't somehow mention his name or give us a hint that he was always close to her heart and on her mind.

Evangeline had her own way of letting off steam about him. She threw herself into fighting invisible enemies, chiefly pretending she was Mighty Mouse fighting the evil, dastardly cat Oil Can Harry.

After the broadcast at station KOFF had drawn to a close, I moseyed on down to Densesky's while Ruby and Evangeline tidied the studio. As I walked out the door, Ruby was snapping her violin back into its case, and Evangeline was alternately rolling around on the floor and leaping off tables, pretending to sword fight Oil Can Harry. Oh, she was a lot of help to Ruby, all right.

That Ruby had sent me on to meet William, even when she could have used my help, was an endorsement of sorts. Of William. Of wanting me to be a normal eleven-year-old who needed a space for herself that was apart from just being a member of the Cranbourne family.

When I arrived at Densesky's, William was in the midst of both selling his chicken eggs to Norman and paying for an ID bracelet. I had meant to buy my own, but he had decided he wanted to make me a gift of it. I would have done the same for him.

"Sugar, Sugar" by the Archies was playing on the radio through the store's loudspeakers. It had just been released that week, and listening to it made me want to dance on the spot, so I did. It beat feeling blue about my father and the upcoming Memorial Day, so I threw myself into it. I didn't much care whether I made a complete idiot of myself. It beat crying, didn't it? I smiled at William, giggled, and danced a couple of steps toward him, pretending to be part of the act. He took the bracelet and money from Norman, set them down on the counter, and danced toward me, likely so I didn't have to look the only fool. That's what love will do for you.

Norman chuckled. "You crazy kids." But when Selma came out from the dry goods section of the store and spotted us having such a good time dancing, she grabbed Norman's hand and pulled him into the scene and started dancing too.

Then, when Ruby and Evangeline finally walked in, they started laughing at the four of us.

"Y'all got ants in your pants," said Evangeline, starting to belly laugh.

Selma and Norman just kept on dancing when the music changed to "You've Made Me So Very Happy" by Blood, Sweat & Tears.

But William picked up my bracelet off the checkout counter and said, "Here, this is for you." I took it out of his hand and looked at my initials.

"If you want, you can give it back to me, and I'll give you mine. But if not, just enjoy wearing it. Either way, it's my present to you."

"It's beautiful. Thank you."

"Would you like to go steady?" he asked.

"Yes, that'd be groovy."

"Swell," he said. "So you're my girlfriend now. Far out!"

"Far out," I said.

Suddenly, Selma and Norman stopped dancing in the background. She leaned over and looked at her sandals. A red line of blood had trailed down her leg and into her shoe. "Oh no," she said.

"What's wrong, sugar plum?" asked Norman, not seeing the problem at first.

"This can't be good," she said. "Now I'm really worried about the baby."

His eyes grew wide, but he quickly regained control of himself and hugged his wife.

"I'll take you to the doctor. Don't let a little blood scare you. Denseskys are tough. This baby will make it."

"Time will tell," said Selma as a tear slipped down her cheek.

It occurred to me that I'd never seen Selma Davis Densesky cry, although she'd dried many of my own tears. She always had an answer to virtually every problem, her ear tuned to every heart. Never appearing to be afraid of anything, she'd roared through life like a biker on a hog down Route 66, yet always dressed to the nines and with teased and sprayed hair that became another kind of helmet. She was a contradiction in nearly every way a woman could be. Yet her heart was no different than many other women's: among the most important of her goals, she wanted to bring one little child into this world and finally had been given the chance. Was this too much to ask?

"Let me drive her to the hospital while you close up the store," said Ruby. She put her white straw purse over one arm and reached out to take Selma's hand.

"That's a good idea," said Norman. "I need to make sure there are no customers in the back before I lock up. I'll be there as fast as I can."

We took Selma to the Fireside Hospital as quickly as we could. Selma didn't say a word, but tears flowed down her porcelain face. This was the first time I'd ever seen her without a smile, and to see her expression so full of fear was startling.

Selma was quickly taken back for examination. All the while, we sat in the waiting room, hardly speaking. Even Evangeline slumped in her chair, kicking at the floor with scuffed tennis shoes but saying nothing.

After Dr. Glasgow finished examining Selma, he came out into the waiting room to convey his findings.

"She's resting at the moment and will recover. However, she could lose the baby. For now, she needs to remain with us overnight for observation."

"Do you know what's causing the problem?" asked Norman anxiously.

"Not as of this moment. Her advanced age may be complicating the viability of this pregnancy."

"She's only forty-five and doesn't even look that."

"Looks have nothing to do with it. Medically speaking, forty-five is quite a bit older than most of the expectant mothers we see here in Fireside."

By the time we left Selma in a private room, she was tucked in a bed and wearing a hospital gown. Her hair was flattened out against the pillow, and tears were still silently sliding. I wondered how many moments it had actually taken to go from dancing, cutting up, and acting silly, without a care in the world, to lying in a hospital bed, crying as though the world was ending? Hardly any, and yet mostly all. It seemed all she had both ever and never wanted lay ahead.

I thought ahead to the things that would come into my own life. In the short term, the Memorial Day picnic at Fireside Shore, helping Jewel grow up, sharing lunches at school with William. What I didn't know was whether seeing my mother lay ahead in the near or distant future. It occurred to me that perhaps it was best we didn't always know the particulars of how or what we would face. Minute by minute was the only way to live it.

Twenty-Two

Even today, years after we buried Sport out near the chicken coop, I can tell you exactly where his grave lies. I can no longer look at chocolate Kisses without thinking we shouldn't have fed him them. On occasion, Evangeline and I will speak of our beloved dog, usually when we sit up late at night preparing for our radio program on station KOFF. What I'll tell you is I can no longer stand the sight or smell of waffles. Like a stuck record, my conscience still grates on my nerves. Of all the people I need to forgive the most for transgressions, including my mother, I still need to learn to forgive myself.

One morning in February 2003, I woke up and decided to try my best to pull myself out of the quagmire of perpetual guilt in which I was so often stuck. Instead of constantly beating myself up over what had happened to Jewel and Sport, I would do something positive.

William Bartlett called me up on the telephone, asking whether I'd remembered I was to go with him; Selma and Norman; Evangeline; and, of course, Jewel over to Diamond's Dance Hall to practice the Lindy Hop on Saturday night. I said, "Well, of course."

It wasn't a Fireside minute before my wheels started turning. "What if we could encourage all the burg to learn the dance and then host an international Lindy Hop to raise money for children with spinal injuries? How much fun would that be? More importantly, how many families would be helped by it?"

"Just enjoy yourself on Saturday. You needn't worry so much. You don't have to save the world."

"Well, there's a thought," I said. "But I'll likely take this on anyway."

"What I meant was I want us to enjoy our time together," said William. "And I only want you to dance with me. Not some Joe Schmo," he said and laughed.

"I'll keep that in mind," I said, teasingly.

"Why don't you call up Jewel and tell her we'll pick her up at about seven, go over to visit Charles Wesley, eat some barbecue, maybe play him a game of pool, and then head on over to dance?"

When I called Jewel, I had to let the phone ring a long time until she picked it up. It wasn't easy for her to move her wheelchair around Pearl's house on account of there being so many corners between the rooms that required tight maneuvering.

"Hello," she said. "Hope you're having a jewel of a day."

"It's just me," I said. "You still want to go out to Diamond's on Saturday?"

"You bet," she said. "I love to watch dancing. And it's been years since I've been to a Texas honky-tonk. Are you sure they have swing music there? Not just western swing, but something like Lionel Hampton would have played?"

"Jewel, you know me. I'm a good Girl Scout. I always go prepared. All I have to do is borrow some records from the radio station. There are stacks of records a mile high. I just need to dust them off and maybe get rid of a few silverfish."

"In all my years teaching at Cambridge, I don't believe I've ever seen a silverfish up there."

"Welcome back to Texas, cuz. If we can't do everything bigger here, we just do more of it. By the way, when are you going to give Charles the picture of him posing next to Chuck Yeager in front of Glamorous Glennis?"

"Might as well be on Saturday; that way you and Evangeline can see it too."

"Why don't you call Charles 'Daddy'?"

"Sometimes I do, Juliet. When we used to sit out on the porch drinking iced tea and listening to the cicadas, I'd call him Daddy. We don't sit on the porch like we once did, not anymore, since he's spending his nights at assisted living and getting a little hard of hearing. Anyway, I just grew up calling him Charles because Mama did."

"Now how come he's in assisted living but still drives to work every day?"

"Two reasons. First, he didn't want to live in this empty house anymore without Mama. Second, he likes his shirts done with heavy starch and hates to iron. They do all that for him at the Fireside Sentinel House."

"I hate to iron too," I said and paused before continuing. "Have you thought about moving back to Fireside?"

"Someday, when I'm tired of teaching or can no longer take care of myself. In the meantime, I need to pack up Mama's things and sell this place. It'll just go to ruin with no one living in it."

"Let's all go out and have a good time tomorrow night, and come Monday, Evangeline and I will come help you pack up Pearl's belongings."

"How do you pack up a lifetime?" asked Jewel. Her voice became barely a whisper.

"One memory at a time. . . with the help of cousins who love you dearly."

The following afternoon, I walked into station KOFF for our Saturday radio program. The previous December had marked the thirty-fifth anniversary of *The Cranbourne Variety Hour* broadcast. The station walls were filled with so much memorabilia from years past that I couldn't help but feel sentimental as I passed the picture of an eight-year-old Evangeline pressing her cheek against Ruby's.

There was a photograph of Walt and Miss Alma Webster, snapped the afternoon he'd helped her rescue her white puffball of a dog, Little Bit. It was the same day, due to her puppy's escapades through Fireside, that had presented us with the opportunity of having our own radio show. What had initially seemed like a disaster turned out to be one of the best things that ever happened to us. Had it not been for one little wild pooch, I might have someday moved up north to Waxahachie and become a gumball machine repairwoman.

Evangeline was waiting for me in the station KOFF office and was bent over the desk editing a small stack of papers. She had fastened the paper clip that had held them to the collar of her blouse, a habit left from her years of conducting research at Oregon State University. She was working on an article about "Peach Tree Bark and Its Hidden Mysteries" for *Sunset Magazine* and was wearing blue jeans with ragged cuffs and a white T-shirt and denim jacket. Wire-framed sunglasses with small rose-colored lenses were perched up in the crown of a hairdo that was coming apart from the updo I'd seen her create in the bathroom mirror early that morning on the ranch.

"Ten minutes to showtime. I thought I might have to start without you," said Evangeline, looking a tad miffed.

"Really? And what would you have said?"

"That you were late on account of having a wart burned off your nose. That all our KOFF listeners ought to drop by a large box of bandages and monkey blood due to the sheer enormity of the catastrophe. Then I'd have to start a fund so you could have plastic surgery to fill up the crater it left when they burned it off. Next, I'd have everyone call up Oprah and demand she do a story on what it's like to make a comeback after wart disfiguration. . ."

I playfully plucked her sunglasses off her head and popped them on mine. "Oh, you would, would you? Maybe today I'll have to put in a word about the Martian from Marfa who lives in your bedroom and makes sculptures out of the trash you leave lying around on the floor."

"You're not funny," said Evangeline. "You're a sourpuss. Guess I'll put up with you for one more show, considering you're the only sister I have."

"You better thank your lucky stars you've got me to keep you in line," I teased. "Good luck with your article, by the way."

Evangeline followed me into the soundproof room and began helping me set up to broadcast. Within five minutes, we were ready. She gave me the thumbs-up, hit the red button, and then retreated back into the office to check for any late-breaking news feeds.

"Welcome to Fireside, Texas, home of the free and the brave and the everlasting polite persons. We never take the last cookie, but Evangeline will eat the last doughnut in any box; that is for sure. No one in this town eats beets, but we thank the hostess for them anyway.

"In today's local news, I'd like to say that some of us are tossing around the idea of having a Lindy Hop dance contest to raise money for kids with spinal injuries. If you can, come on down to Diamond's Dance Hall tonight at nine o'clock and learn how to dance the Lindy for a good cause. Our very own Selma Davis Densesky will show you how it's done. Remember, that's tonight at Diamond's. Get ready to dance your shoes off."

A sad-faced Evangeline came into the studio and handed me a message she'd printed on white paper. Tears filled my eyes as I read it.

"I have just learned some tragic news. At eight fifty-nine EST this morning, Space Shuttle *Columbia* and its entire crew were lost during final approach. They were somewhere over Dallas when all communications failed.

"While we don't yet know what caused this accident, those of us at station KOFF send our deepest sympathies to the families of the deceased. In recognition of this sad occasion, the flag at the station will be lowered to half-mast. What a devastating day for these families. What a tragic loss for mankind."

The sadness of that morning's events cast a pall over our group as we gathered later at Wesley's Barbecue Heaven. William had come to the ranch to pick us up in his Suburban for the evening, but I just said, "Thanks, but no. Let's drive Ruby's Thunderbird tonight. The old girl is still in mint condition. Perhaps it will cheer us all up. Furthermore, there's plenty of room in the trunk for Jewel's wheelchair."

We carefully tied Jewel's framed gift of the gigantic picture of Charles with Chuck Yeager to the top of the Thunderbird. Evangeline, lead footed as always, started out in a streak, but after we picked Jewel up, she put her foot down when the picture got to shifting in the wind.

"Slow down. Don't even think about ruining his gift. I brought that thing all the way from Cambridge in one piece, and I don't want to have it smashed to bits now."

"Spoilsport," said Evangeline and looked slyly at Jewel but immediately took her foot off the gas pedal. "I'll do anything for you, cuz, even straighten up and drive right."

When we arrived at Wesley's Barbecue Heaven, William popped the Thunderbird's trunk and lifted the wheelchair out for Jewel and then untied the large framed picture from the roof.

"Thank you," she said. "I'm not used to having anyone wait on me. I am growing a little weaker than I used to be, so it's appreciated."

William held the door to Wesley's open, let us all pass inside, and then pulled the door closed against the February damp. Charles moved away from behind the counter where he'd been sharpening knives. His face lit up when he saw us, but the wrinkles around his eyes and the lines around his mouth seemed deeper somehow.

While it hadn't been all that long since I'd last seen Charles, he looked older to me than usual. He wore hearing aids and stooped a little as he walked. But when he reached out to hug Jewel and then the rest of us, we felt his love, steady and strong as it had always been.

"Look what I've brought for you," said Jewel, pointing to the picture that William held for Charles's examination.

"Well, I'll say." Charles stood close to it, inspecting every inch, and then backed away for another perspective. One tear slipped down his cheek, but he wiped it away with a corner of his white apron. "Thank you. Where'd you come by this, baby girl?"

Jewel's face lit up when he called her that. "Found the original in the *Boston Globe* archives. Had it blown up for an early birthday present."

"Them was good days. Mighty good. Though not half as good as the day I met your mother. Uh, huh, huh. Sure was an important time. Though war is never something to remember lightly."

"You were one of the world's best pilots ever on record. You do know that, don't you?"

"That's what they say. Well, I just applied myself and never took no for an answer." He smiled and reached out for Jewel's hand. "Sure am proud of my daughter. Teaching quantum mechanics at MIT. I can't hold a candle to you, that's for sure."

"Thanks. . . Daddy," said Jewel, pulling his hand to her cheek. Charles reached down and kissed her on her cheek. "How about you come dancing with us this evening?"

"Dancing? What do I want with dancing now that your mother's gone?"

"Come with us. You can twirl me around in my wheelchair."

Charles looked at Jewel and then smiled. "Why not?" he said.

"Come on then; time's a-wastin'," I said. "Let's go see if any of our local Fireside residents have arrived. Let's show them how the Lindy Hop is done!"

"I'm not one to brag, but I am a pretty talented dancer," said Evangeline.

"Like the time you wiped out and took three couples down with you?" I said.

"Except that once," she said and giggled.

By the time we all managed to get to Diamond's, we had whooped one another's spirits up into a frenzy. I carried the stack of old albums to Jack the Knack, the honky-tonk's disc jockey.

"Here, Jack. Thanks for letting us take over your place."

"From one disk jockey to another, I'd like to say I'm proud as peaches to do it." Jack was wearing a black western-yoke shirt with pearl snaps and a white scarf around his neck. He wore a white Stetson and a huge smile that revealed tobacco-stained teeth. His head may have been bald for years, but no one in Fireside knew for sure, because Jack had never been spotted without his hat.

"Hopefully, you'll have a good turnout tonight."

Selma arrived, wearing a red-sequined bodysuit, red tights, a white skirt, and fancy red Keds. Clearly, she was dressed for action. Although no spring chicken, Selma's youthful spirit had wrestled old age down to the floor and stomped it to death.

"Don't you look a picture?" I said, hugging her around the neck.

"Like Jerry Reed says, 'When you're hot, you're hot.' Now, if I can just remember all the moves to 'In the Mood.'"

It wasn't long before Norman, who was dressed in suspenders, pants, a white shirt, and a 1930s'-era vintage cap arrived too. In the corner of his mouth was an unlit cigar, but that was part of what made him Norman. Since Walt's death, it made me kind of sad to look at him because he

216

reminded me so much of the grandfather I'd adored. He was a kind man with a generous heart who'd been good to so many.

Let me just say, despite their ages, Selma and Norman could shake a leg like no one's business. Although they didn't do any aerials, their movements were impressive and as smooth as silk. Just as soon as they'd finished their first demonstration and the crowd who'd gathered around them had quit clapping, William hugged me and said, "Come on, Juliet, we're gonna whip this dance."

"How so?" I said, looking up into his handsome face. He reminded me so much of Clark Gable but was truly even better looking.

"Don't I remember that back in high school, you were on the dance team?"

"Well, that was eons ago, but I do love to dance."

"That's my girl."

"And you played King Boogie in our high school musical."

"Oh, I hoped you wouldn't remember that."

The next record played was "Wham (Re-Bop-Boom-Bam)," and as Selma later pointed out, William and I were hot as firecrackers on the dance floor.

"I didn't know you could do that," I said.

"There's a lot of things you don't know about me."

"For instance?"

William pulled me up close to him, "That I'm in love with you, Juliet. That I'm so thankful you're back in my life." He paused and held my hand. I could sense his nervousness, which transferred directly to me. "What I need to know is whether you feel the same way."

William took my breath away, and I flat-out lost my head and composure. "Excuse me for a minute," I said. Who's to say why I reacted as I did when he said that, but it was the same way I'd always responded when terrified. I just took off running and running and running. Past Charles twirling Jewel around in her wheelchair, past Selma and Norman shaking a leg better than anyone else in the room, past Jack the Knack in his booth, and straight into the men's restroom. Then I had the biggest, fattest panic attack I thought possible. My heart was pounding, my breathing choppy, and I was crying like a banshee. I didn't realize I was in the wrong room until I'd finished washing my tear-streaked face with water in the sink, looked up, and saw a man standing behind me.

"You're in the wrong restroom," I said.

"No, ma'am. You're in the wrong restroom. I can read. The sign says 'Caballeros.'"

"No matter where I am, it seems I'm always in the wrong place at the wrong time. That's the story of my life."

"You all right, miss?" he asked.

"Oh, 'bout like always."

When I exited the men's room, a crowd who'd seen me dash inside had gathered outside to enjoy the outcome. Imagine my embarrassment when so many of my Fireside KOFF listeners started roaring with laughter, clapping, and then cheering when they saw the horrified look on my face.

Eventually, I wound my way back to William, who was leaning up against the bar with a stricken look on his face.

"Oh, William, I'm so sorry."

"I guess that means your answer is no."

"No, it doesn't. You just scared me. I wasn't expecting it. I just need a little time to get my thoughts in order."

"There's no rush. After all, I've been in pursuit of you since grammar school."

"No, you haven't."

"Oh yes, I have."

"Then why didn't I hear from you until last year?"

"After our wild finish during high school graduation practice, I thought I'd busted my britches with you forever."

"Maybe we just needed time to grow up."

"Could be. Actually, there's something more I need to talk to you about." William looked down at the floor and then back up at me. "I've been awarded a contract to design two new American embassies, one in Gaborone and the other in Jerusalem. I'm trying to decide whether to accept or not. I'd have to be gone for a long while if I do."

"And leave Fireside? Leave me?"

"Unless you were to ask me to stay or come with me."

"Go with you? Leave Fireside?"

"Won't you think about it?"

"Like Ruby would have said, 'Oh my stars. Just wow!'" I swallowed hard. "I will think about it, but for starters, I wouldn't want you to give up something important like those amazing contracts. You've got a business to think about. Making a living in this town is hard. Look at what I have to do to make it. I have my House of Cranbourne store, the radio show, and the money Evangeline and I eke out of the ranch. It takes all those things combined to make a decent living."

"Of course, my business is a little different," said William thoughtfully. "Much of mine comes to me through the internet. Building a good reputation took many years, but I did it, and I'll continue enhancing it."

"Yes, but wouldn't building those two new embassies be quite a feather in your cap?"

"Well, I'm no I. M. Pei, but I'd be in a different league than I am now."

"How can you not go?"

"I don't think I want to leave you, Juliet. Give me a reason to hope for our future."

William kissed my cheek and pulled me back onto the dance floor. Deep down, I knew I loved him and always had. We'd had so much fun together; a part of me never wanted the evening to end. But didn't all good things have to come to a halt? Relationships? Life? Wasn't there always a final record to play or one last bow to take before life's curtain call? How could I even consider leaving Fireside, my sister, and the family ranch? Wasn't that practically unthinkable?

Twenty-Three

On Monday, Evangeline and I left the ranch in my Avalanche truck and headed to Pearl's house. It was our privilege and duty to help Jewel begin the painful process of closing up the house where her parents had lived for so long. Even Sapphire, the only living sister of the Gemburrees, no longer wanted to live there. She had moved to San Angelo years before and had sold Pearl her half of the house after she and Charles married. Evangeline pounded on the front door and slowly pushed it open.

"Yoo-hoo!" I called, so as not to frighten Jewel. In a moment, she wheeled into the living room.

"Good morning, favorite cousin," said Evangeline.

"I'm your *only* cousin," she said and laughed.

"Your friendly packers and movers are here. Just call us the Mayflower girls," I said. "May I tag the boxes as we pack?"

"Squirrel, you nutty girl," said Jewel. I thought about how many times Pearl had called me that and felt moved to tears. We'd all shared such good memories together in this house, and now to see the era draw to a close was almost more than I could bear. Furthermore, that she could speak to me with love in her heart after what I'd let happen to her spoke of her ability to forgive those who'd caused damage.

We started in Pearl's sewing room, the place where she'd created such stylish outfits for herself and Jewel and many of the costumes worn on stage by the Gemburree Sisters. Like Ruby, Pearl had once used a treadle machine but then had bought a new portable Singer model that was a virtual dream machine. Now the newer model rested on top of the old

220

cabinet, and a dress pocket made of hot pink fabric lay underneath the presser foot.

"Mama was making herself a new dress when she flew up to visit me that last time. She didn't finish it before she left, and of course, she never got the chance. I haven't had the heart in me to take it out. I'm not sure what you do with things like that. Odds and ends so sentimental you can't throw them away but that would mean nothing to anyone else."

"I definitely know what you mean, Jewel. It took me many years to clean out Ruby's cellar after she died," I said. "What are you going to do with jars of expired jams and jellies? Jars filled with fruit that was grown, picked, peeled, and canned by her hands."

"Whoa, y'all. We're all going to end up in tears, and what a mell of a hess we'd all be. Let's keep on track. Where do you want us to start?" asked Evangeline.

"There's a metal box that had a lock on it. I've found the key, but the lid is rusted shut. Can you pry it open? I've been trying to find the deed to this house and I'm hoping it's in there. I don't have the strength in my hands anymore to get it open."

"Sure thing." Evangeline got a long screwdriver out of the utility drawer, came back into the sewing room, made a lot of racket, and then prized the metal box open. She passed the open container to Jewel, who sat in her wheelchair, going through its contents.

"Well, here's the lifetime guarantee from Sears for the silverware she bought and a wedding picture of Mama and Charles," said Jewel. "And there's a snapshot of me as a baby being held by a woman I don't know."

She handed the picture to Evangeline and me, and I was instantly struck by how familiar the woman looked. "Do you know who she is?" she asked.

Then it dawned on me that of course I knew who she was. "Evangeline, you remember who this is, don't you?"

Evangeline reached out for the photograph and then put her hands over her mouth. "That's our mama," she said. "Why was she holding you, Jewel?"

"I have no idea. How weird is that? I guess Pearl must have kept in touch with her after she left. They were such close friends at one time."

While Evangeline and I struggled to cope with what we'd just learned, Jewel kept digging through the box, methodically poring over each piece of paper. "Here's the receipt for the wedding ring she bought for Charles. She had their wedding date engraved on the inside of his band, and it cost her ten extra dollars to have it done. And this looks like a birth certificate. Let me see, this one is for a baby girl named Elspeth Darajani, born to Marguerite Cranbourne Darajani, a citizen of the United States, and her husband, Mukiri Darajani, of Kenya, East Africa." She looked at us with wide eyes and asked, "Isn't that your mother?"

"Marguerite Cranbourne is our mother, but I don't know nothing about the Darajani part," said Evangeline. "Look at the rest of those papers while we mull this over."

Behind the birth certificate was a paper-clipped stack of official-looking documents. Jewel picked them up and said, "These are adoption papers. I can't believe what I'm reading. Pearl adopted me from Marguerite when I was a baby."

"Our mother had another baby!" said Evangeline as her voice rose shrilly.

"And Mama never told me?" said Jewel. "Or Daddy or Selma? Not even Ruby or Walt said a word. They lied to all of us by omission. Why would such wonderful people do a thing like that? I know they were bound to have a reason."

"Maybe they were protecting somebody," said Evangeline. "I'm remembering that day I overheard Pearl, Sapphire, Walt, and Ruby in the kitchen talking about the rabbit having died. I thought they were talking about this Rabbit." She tapped her chest.

"I'm realizing they just couldn't bring themselves to tell us, fearing it would cause more harm than good," I said. I leaned over and hugged Jewel and then Evangeline. "Do you girls realize this means we're half sisters. . . not cousins?"

"Jeez Louise," said Evangeline. "This is making my head spin. I'm not sure I can take too many more secrets today. Quit looking in that box, Jewel!"

Jewel ignored Evangeline and continued picking through the documents, newspaper clippings, and photographs in the box. "We might as well get it all over with today. The future is uncertain—all we really have is now. Look, here's an obituary from the *New York Times* for Mukiri Darajani. He designed sets for Broadway productions. I guess that's how they met. What a good-looking man he was and apparently really talented. He died at age thirty-six from a rare form of muscular dystrophy, the same thing I have."

"You have muscular dystrophy?"

"Oh yes, I always have had it, but we didn't know what it was until I was grown and gone from Fireside and saw a specialist in Baltimore. I just haven't felt like telling anyone about it because I've been afraid my relationships with friends and family would change. I just don't want everyone to focus on the possibility that I won't always be here. And I don't really don't want my remaining time to be filled with sadness. Joy feels quantitatively better."

"All these years I've thought it was my fault. I've blamed myself for the fact that you couldn't walk," I said. "Why didn't Walt or Ruby tell me that, either?"

"They did, egghead. They told you it wasn't your fault over and over and over again," said Evangeline, batting my forehead with a piece of paper. "You've just got a thick skull. Just one more reminder that you are a squirrel of a girl."

"What a strange thing to suddenly find out that all these things we believed were true for so long really never were." I glanced over at Pearl's wall clock that had stopped keeping time years ago and shuddered.

"I'm so sorry. I didn't realize. For years, we all thought it was due to Sport knocking me off the porch, but no. I wish it were that simple," said Jewel.

"What are the doctors saying?" I asked, almost afraid to hear the answer.

"That time for me is short. It's why I've made my life's work teaching about time. It's such a precious thing. I want everyone to realize it. To make the most of their lives in the amount of time they have."

Evangeline and I reached out to hug Jewel as tears slipped down our cheeks.

"Oh no," said Evangeline. "We love you bunches and are sad to hear this. Sad you didn't tell us what was really going on with you years ago."

I picked up Jewel's hand and pressed it against my cheek. "Then why don't you stay in Fireside with those of us who love you? We can be here in a flash when you need us."

"I hadn't really thought about it," said Jewel. "Maybe I shouldn't sell the house just yet."

A thought suddenly occurred to me. "Jewel, in what state were you adopted, New York or Texas?"

"Let me see. . . the great state of Texas, it says here. Why?"

"Because maybe our mother came back to Texas to sign away her rights."

"Why do you think that?" asked Evangeline.

"Because I think I saw her on Groundhog Day all those years ago. She was smoking a cigarette, and I could see her from the courthouse lawn when we were having our sister city celebration with Austin. I took off running after her, which is what I generally do when something pushes me over the edge. My legs have a mind of their own, and they don't listen much to my head. Just my heart."

"If that's true, and it was Mama, it makes me mad enough to fight, just thinking she wouldn't let you get up close enough to talk to her. That she would hurt your feelings that way, Squirrel," said Evangeline.

"This is all quite a shock," said Jewel. "There's nothing in the world of physics or mathematics that prepares one for this."

"All these years, I've thought that Charles Wesley was your biological father," I said.

"Come to think of it, he never said he was. He just always told me I was his special girl. That he loved me more than the moon he admired so often. All those years, flying in the same league as Chuck Yeager and the others. . . Oh snap! Just talking about this makes me wish I could have been an astronaut if my body had cooperated."

"You're the rocket scientist in the family," I said. "The youngest child. The one with serious brain power."

"Hold on," said Evangeline. "I am pretty smart—the other brilliant scientist in this family."

"We all have unfulfilled wishes. A part of me wanted to become a dancer, not the guitarist and singer Walt wanted me to be. Heaven knows, I was destined to fail at that," I said.

"Squirrel, don't feel bad. We all knew you couldn't sing a note or play the guitar, even if your life depended on it," said Evangeline. "You just didn't get that gene, but I wound up with a great guitar."

"You're right," I said. "I guess I didn't come out with any talent except talking, now that I think about it."

"Sure, you did," said Evangeline. "You have the talent of being wacky. Wacky on the air, wacky in person, wacky as a sister." She smiled and tweaked my nose. "Look, I've got your nose." She stuck her thumb between two fingers. "Remember when Walt used to do that and wink?"

225

Twenty-Four

As time drew closer to the Lindy Hop dance competition, I realized even in a wheelchair, Jewel knew far more about it than I could ever learn. I picked her up from Pearl's house and took her in to have lunch at Wesley's Barbecue Heaven, where all pigs can fly.

"You know the story about all those flying pigs, don't you, Jewel?" asked Charles when we sat down beside him to eat. "Here, have some more dills." He passed her a paper container filled with ridged pickle chips.

"If I've heard it once, I've heard it a thousand times," she said and laughed. "Mama told me at least once every year until she died."

"She still lives in here," said Charles, pointing to his heart. "Always will."

"I can't believe you never told me I was adopted," said Jewel.

"I'm sorry you found out that way." Charles eyes filled with sadness. "I wanted to tell you, but Pearl wouldn't have it. Wasn't my news to tell anyway. The ball was in her court, but she never could quite bring herself to say the words."

"Same with Ruby and Walt," I said.

"That's right," said Charles. "But don't judge the folks who truly loved you too harshly. We all tried our absolute best to do right by you."

"And they did," said Evangeline.

"It was the rule set by the Fireside Gem Society," said Charles.

"Were you made a member like Walt?" I asked.

"Oh yes," he said. "We held parenting meetings and played forty-two afterward. We were a society of family, engaged in the business of

226

protecting and raising you three girls. A secret mission, as important as those I flew during wartime as a young pilot."

"What were you protecting us from?" asked Jewel.

"From more suffering than you'd already been through. From cruel talk in this town. From abandonment issues."

"Too late," I said. "Way too late for Evangeline and myself. I just hope Jewel is OK. Are you?" I looked at her as I asked.

She smiled and shrugged her shoulders. "I am. I wound up with the best mother in Pearl and father in you that a girl could ever have had. But, Daddy, was it worth it? Were we?"

"You betcha, baby girl. Worth every single moment." He reached out and took Jewel's hand.

"The Gemburree Sisters were something else. I think we were all lucky to have been raised by them. No telling what might have happened otherwise. We're also grateful for Walt and Charles," said Evangeline.

"Both of us married up," said Charles. "But there was no finer man than Walt Cranbourne."

"Or you, Daddy," said Jewel. "No finer men."

None of us could think of anything to say to add to their words because we all felt the same way. When I noted that Jewel's eyes had teared up, I changed the subject.

"Jewel Bug, how about you serving as presiding judge for the Lindy Hop contest? We've got contestants flying in from as far away as Germany and Italy. You're the local authority on deciding who would be the best couple on the floor."

Jewel raised up a little straighter in her wheelchair and smiled. She pushed back a purple sleeve on her cotton blouse and said, "I guess I am. All those years of watching from the sidelines have given me a pretty good eye. Yes, I'll do it."

"Just two weeks until it begins. So many details still to take care of, I can tell you that for sure. But I'm so glad to have you lined up to judge. What a relief."

"Anything for a cuz, uh, sister," said Jewel.

That evening, Evangeline and I sat around the kitchen table planning the live broadcast we were going to make of the Lindy Hop dance competition. A portable dance floor was going to be put on the city park grounds in central Fireside. It was the same site where William and I had roller-skated so many years before.

"What do you think?" she said. "Should we limit the broadcast to two hours? Maybe get KTBC coverage too?"

"No more than two. Geez, I wish Uncle Jay could come down to say a few words for old times' sake. What I wouldn't give to hear 'Hello, boys and girls' one more time."

"I need a hug from Packer Jack," said Evangeline. She spread peanut butter on a graham cracker, took a bite, and managed to get it on her nose.

"What?" she asked as I pointed to her face.

"Some things never change," I said and handed her a napkin.

"But some things do," she said. "For instance, who knew Jewel was really our sister?"

"You've got a good point." Changing the subject, I said, "I'm worried about her health. I wonder how much longer she'll be able to live on her own. She seems to be getting weaker by the day."

"I'm worried too. Whatever happens, we'll be there for her."

"Cranbournes and Gemburrees stick together."

"Like peanut butter to a graham cracker," she said and took another bite.

When the Fireside International Lindy Hop Contest rolled around in the middle of June, I brought Hadley King Hammerschmidt to help produce the event.

"What can I do you for, girl?" she asked. As usual, Hadley was wearing Mary Kay's Ravishing Red lipstick. She'd recently gotten her dark hair frosted, and a large blonde section curved from her part and dipped low over her forehead.

"How dramatic!" I said, admiring her new hairdo.

"Do you think I favor Anne Bancroft?" she asked, turning to show me her profile.

"Yes, I see a resemblance."

"That's what my husband told me last night at dinner. He said, 'Hadley, you look just like Anne Bancroft in *The Graduate*.'"

"Oh no, you mean as Mrs. Robinson?"

"The very one."

"That's scandalous. Don't tell anyone else in Fireside that. Rumors will catch on fire, and the whole place will go up in flames."

"Let them talk," she said and laughed. "Obviously, they don't know how boring my life really is."

"Nonsense. After all, you do get to work at the best store in town."

"I do! Come to think of it, selling embellished garbage bags, Elvis Christmas ornaments, and Phyllis Diller wiglets should be considered a high calling."

"The highest." I laughed with her and then said, "How about you read the copy I wrote for the broadcast while William and I dance one dance together? We're not official contestants, but we can demonstrate the Lindy Hop to our Fireside friends."

"I'm not a broadcasting whiz, but I do look the part," said Hadley.

"Yes, you definitely do."

By the time the event arrived, I was aflutter with angst. While I felt good about the effort Evangeline and I had put into organizing it, I couldn't help but worry that something was missing. I put on my 1940s' vintage dress that had been Ruby's costume when she performed at USO shows with Bob Hope during World War II. It had a white bodice with black ribbon woven through the neckline and the cuffs of the puffy sleeves. Its skirt was black, with a V-shaped belt and white ribbon at the hem of its skirt. While I was several inches taller than Ruby had been, the skirt was long and so still worked for me. With the help of an old jar of Dippity-do and bobby pins I found in the bathroom cabinet, I parted my hair in the center and created victory rolls out of the front section, just like Martha Raye used to wear.

"My, my," said Evangeline. "If you don't look like you've got two cinnamon rolls stuck to the front of your hair."

"Gee, thanks. I'm trying to get into character for a 1940s' swing dancer. Don't you recognize the dress?"

"Oh yes, all those pictures of Pearl, Ruby, and Sapphire with Bob Hope in the Pacific. You need some stockings with seams down the back."

"I don't have any, unfortunately."

"Well, you could paint a seam down the back of your legs like they used to when stockings were hard to come by."

"I could, but I think I'll let that slide. If I were on a movie set, well, then, things would be different. Besides, I'd paint crooked lines and ruin the effect."

Evangeline was wearing jeans, just as she usually did. "Aren't you going to get dressed up?"

"No. I'm not going to dance. I'd rather stand in front and get a bird's-eye view of you, William, Selma, and the others. At the age of forty-three, I've decided if I can't wear jeans, I don't really want to participate."

I looked at her suspiciously, "Are you up to something, Rabbit? Are you hiding something?"

She showed me her empty palms. "What makes you ask a thing like that? Don't you trust me?"

"Well. . ." I said, shrugging my shoulders.

The Fireside Lindy Hop International Dance Contest area looked so festive, what with all the red plastic geraniums winding through white trellises along the stage where the band would play in the background. The countries of the contestants were represented by flags suspended from the eaves above the stage.

Right away, I did a sound check. The microphones were in working order, the temporary dance floor was perfectly aligned, and the space for spectators was filled with round tables, white folding chairs, and white lanterns.

"Looks like a picture, Evangeline. You did such a good job," I said.

"I found muscles I didn't know I had," she said. "But Squirrel, we're a pretty good team."

"Yes, we are." I hugged her and laughed. "Most of the time."

"You goofball," said Evangeline, tenderly. "I love you."

"Love you too, Rabbit."

I rolled my eyes and moved on to the next item on my list, a briefing of the evening's events. "I'm going to open the broadcast with a dedication to the Gemburree Sisters. I thought it was fitting, due to the countless hours they performed for the USO and danced their feet off for the troops. Then Hadley Hammerschmidt will introduce William and me. Then William and I will give a demonstration of the Lindy Hop at the beginning to warm things up, and shortly after that, the dance competition will begin."

"I've got the trophies ready," said Evangeline. "First- through third-place trophies and the honorable mention jelly bean cupcakes."

"I should have known you'd pick dessert as a reward. . . but jelly bean cupcakes?"

"Don't knock them until you've tried them."

At six o'clock sharp, the crowd was gathered and helping themselves to glasses of lemonade and iced tea. They'd filled clear plastic plates with pimento or chicken salad sandwiches, chips, and oatmeal cookies that had been donated by Davy Ottmers, current owner of the Fireside Café.

I went up onstage, smiled at the excited crowd, and started my spiel. "Welcome to station KOFF's first Lindy Hop International Dance Competition," I said. William stood nearby, looking as handsome and polished as ever. He wore khaki trousers, tan suspenders, white dancing shoes, a white shirt, a blue tie, and a fedora.

"Doesn't this crowd look swell?" I said, surveying the several hundred guests who'd scurried to find seats at the tables, placing their plates heaped with food and their drinks down on the linens. Several people started clapping.

"Yes, you should clap for yourselves indeed. This is a fine group of the best of the best, both of Fireside citizens and of the Lindy Hop international dance set. On behalf of station KOFF, I'd like to dedicate this evening to Ruby, Sapphire, and Pearl—the Gemburree Sisters—who gave so much time during World War II to entertain the troops in Europe and the Pacific. Tonight, I'm wearing an original costume used in several of their acts that belonged to my cherished grandmother, Ruby Gemburree Cranbourne. I can't help but feel she's smiling down from heaven and dancing along with us this evening. One thing's for sure, I know she'd be delighted to help raise funds for the Fireside Children's Fund, serving disabled kids everywhere. And now, please welcome my longtime friend and yours, Hadley King Hammerschmidt!"

Hadley sashayed up to the front in a swishy satin skirt and white blouse. Her dark hair with its dramatic frosting made everyone sit up and take notice, even if they hadn't before. She took the microphone from my hand and said, "Well, everyone knows they're clapping for me, Juliet." She laughed good-naturedly along with the audience. "You all know me: I'm Juliet's long-suffering best friend and employee. While she's on air getting more famous by the second, I'm at the store selling precious egg-decorating kits to keep refrigerators looking their best. If your eggs just sit in the carton and give you that ho-hum feeling, come on down to the House of Cranbourne. We'll give all attendees a complimentary set of feathered egg tiaras, duck bills, or frog and violin egg hoods. Remember, we're the only distributors in Texas for banana-flavored toothpaste, licorice-scented hand soap, and safe beet-free smelling salts.

"Allow me to introduce the first dance of the night, a Lindy Hop demonstration by our very own Juliet Cranbourne and William Bartlett, for those of you who've never seen it before. Please also welcome the Fireside Orchestra with Benny Bachman on the clarinet as they play 'Just Kiddin' Around,' originally recorded by Artie Shaw and his orchestra."

My heart skipped a few beats as William held my hand and pulled me to the dance floor.

"Are you ready?" he asked.

"Ready as I'll ever be."

We danced across the stage, sliding, strutting, and twirling to our hearts' content. When William lifted me during an aerial, the audience went wild with excitement, cheering and clapping like nobody's business. When the music finally ended, we held hands and took a bow.

That's when Evangeline ran toward us, holding out a small box for William. He thanked her, took the blue velvet box, and said, "I'm not 'Just Kiddin' Around,' Juliet." He got down on one knee and opened the box's lid, revealing a vintage diamond engagement ring. Holding it open before me, he said, "I tried awfully hard to find the perfect ring surrounded by rubies, sapphires, and pearls, just the way you were surrounded by your wonderful grandmother and her sisters, but frankly, it would have looked a little gaudy. If Walt or Ruby were still with us, I'd have gone to them first for permission. Failing that, I spoke to Evangeline and Jewel, and they gave me their blessings. So, in the company of our friends and family, I'd like to say that Juliet, you are the love of my life. Will you marry me?"

Acknowledgments

I am truly grateful for the kind words of encouragement from Linda Amey, without whose friendship the business of writing would be far too solitary. During the past thirty-two years, our discussions about the craft of storytelling have been extraordinarily meaningful and have made the journey more fun.

Furthermore, I send my heartfelt thanks to Kathy L. Murphy, founder of the Pulpwood Queens Book Clubs, who has worked miracles for authors across this great nation and beyond.

Thanks a million to my mother, Carolyn, who taught me to love to read and who helped me make the book trailer for *When We Last Spoke* that ultimately led to the making of the feature film based upon this work.

So much of my inspiration comes from loved ones, family, and friends. I want to especially thank my children—Dustin and his wife, Ashley; Lauren and her husband, Sean; Elizabeth and her husband, Tim; and Patricia and her husband, Mark—who give such joy.

Special appreciation goes to my talented siblings, Kit and Colin, who crack me up with their beet jokes and provide much support regarding the worlds of publishing and film. No doubt, our brother Mike is looking down from heaven and helping them plan the next practical joke.

I am truly blessed by the love and prayers of my precious sister-in-law, Ruthie, and brother-in-law, Bob. They have made such a difference throughout all these years. I deeply appreciate my Aunt Penny's encouragement and enthusiasm during the writing of the Fireside, Texas series. Family makes all the difference.

Marci Henna

Thanks to my high school English teacher Bill Voron and his lovely wife, Beverly, who taught me with such patience and skill. Yours is a gift that keeps on giving.

None of this would be possible if it hadn't been for my father, Jules, and my grandparents, Max, Opal, Marie, and J.C. I benefited from their rich stories, and the education I received by the examples they set. Blessings and love to all of them and the angels they entertain on a daily basis.

Made in the USA
Coppell, TX
10 October 2020